All Access

Liberty Kontranowski

To the Big Dreamers: Go for it. No regrets.

CHAPTER ONE
Text Me, Maybe

Ever been on the receiving end of a text from your celebrity crush?

Yeah, neither have I.

At least, I don't think I have.

I stare at my phone, where all kinds of letters are lined up to make sentences that would normally be pretty benign. But when I see they're from a number I don't recognize (with a New York City area code) and they say, "So is it true? Did you write your book about me?" they go from benign to *what the hell?!* in a hurry.

Because my book was written with someone very specific in mind—as in Niles Russell, the lead singer of my favorite band—and it's highly unlikely he's at the opposite end of this texting conversation.

Isn't it?

God, Kallie, get a grip. Of course it's not him. No question this is just a prank and I should definitely ignore it. But, not gonna lie, I kind of have the flutters here. And I'm a little intrigued. So, I take a deep breath and type, "?? Who is this?" and hit send.

Oh, God. Did I just do that? Seriously, why am I engaging with someone who A) seems to know they're talking to someone who wrote a book and B) also seems to know said book was inspired by someone real? I must be a special kind of crazy. I roll my eyes at myself and toss my phone back on the coffee table.

An instant later, my mystery texter's response comes in.

"You've written books about other people?" it says, complete with a winky face.

Uh, no. No, I have not.

I shake my head and laugh because, duh, I get it now. This is obviously Sara, my "best friend," clearly taking pleasure in messing with my head. She knows that even though I'm wedged firmly into thirty-something territory, I become a complete and utter fangirl whenever I talk, think, or speak about Niles. Sara's a total goofball and she must be bored, so, hey, why not borrow someone's phone and pretend to be Niles, just to blow my mind? Awesome.

"Sure, I've written tons of them," I respond.

Let's see how long she'll play this out before coming clean. Hopefully not long. I have laundry to do.

"Aw, then I'm sad. Thought I was the only one." Another winky face. "Saw a lot of myself in the Nash character and was kinda flattered. Just wanted to let you know."

My eyebrows pop up and I look around to be sure there isn't a hidden camera somewhere, capturing this terrible joke. She's starting to be a little convincing, which is honestly kind of mean. You know what I would give to hear from the real Niles? I sigh and, against my better judgment, keep playing along.

"Okay, you got me. Now send me a plane ticket so I can come manhandle you and we'll call it a day."

Ha! If that doesn't make her squirm, I don't know what will.

My phone stays silent for a minute, maybe two. Yep, I got her. She has no idea how to respond.

Bloop. "So . . . about your book . . ."

Oh, okay. This is how it's going to be? She's going to keep going? *Blerg.*

"What about it?"

Sara, more than anybody, knows all about my book—the book that started out as an outlet for the fangirl crush I have on Niles and totally took on a life of its own. When I finished the thing (Shocker #1, because writing a novel is *hard* and takes a *long time*!), I reached out to my dream literary agent, who loved my book as much as I did and signed me fairly quickly (Shocker #2). The next thing I knew, she was shopping my novel to some of the biggest publishers in New York City and ultimately secured me a deal that slightly squelched the monetary fears I was having as I navigated my way through the dissolution of my twelve-year marriage (the book deal was Shocker #3; the ending of my marriage was of my own doing).

"It's creepy," the mystery texter says. "And awesome. Good job. But weird."

Okay, *that* line twists my stomach. Sara doesn't speak like that. She would never, ever start a sentence with "and" or "but." And she really wouldn't do it two times in one text. For a minute, I let myself believe it really is my muse.

Okay, minute over.

"Hey, Sar. You're super hilarious, but quit playing with me, k? Aren't you supposed to be heading to dinner with Jack?" Sara is going through a divorce, too, but instead of swearing off men for the next six lifetimes like me, she's diving right back in with a guy from high school. From high school! Ack!

The next response is instantaneous. "Sara? Uh, nope." A few seconds pass, then, "It really is me. –NR"

Okay, if my stomach had the flutters after that very first text, it's hosting an entire community of butterflies, hummingbirds, whatevers after this one. NR. NR. NR. No freaking way! It *cannot* be Niles Russell! I feel woozy. If this is a game, I am so done with it. My hands shake as my fingers slowly type, "Okay, if you really are NR, then where are you right now? I know . . . but do you?"

This will definitely bust Sara—or *whoever* is yanking my chain. Niles and his band are on tour right now, not too far away from me. I know this because in five days I am going to see them live. Again. I know every single stop on their tour, and if I somehow can't remember where they are on a particular day, I dash straight to their website to check. I am like a high schooler who knows every class her crush has, what halls he goes down, the drinking fountain he stops at before each period, everything. If Niles is doing it, I know about it. It's become like a game.

"Just sound-checked in Chicago. Barely made it in time. They're starting to let people in. Oops." Another smiley face.

Whoa. Niles *is* in Chicago. I was *thisclose* to going there myself, but chickened out on driving alone. Nobody knows that. Not even Sara.

"Hang on. Sending you a pic."

As I wait, my stomach flops, my heart races, and my lips hurt from clenching them so tightly together. If this really is Niles, what in the world does he want with me? How would he have gotten my number? Yeah, he was the inspiration behind my book, but it's not like I actually called him out in there. How would he know? Why would he care?

My phone blips and my shaky hands raise the screen to eye level. The air leaves my lungs as I focus on those funky blue/green/gray eyes that have lured me in during every music video, those lips with the perfect bow, and those super white teeth that are a bit too big for his slender face. This *can't* be real.

My eyes travel up to his hair—that telltale floppy brown hair that's short on the sides and all crazy on top. It is the exact same hair

I've seen in a million pictures and subsequently fantasized over. I want to reach through the phone to touch it.

He's not smiling, but he's also not *not* smiling. He looks exactly as quirky as I expected him to. I'm smitten all over again.

"See? Told you it was really me."

I can't even feel my fingers as they type, "Holy shit," and then press send.

In an instant, my mind is plotting whom to tell first. No one will believe me. But, wait, they'll have to. The picture is right here. The picture of Niles. Niles Russell. Right here on my phone.

I'll tell Sara first, of course. After all, she is the one who encouraged me to write the dang book, knowing full well it was stirring up some major dust in my head and my heart. Then maybe I'll go to the library or Target or somewhere. Just whip out my phone and say, "Oh, hey look. A text from Niles Russell. Oh, and he sent me a pic, too. Huh, isn't that something?"

Half the people won't know who he is, because even after winning three Grammys, he's kind of nondescript. They're the band that is all over the radio and TV, and everyone knows their songs, but hardly anyone knows their name. Which I love because they're kind of like "all mine."

Of course, I'm not their only real fan, and their real fans are diehards. We know every word to every song, every funky inflection of Niles's voice, every pause where he takes a breath in preparation for his trademark belting. We know that he shows up to concerts in whatever he has clean—usually black jeans, a way-too-big sleeveless shirt and some cool jacket. We know—and are okay with the fact—that he often takes his shoes off mid-concert and runs around barefoot. And we know that no matter how many shows they've done in the nights, weeks, and months before, every single performance is like it's their first and last. There is so much heart in them, it makes my breath catch.

"Sorry if I freaked you out," he says. "Read your book. Thought it was trippy. If it's really inspired by me, I'm super flattered. If not, then pretend this never happened."

I'm not sure I've ever had a harder time breathing. If Niles Russell truly read my book, then he truly knows exactly how I feel about him, and that is truly insane. Truly. Because, let's be honest here, things definitely got pretty steamy in a few parts. Within those pages, Niles and I got naked together, bore our very beings to each other, and ran off into the sunset, living happily ever after. It was a magical, electric, beguiling, and mesmerizing journey. And now he knows all about it.

My phone startles me when it dings again. "You still there?"

My face is scorching hot. Not only does he know my deepest and darkest feelings, but five seconds ago I told him to send me a plane ticket so I could come manhandle him. Oh my God. This is the opportunity every fangirl dreams of, and here I am, totally blowing it. I'm paralyzed, deciding whether to pretend our connection got dropped, tell him the book wasn't about him, or hell, just ignore him altogether. Sure, it's one thing to fantasize about someone when they're nothing but a few pages of Google images and some concert viewings from the first few rows, but it's quite another when the real deal sends you unsolicited text messages and you suddenly have to own up to your obsession.

I wonder what he's thinking right now. Is he seriously flattered? Or is he totally freaked out? In my wildest dreams, I didn't expect my book to find its way into Niles's hands . . . or for him to figure out he was the inspiration behind it. This is so crazy.

After the next ding—a picture of him with a big, genuine smile, raised eyebrows, and the heart-meltiest look in his eyes—I know what I have to do.

"I'm here. And I wish you were, too."

CHAPTER TWO
Reality Rocks

I stare at my screen in horror. *Horror.* What am I doing? Am I flirting with him? I tell myself, no, of course not. I'm just fangirling over him. What self-respecting fangirl *wouldn't* fangirl over her biggest rock star crush with whom she just happens to be texting?

Yes, I am definitely fangirling.

But maybe also flirting.

I think fast, trying to come up with a response that will make me seem a little less like a freaktastically-forward ho-bag. Too late. I hear a ding.

"Is that right?" he asks, adding a surprised-mouth emoticon. "Well, maybe I wish I were there, too." Wink.

Have mercy. Niles Russell is totally toying with me.

As every single winged creature in my stomach explodes into flight, I inhale a huge breath, thinking about how well I "know" him thanks to my book. I've tracked down every interview I could find, covering everything from his punk scene high school days to his random quote to a fan who saw him in a Tim Hortons just yesterday. I've watched more videos of him than I can comfortably admit. I know details about his family (including his sister, Kallie, who shares a name with yours truly!), his current and past relationships, and the fact that he hasn't driven a car in over a year because, well, he doesn't have to.

Of course, I twisted some of these facts when I created the character of Nash, but he obviously sees right through that. Obviously.

Ding. "You going to our concert on Friday? Maybe we can say hi after the show or something. I can sign your book, haha." *Pause.* "Wait. Is that narcissistic? That's probably a little narcissistic. Sorry." Sad face.

Is he even kidding me right now? Seeing him in person. Having his name hand-scribbled in a book I wrote based upon my hella-hot fantasies with *him.* If he wants to call it narcissistic, he can go right ahead. I call it *pinch-me-I'm-dreaming*!

I catch a glimpse of myself in the reflection of my laptop screen. It's hard not to notice my smile has just about taken over the entire circumference of my head. I'm nervous, but excited. Freaked out, but stoked. In five days, I'll not only see Niles in concert again, I'll actually meet him, too! Eek!

"Of course I'll be there," I type, finding my composure. "Sixth row this time. All that was left. Somebody is getting pretty popular." I almost erase my winking emoticon but, given how many he's thrown out there so far, decide to keep it.

"I'll get you up front. Let's see if I can pick you out of the crowd. If I reach for your hand, you'll know I know it's you."

My stomach flops again as I think of Niles on stage, looking out over his adoring crowd. Lights in his eyes, sweat pouring down his face, his earpiece dangerously close to falling out, as it seems to at every show. What a thrill that must be (except the earpiece part).

I wonder how often he recognizes faces in the crowd. I've seen him make eye contact with people before—even me once when I was in the second row—but he never touches anybody. Ever. He's a total germophobe and never executes "the reach." A lot of fans don't know that about him and get pissy because he doesn't go crazy making friends with the crowd. But I secretly adore it. Especially now that I might be the lucky one who *will* get to touch him in just a few days.

"I thought you hate touching fans during your shows," I challenge.

"Yeah, your right. But I feel like I could probably touch a girl who seems to know me so well." *Pause.* "Wait. Make that *you're. Better step it up a notch when I'm texting an author."

As if I weren't already, I am now officially dying. I seriously can't even feel my legs. I am floating—levitating—above my chair. I don't know much about music, but I do know that Niles is one of the most incredible songwriters in the business. His lyrics are bold and touching and raw and real. He's had some of the biggest-named recording artists recruit him to write with them. A few have even convinced him to record duets and/or features. In my little word-nerd world, having someone like him refer to me as a legit *author* is nearly as incredible as actually conversing with him.

"Make sure you save my number," he types. "My memory is shit these days. If you haven't heard from me again by Thursday, give me a yell. And watch your email for tix. You bringing your husband?"

Dude, please. If he read my book, he knows damn well I don't have a husband anymore.

"I think you know the answer to that."

"Right. Good. One ticket. Watch for it."

One ticket. Niles Russell wants me to watch for one ticket. To his show. Where I'll see him. And touch him. And—ermergerd!—meet him. How is this even happening?

I know I'm pushing it, but dammit I'm on a roll, so I gather up my big-girl bloomers and ask the one big question that's been on my mind since the minute he texted.

"So, how did you get my number, Niles? And why?"

"My people called your people, LOL. We had to jump a few hoops, but we got ahold of your agent who had a pretty good feeling you wouldn't mind hearing from me." Winky face.

"She was right. Really, really right." I make a mental note to call Lucy first thing in the morning. She was already my hero to begin with, but now I might have to propose marriage or buy her a house or something as a thank-you for this one. Seriously. I really might.

"What you did was cool. Freaky and trippy, like I said. But cool. So thanks." Blushing smiley. "See you at the show Friday. Later."

I set my phone face down on my leg, my mind trying so hard to process this whole thing. But it can't. I can't even breathe, let alone understand what just happened.

My phone dings again, and since I'm sure it's Sara and she is going to *die* when she hears this (after I actually get her to believe me, of course), I flip that puppy over and get my typing thumbs ready.

Except it's not Sara. It's yet another selfie of Niles. This time, he's holding my book in his left hand while giving a thumbs-up. His hair is flopped over his left eye, his right eye is clear and twinkly, and I see just enough of his shirt and jacket to know exactly what he's wearing to the concert tonight. He is so sexy, I die on the spot.

What. In the hell. Am I getting myself into?

CHAPTER THREE
Let's Make a Deal

As predicted, Sara doesn't believe me when I call to share my news. Even after I send her Niles's first two selfies, which, she claims, I lifted off the Internet. Nope, instead of freaking out with me like I hoped she would, she insists I am finally off my rocker and that my obsession with Niles has morphed from "healthy outlet" to "next stop: Psychoville."

"Okay then, watch this." I send her the last thing in my arsenal: the picture of Niles with my book. If this doesn't work, nothing will.

I wait a moment then hear her squeal. Bingo!

"Kallie, where did you get that?! That's incredible. Is that really him? With your book?"

"Told ya."

I have a totally captive audience for the next hour as Sara hangs on my every word. I recap our whole texting conversation, and the fact that I'd already heard from him again this evening. He wondered what side of the stage I prefer and if I could text him my email address so his people could send the ticket. I told him I didn't care where I sat, that every spot within ten yards of him was perfect. (I nearly puked in my own mouth after I sent that one.)

For sure, I am bordering on crazy. He's just being nice. He wants to know where I want to sit to increase his chances of finding me in the crowd. He's trying to act like he cares about my silly book, but no doubt this is something his PR people think is necessary since I devoted an entire tome to him. Not that most people would know it's about him. But still. I need to talk to Lucy to see what she knows about all this.

Of course, I don't sleep a single second all night. Not one. Thoughts of our conversation, thoughts of meeting him, thoughts that both his email address and cell phone number are now permanent residents in my electronic devices—seriously, I can't even handle myself! This is so beyond real, I swear I must've dropped dead at some point without knowing it and this is my little sampling of heaven.

Finally, *finally,* after a night of everything but rest, it's morning. And the second nine o'clock hits, I'm on the horn with Lucy.

"So, uh, I got a text from someone kind of interesting last night," I tease after an as-professional-as-I-can-manage hello.

"*You did?*" She knows exactly who I mean. It's written all over her voice.

"Any idea who?"

"Oh my gosh, Kallie! He really texted you?" It's hard not to notice that her voice registers even higher on the squee-meter than Sara's did. I love it! (Lucy's a huge fan of Niles now, too, thanks to my excellent sales skills—as in, every conversation we have, I sneak something in about Niles or the band). When pressed, she assures me that if this is a PR ploy, she's not aware of it. And she can usually smell stuff like that from a mile away.

"I promise. I have never talked to his people before. This came out of nowhere. I thought it was a joke, but then they put him on the line and his voice is, well, pretty recognizable. Under most—well, pretty much all—circumstances, I'd never give out a client's info. But in this case, I kind of thought you wouldn't mind."

What would ever give her that idea?

Now, please excuse me while I go pass out.

***

For being so busy and having a "shit" memory, Niles seems to have figured out the art of keeping in touch. He's currently blowing up my phone, telling me that they always have food after the concert. Mostly junk food, since he likes to binge after burning off somewhere close to a bazillion calories during his shows.

I've always marveled at his energy level. He's not a stand-there-and-belt-it-out kind of guy. He's everywhere. He bounces and jumps and runs and sometimes even slides. One thing he doesn't do is dance. I hate to say it, but I don't think he has a lick of rhythm in that super-fly body of his. But, for sure, they (whoever "they" is) should do a study on his pipes. Even after all that gallivanting on stage—and the fact that he just quit smoking after a fifteen-year habit—he somehow has the lung capacity to carry a note for ages. It's pretty incredible.

He asks me if I want something special after the show. Any type of drink or salad or smoothie or whatever. He tells me he likes to down some Scotch on the rocks before his concerts (I already know this), but usually sticks to beer after. I say beer is just fine, and no food is necessary. He tells me there will be jalapeño poppers, since those are his favorite, and I promise to eat a few with him. This must make him happy because he responds with a series of seven smiley emoticons.

Who knew rock stars had such a penchant for emoticons?

But let's get serious for a minute here: the idea of sipping beers and eating poppers with my rock star obsession? Yeah, I'm kind of tingling all over. And the fact that he keeps texting me? Even more tingling. True, the texts usually start out as business-type inquiries (tickets, backstage food, etc.) but in no time they develop into borderline we've-been-friends-for-ages chats that go on longer than they need to. Over the course of Wednesday and Thursday, we chat five more times, in between me visiting the hair salon for a highlight refresh and lounging outside to catch a tan.

I am grateful now more than ever for my flexible writer's schedule, though the mom in me feels sad that I'm not with my girls. For years, I coveted a schedule like this so I could be home with them during the summer and on snow days, baking cupcakes and making Etsy-worthy crafts. Now that I'm finally around, they're staying with Brad at his parents' in North Carolina. For the whole freaking summer.

My stomach turns over as I walk past their bedroom. It's nothing special, especially since Brad kept the house and they have to share a room here. But it's cute, anyway. It's a mix of princesses and ocean life, true to each girl's personality. It's tidy and colorful and looks like a nine- and seven-year-old girls' room should.

Seeing it makes me miss them. A lot.

I think about our lives now, and yes, it's different and hard sometimes, but I know I didn't make a mistake. Since Brad and I split, the girls and I have gotten along so well. I'm happy now, joyful and (pretty much) carefree. We take off and shop until someone has a meltdown, sometimes never buying a thing, but always enjoying each other's company (until said meltdown occurs). We eat ice cream for dinner, then make up for it the next day with vegetable omelets and whole grain toast with organic honey. They giggle nonstop and I do, too. We paint each other's toenails and comb each other's hair. When Brad and I were married, it was one strained Family Movie Night per week and the rest of the time we spent avoiding each other. It was no way to live and I think the girls can see that now.

I flop on my couch and reach for my laptop. I really need to send Lucy the first three chapters of my next book—the highly anticipated sequel to Emily and Nash's story—but my mind is a little, um, preoccupied. I check my phone, hoping for a text from Niles, but there isn't anything other than a missed call from my dentist, confirming my cleaning appointment for Monday.

I lift the lid on my laptop and am immediately lured in by the number on my inbox. I dig right in and see not one, not two, but *three* emails from Niles and his "people." The ones from his people are confirmations of my front row ticket and backstage pass. I am allowed to bring a camera, but no backpacks or anything else aside from "my person." Sure, fine, that I can do.

The one from Niles starts out innocently enough but gets personal in a hurry. He tells me he's excited to see me and that every time he starts envisioning what I look like, he pushes it out of his head because he doesn't want any preconceived ideas.

For real? That's kind of adorable.

As I think about how to respond to his email, a text from him comes in asking what I think he should wear to the show on Friday. My poor mind can't keep up with him. He's all over the place.

But, hey, I know what you should wear, Niles.

How about *Not. A. Thing?*

After my cheeks catch fire thanks to my naughty thoughts, I yank my mind back out of the gutter, pull myself together, and tell him that I love the black jacket he's worn in the past, but I think it will be way, way, way too hot for that. As in, 90 degrees hot. He says he'll wear it anyway and ditch it when the sweat starts pouring. I shiver. Niles Russell is wearing my favorite jacket. Because I asked him to. Wow. I couldn't even get Brad to wear a shirt without holes in it on the rare occasions we went to the mall.

"Kallie, I just want to prepare you . . ."

Uh-oh.

"I'm not the most outgoing guy IRL. So if I'm a little awkward after the show, don't be surprised. I figured I'd better just apologize in advance."

Not outgoing? That makes no sense. All of our conversations, his stage presence, the zillions of interviews I've seen him do. If he's not outgoing, then he's a darn good faker.

"I hide behind my music. But you probably know something about that, don't you?"

I let this digest a second, then shake my head as if he can see me. I have no idea where he is going with this.

"You don't need to hide behind your words with me, Kallie. When we meet on Friday, be yourself. And I'll be me. Let's at least try. Deal?"

Oh. So *that's* what he meant.

Okay, then.

"Deal."

CHAPTER FOUR
Ring My Bell (Or, My Cell)

It's finally concert day, and I'm on my way, gripping the steering wheel as if it will fly out of my hands if I dare loosen up. I hate highway driving and the venue is a good hour and a half away. Not good news for me, right?

The only thing squelching my fears is my brain's constant replay of our last conversation. In the few days we've been talking, Niles has apparently gotten to know me better than I know myself. How could that be? He didn't watch a hundred interviews of me, like I did him. He doesn't know my friends. Or my family. Or the really real story behind my relationship with Brad. I don't think he even knows I'm a mother. Yet, he knows how to pull me out from behind my own curtain. He knows how to get me to flirt, how to let myself be more vulnerable than ever, how to twist my guts by calling me out for something he's guilty of as well.

Hiding.

I never thought of it that way, but that's exactly what it is. Instead of talking through my problems with Brad, I hid from them by creating a fictional world. A world where I was in control and I called the shots. Where I could make anyone do what I wanted, when I wanted, and I could dictate every second of my own destiny.

In my book, Nash and Emily weren't perfect, but they were close. The few hiccups they had (every book needs tension!) were solved within a chapter or three. The overarching plotline was dreaming big and being lucky enough to have those dreams come true. That was much simpler than real life and it made for a better story.

As I went to bed last night, I thought of Brad. Was it unfair of me to end our relationship without trying harder? Were we that far off? Was what we had really unsalvageable or could we have stuck it through?

I flopped around for a while, thinking I should feel sad about the empty sheets beside me. But, I don't. I don't miss his snoring or his grunting or the way his breath encased me as he rolled toward me while he slept. I don't miss seeing him at breakfast or dancing around him as he fumbled in the kitchen. I don't miss faking our good-bye peck or the emptiness of the "Love you" I'd obligatorily fire at him as he left for work each day. I don't miss any of it. I don't miss him at all.

He's not a bad guy. He really isn't. He loves our girls in a crazy way and is a really great dad. It's just that somewhere along the way we stopped trying to impress each other, stopped having fun with each other, stopped wanting to learn more about each other. Each day was the same. We were on autopilot. There were no date nights, no weekends away, not even a quintessential princess-filled trip to goddamn Disney World with the girls. He likes predictability and I like excitement. We just weren't a good match anymore, and carrying on as if time would fix that was just completely unrealistic.

When I woke this morning, my first thought was of Niles. He *knows* me. Already. Brad no longer knew me. To me, that speaks volumes.

The second I knew she'd be at her desk at work, I called Sara to share my big revelation.

"You want my two cents?" she asked after I finally shut up.

"Yeah, of course."

"Niles is a smart guy. He's a writer, too, so he gets it." I nodded as a smile broke across my face. I knew she'd agree with me.

"However . . ." *Uh oh.* "Just because he 'gets' some of the stuff you're going through doesn't mean he knows you, Kallie. He's still just a guy you 'met' a few days ago. You've spoken over text and email. That's it. You haven't even shared air with him yet. I mean, right?"

Of course she's right.

"I know you don't want to hear this," she continued, "and maybe it's possible you two will have some sort of insta-bond. But just remember, this guy's been around. He's a professional performer who's met a lot of people. Maybe not one who's written a book based on her wildest fantasies with him, but still."

To her credit, she tried to laugh and lighten the mood, but when I wouldn't play along, she said, "Just be careful, Kal. You're my best girl and I don't want to see you get hurt. Hang tight before giving your heart away again, okay? Even to a rock star."

"Yes, Mom."

"Good. I'm done lecturing now. Have fun tonight, take a million pictures, and call me first thing in the morning."

"Of course."

"And Kallie?"

"Yeah?"

"If he tries to kiss you—or more—don't let him. Not yet."

Uh, right.

"Sure."

"Good. Now, go get yourself together and get on the road. Your granny ass will take twice as long to drive there as a normal person."

***

What can I say? The girl knows me. As she predicted, the hour-and-a-half drive turned into two hours and twenty minutes. But that's fine, since I left plenty early. Now I'm here and I'm in one piece, and holy crap, I'm about to see and meet Niles!

I clench my ticket to within an inch of its life as I trudge through the open field that serves as the parking lot to the outdoor venue. Five minutes into my walk, the sweat is already trickling down my temples and my shorts are sticking in my crotch. Thank goodness I spent so much time toning my legs this winter, though, because crotch-intrusion aside, I am rocking the hell out of these white cutoffs.

I adjust my shirt, careful to show just enough of the The Ladies to be intriguing. (That was one of our final joint investments—new boobies—but even those couldn't save Brad and me.) I've played with this shirt in front of the mirror so many times today I know exactly how much to yank before I get into the danger zone. Once I'm satisfied, I smooth down my humidity-destroyed hair to the best of my abilities and take my place in line.

As I stand there, my eyes sweep across the gobs of people that I fully consider "my peeps." I can tell instantly who the old fans are and who are new. Those with concert tees from tours past feel like long-lost relatives to me. I'd love to embrace them all, one by one, but that might be a little weird.

Then there are the girls. For certain, at least half of them crush on Niles nearly as hard as I do. Each of the main band members are cute in their own right, and each has their own following, but Niles attracts the most attention, by far. (As the lead singer often does, I suppose.)

I eye up one particularly cute blonde, feeling smug because I will be touching Niles later and she won't. She catches me looking at her and flashes a sweet smile. I flash one back, then reach for my phone as a distraction. It takes all my restraint not to run over and show her the many lines of text chats between Niles and me. Or the selfies. He's only sent the original three, despite my telepathic encouragement for him to send more. But it's three more than Blonde Girl has on her phone, so I still rule the world.

As I scroll through the extended weather forecast in an effort to keep my mind busy, my phone buzzes. I nearly leap out of my skin as Niles's name and picture overtake my screen. I stand frozen with my eyes bugging out, not knowing whether to show the universe or hide my phone for privacy. It takes me a second to realize this is not a text. He's calling me. Like, seriously, really calling me.

"Hello?" I hiss. There are people everywhere. And being loud and discreet at the same time is kind of a challenge. This is so weird.

"Hey. You here?"

In a flash, everyone around me disappears and I breathe in and savor his voice. It's unmistakably his and I love hearing it even more than I thought I would. Just listening to his three-word utterance is like hearing a chorus of angels at the Pearly Gates. Okay, maybe that's a little dramatic, but to me, it's the most incredible sound. And it's coming right through my phone.

"Yeah, me and the rest of the world," I laugh.

"Awesome! What's the crowd look like?"

"Hot and sweaty and ready to party."

"Perfect. That's just how we like 'em."

There's some fumbling around in the background and the squeal of a guitar being tuned. Niles laughs at something someone says, goes quiet for a second, then lets out a loud, long breath.

"You okay?"

"Yep. Shot number two, down the hatch."

Oh, man. He's doing his preshow shot ritual. While he's on the phone with me. What I wouldn't give to be back there with him right now.

"So . . . are you nervous?" I try to keep my voice calm and even.

"A little. Wait. About the show? Or meeting you? The show, no way. It's what I live for. Meeting you, yeah, a little."

Awww.

"I, uh . . . I'm a little nervous, too," I stammer, shuffling forward. If being smooth is my goal, I am failing so hard right now.

"Don't worry. We'll have fun. See you in a little bit?"

Oh, yes. Yes, you will.

"Can't wait," I breathe, as I push through the turnstile.

Holy crap, here we go!

CHAPTER FIVE

Backstage Pass

Backstage is not at all as glamorous as it should be. It's a bit musty and surprisingly chilly, given the steamy summer night outside. Eight-foot tables are pushed together in a C-shape with food, beer, energy drinks, and disposable tableware covering every inch. I lean against a wall, not knowing what to do with myself. There are a few others trickling backstage, but Zeke, the bouncer, took only me to the part of the room with the food.

There's some commotion and laughter, but it still sounds far away. My pulse picks up and there is no question that anyone within a ten-mile radius could hear my heart thump if they listened hard enough. This is getting too real. This isn't words on the pages of a book anymore, or even some texts and a quick phone call. Niles is a real human being who just walked through the door backstage and is heading straight toward me. There is seriously nowhere—and no time—to hide!

He immediately catches my eye, and I lose my breath. I am one hundred percent sure my face rivals the color of red velvet cake. I break into a cold sweat so bad it feels like my skin is melting.

He slips past everyone else and, in an instant, is less than a foot away from me. "I got you on the first try," he announces, clearly proud of himself. "I knew it was you. I knew you'd be blonde. Knew it!"

His lips part to reveal those teeth! I read once that he had veneers applied after busting a tooth at a show a few years back, and now I truly believe it. They are Colgate-commercial straight, pure white, and all lined up like little soldiers in his wide mouth. I'm dying.

From the first row, I could see every one of his fillings (there are four) and I quickly became fascinated with how he could sing and smile at the same time. When his eyes fell on mine, not five minutes into the show, I knew he knew. He didn't reach for my hand until over halfway through, but we made eye contact several times. When his fingers finally clasped mine, it was electric. I was touching Niles Russell. He held on longer than he should have, making the fans around me—guys and girls alike — that much more determined to get their own piece of him. He surprised us all by grabbing a few more hands, but only mine did he grab a second time.

Now, he's so close to me I can smell him. His hair is wet and messy, but his face is no longer sweaty, as though he stuck his head under a faucet on the way back. He has a towel wrapped around his neck and his concert T-shirt has been replaced with a clean, dry one. He smells of deodorant and hot skin. It's intoxicating.

"Have fun?" He hands me a half-empty water bottle. "Shit! That one's mine. Here's a full one." He shakes his head in embarrassment and switches the bottles, which is disappointing since I would have gladly taken his.

It occurs to me that I have not yet uttered one word—only smiled stupidly—so I take a breath and give it a try.

"You positively killed it tonight," I say, my voice shaking as it finds its legs. "As always." He beams.

I can tell I touched a hot spot, so I keep going. "Every

performance gets better, I swear. And I've seen many."

"Thank you." He reaches out like he's going to touch my arm, but his hand just kind of airballs and falls back to his side. "Much more fun than real life." He winks.

As I attempt to collect myself (how am I still breathing right now?) he nods toward a group of people gathering near a doorway. It's clear he wants to tell me something about them, but nothing's coming out. He looks at me helplessly, then gestures and nods toward them once more. He looks so flustered, I wish I could reach into his mouth and pull the words out for him.

"Jesus," he finally says, throwing his hands up. "I can't talk. I warned you about this." He laughs and unscrews the cap on his water bottle, only to replace it again without taking a drink. I smile and raise my eyebrows as if to tell him it's okay—and that he's absolutely freaking adorable for being so shy and awkward around me.

"Okay, let me try this again," he says, extra slowly. "Bottom line? We have a lot of great fans who pay good money or pull a lot of strings to get back here. The other guys keep them pretty entertained, but I do need to sneak over to say hi. I won't be gone long, okay?" He looks at me with wide eyes, as if half-expecting I might freak out if he goes.

"Oh, of course. Take your time. Really." I hope my voice doesn't reflect the burst of relief I feel, but we've already interacted more than my heart can handle. Him stepping away for a minute will give me a little time to regroup.

"Want a beer?" He motions to one of the tables sporting ice buckets filled with Coronas and local crafts.

I don't hesitate for a second. "I'll take about ten of them!"

He eyes me up and lets out a loud, sincere laugh. "You're my kind of girl. Corona with lime okay?"

"Perfect!"

He pops open the top of my beer and slips a lime inside. A simple task, but it has me absolutely mesmerized. Niles Russell is fixing me a drink, for crying out loud. How whacked is that? He prepares one for himself and holds his toward mine.

"Cheers?" It comes out as a question rather than a statement. His eyebrows are cocked and a half-smirk pushes in the dimple on his right cheek.

"Cheers!"

We clink our bottles together, then with a departing smile, he turns and walks toward the crowd. After about three steps, he spins around and mouths, "Be right back." I nod. And then die.

Once I resurrect, I take three deep breaths, just as *Shape* magazine suggests you do when you're in a stressful situation, and try to quiet my heart. I watch him across the room, posing for pictures and making small talk with fans. He's not as loud and chatty as the other guys, but he doesn't look awkward at all. He's in his element. He's in control.

At one point, his eyes lift toward mine and he gives me a small smile. He tips his bottle back, draining it of its beer and I can't help but think he's onto something. I polish mine off like I'm trying to win a high school drinking game and instantly feel a little calmer. I grab another from the table and pop it open. It's ice cold and feels amazing on my burning hot hands. I mosey around, trying to look natural, but I'm sure I'm not fooling anyone. That's okay. I'm here. And I wouldn't want to be anywhere else right now.

He's gone for what seems like ages, and with my back turned to the rest of the room, I feel him before I see him. I spin around to find him smiling wide, his drying hair all crazy and sexy. My entire body catches fire.

"You are really, really tiny," he says, looking me up and down.

"You're taller than I expected," I shoot back. I was never able to pinpoint his height, but I always kind of assumed he was pretty short. He's not. I'm guessing he's about 5'9", which isn't exactly gigantic, but still seems pretty impressive next to my miniature 5'2".

"Beer's good, right?" He reaches for his second, this time a craft.

"Nothing like a cold beer on a hot summer's night."

"Yeah. Nothing better." He gives me an appreciative smile. "And we booked you a room, so drink up."

He says this so casually I almost think I didn't hear him.

"Wait. You *what*?"

"Safety first," he says, with a wink. I must have the ol' deer-in-headlights vibe going because he looks at me almost sympathetically and says, "These after-parties can last a while. Especially when we're here, since we're minutes from our drummer's hometown. If you think it's crazy back here now, wait 'til his family gets here. Those people are nuts!"

I still have no idea how to respond, so I just stare at him, smiling like an idiot. I expected to have a beer or two, get my book signed, maybe eat a jalapeño popper, and leave. As if to prove me completely wrong, Niles puts his hand on my shoulder and says, "This way, you can stick around and have a few—or a bunch—of beers with me, and you won't have to worry about driving home."

My bare skin ignites under his touch while I attempt to process this new information. Niles Russell wants me to stay and hang out with him? And they rented me a hotel room so I could do exactly that? *Good God!* This is more than what my wildest dreams could have ever expected out of tonight.

I take a long, long swig of my beer and let my mind go wild with the possibilities.

Because this, my friends, is the full-on definition of dreams coming true!

CHAPTER SIX
We Own the Night

Multiple beers, the gift of time, the shots of Jägermeister that just made their rounds . . . whatever it is, it's working. Niles and I are having a great time.

True to his prediction, the backstage party is really hopping. There are people everywhere. I've rubbed elbows with Austin's (the drummer's) entire family, knocked back a shot with Austin himself, and drank off of Niles's bottle when he insisted I sample one of the crafts he was drinking. This night—my life tonight—is a dream.

Jase, the band's keyboardist, was particularly anxious to meet me. When Niles introduces me as his "writer friend," Jase grabs my hands with his, telling me, "You must be one helluva great writer to come up with something interesting to say about this guy." He lets go of my hands and does the guy-nudge against Niles's shoulder. Niles laughs and turns red, and for the first time, I wonder how much all the guys know about my book. Did they read it? Ohmygawd, if they did, what must they think of me? What if Niles is embarrassed by it? What if they think I am some groupie ho who is trying to bed their leader? Gah!

If they are thinking any of those things, none of them let on.

We're all relaxed and behaving as if we've known one another for ages. It's clear that Jase and Niles are especially close. In fact, it's common knowledge that until recently Niles dated Jase's sister, who is a permanent fixture in their entourage. I always thought that was a huge violation of the bro-code, but maybe not. Either way, I have yet to see her backstage tonight, but I keep watch, just in case.

Niles disappears for a moment, so I look around, taking it all in. This is what he lives, every day he's on tour. This is such a departure from life as I know it, I can't imagine what makes him feel like he needs to hide. He has everything he could want. He's crazy talented, he's surrounded by fans and friends, and he's got people willing to run out and restock party supplies at any whim. What's not to love?

"Here," he says, coming up behind me. "This is for you."

I can't see him, but I sure do feel his chest against my back as his arms reach around in front of me. We've been brushing against each other all night, but close contact like this is enough to make me lose my damn mind.

My eyes drop down to his hands, which are holding my book. "I figured I'd better sign it now, before I get too shitty." His breath warms my ear, causing just about every visceral reaction a body can have. I'll be mortified if he sees my skin, which is now covered in goosebumps the size of Texas.

I nod, but don't want to move much more than that for fear he'll back away. Instead, his chin comes to rest on my shoulder. I stop breathing. "There are some pretty personal scenes in here. You're an excellent writer."

My mind flashes to a scene where Nash does this exact thing to Emily—comes up from behind and nuzzles his chin into the crook of her neck. I tried so hard at the time to capture what Emily must have been feeling. But now feeling what I'm feeling with Niles, I know I didn't even come close. My lung capacity has diminished to zero, so all I can do is whisper. "You really read it?"

"Cover to cover. More than once." His weight shifts behind me. I stiffen, hoping to fire up some electromagnetic field that will keep him against me. It doesn't work, but what he does next is almost better.

He turns me toward him and looks right into my eyes. I allow myself to really stare back, and I swear we make a deep connection, right there, right then. "This was a badass thing you did." He nods toward my book. "It took a lot of guts. Putting your soul on the line is never easy. I admire you a ton for that."

"You do it all the time." And he does. Every song he writes is a little piece of himself.

"We get that about each other," he whispers. He is so close to me, I'm certain that if I let out all the air I've been holding in, I'll knock him right over. Our eyes remain locked, except for the moment mine drop to his lips, wishing they'd find their way to mine. What would he feel like? Taste like? My body hums from the mere idea of it.

"Why me?" he asks after a moment, breaking the spell. He steps back a little, leaving my severely deficient brain with no choice but to abandon my kissing fantasy and try to formulate a response.

On the surface, it's a simple enough question. But it's one I figured he'd inherently know the answer to. I had grown so "close" to him during all of my research, every bit of it made sense to me. And my readers all felt like they "knew" him as well. They could see themselves in Emily, pining after a rock star or movie star or whatever kind of celebrity stoked their internal fires. They could see Nash as the object of their desire, turning the pages of a story into their real-life escape.

But, as the *subject* of such an obsession, yeah, I guess I can see where he'd be left wondering some things. I'm suddenly sorry about how clueless he must be feeling.

I look at him quickly and back away even more because now I truly feel like I could cry. Every single emotion and nerve ending is on rapid-fire right now. I have felt everything to the nth degree tonight, and talking about my book makes me emotional even on a normal day. I owe him an explanation, though, so I take a deep breath and fire away.

"You . . . are an incredibly talented songwriter," I whisper, more to the floor than to him. "Your voice is the most unique and amazing voice I've ever heard. You are captivating, and you are seriously, seriously adorable." I glance up and he's smiling ear to ear. Yep. Adorable.

"But most importantly, you are my muse. Everything I do, I want to do better because of you. I work out harder when I listen to your songs, I write better when I'm writing about you, I put in more hours because I know how hard you work for your fans every single night, and I want to match that dedication. You challenge me and encourage me, and you don't even know you're doing it. It just radiates. It's your gift. And it's beautiful."

I take a breath. "That's why you."

His smile is gone. His face is stone, only showing life when he blinks a dramatic blink and pokes his tongue between his closed lips.

"Wow, okay," he says, jamming his hands into his pockets. "We should take some pics and have another beer. Yeah?"

I freeze. Holy crap, did I just massively fuck up? Did I freak him out too much? Jeez, he asked. He shouldn't have asked if he didn't really want to know. Tears sting the back of my eyes, and if my feet didn't feel like bricks, I would definitely make a run for it.

After at least a lifetime of me awkwardly staring at the floor, he takes my chin in his hand and angles it toward him. His posture has softened and he's smiling again. "Kallie," he says, his voice soft, "I told you that tonight I wanted you to be yourself. And you just were.

No hiding. So, thank you." He leans over and kisses my cheek, setting me ablaze once more.

He takes my hand and leads me to the beer table, where we each grab another two bottles. We plop down into some nearby chairs and crack jokes, snap dozens of selfies, and find reasons to touch each other more than new friends should. Whatever weirdness happened after the "why me" question is gone, almost magically. We smash our cheeks together for "silly" pics, rest our heads on each other's shoulders for "nice" pics, and even allow the tips of our tongues to graze as Austin stands behind us, pushing our foreheads together as we stick out our tongues at the camera. I feel his hair against my forehead and shiver. The hair I've wanted to touch for years is now touching me. Damn.

At 2:30 a.m., we're gently encouraged to leave the premises so the grounds crew can clean up. Niles insists on riding in the taxi to the hotel with me. We sit right in the center of the seat, our legs as smooshed together as they can be. We're not holding hands, but we might as well be; our inside arms are kind of draped between our two laps. We don't say a thing the entire time, but my heart beats loud enough to cut the silence. It's the most comfortably uncomfortable thing I've ever experienced.

When we pull up to the door, Niles discovers he has no money to pay the cabbie, so I pull out my wallet and fake-roll my eyes. A rock star without money to cover a twelve-dollar cab fare? Seriously classic.

As we make our way toward the entrance, Niles's hand brushes against mine more than once. There's no way he's not doing that on purpose. I almost think he's going to grab hold, but in an instant, he's migrating away from me as though I just announced I have the bubonic plague. It takes me a second to realize there are several fans hanging around the hotel lobby, waiting for their chance to catch a glimpse. Clearly, Niles realizes it, too. I flash him a knowing look and he nods in my direction and takes off toward the restroom, which totally, totally sucks. I didn't expect such an abrupt ending to our amazingly awesome night.

A few fans look my way, but I pretend not to notice and go about checking in like a normal old schmuck who didn't just spend the evening with her rock star obsession. I make a big show of having my key card in plain sight so that any onlookers know I have my own room and I'm not a groupie simply there to score with one of the guys. Once I make it through the lobby, a pout takes over my face. I mean, shit! Just like that, the night is over. I wish I could have told Niles thanks. Wished him a good night. Gotten one last picture with him. *Something.*

My heart hurts as the thoughts cut through the fog in my head. Will I ever see him again? Will all I have of this evening be pixels on my phone and memories in my mind? If so, I don't think I'm okay with that. At all.

I burst through the door of my room and land in a heap on the bed. My head completely explodes, and so do the tears. Maybe it's the drinks or maybe it's the emotions, but I blubber on and on until I am a mascara-smeared mess.

And I don't even try to fight it.

CHAPTER SEVEN

The Boy Next Door

Ringing. Buzzing. My ears hear both, but my brain processes neither.

My eyes crack open, a paste made of dried tears and not-very-waterproof mascara making it harder than it should be. When I finally focus, I realize I'm in my hotel room and that both the room phone and my cell phone are ringing. Because it's louder and far more annoying, I fling my arm out and swipe at the room phone first.

"Yes?" I croak. I sound and feel like death.

"Morning, sunshine!" With those two words, my pulse immediately quickens. I push myself up and look around my room, all the details from the night before flooding my brain and my senses.

"Hi," I breathe. It is so good to hear his voice.

"Sleep well?"

I look at the clock. 6:45 a.m.! Why is he up at 6:45 a.m.?

"Um, I guess so. Did you?" Jesus, Kallie. Lame response, much?

"Didn't sleep much at all, actually. I wanted to be sure I caught you before you took off."

Whoa, now. He lost sleep? Over me? Because he didn't want to miss out on talking to me? Hm, tell me more.

"So . . ." he continues, "I waited 'til an acceptable time to call. Glad you're still here."

"6:45 is acceptable, hey?" I laugh. "Yes, I'm still here."

"Can I . . . can I come to your room?"

My heart stops. Niles Russell wants to come to my hotel room.

Holy shit. *Niles Russell wants to come to my hotel room!*

I stand up and catch a glimpse of myself in the mirror on the opposite wall. Disheveled hair. Raccoon eyes. Rumpled clothes.

"No!"

"No? You don't want to meet up? Is something wrong?" He sounds genuinely worried.

"No, I mean, yes, you can come. But give me a bit. I seriously look like shit."

"I doubt that, but take your time. Fifteen minutes good?"

I'm thinking it's going to take more like fifteen *hours* to whip myself back together, but I really don't want to wait another fifteen *seconds* to see him again, so I say, "Fifteen minutes is good. I'm in room 224."

"Wait. You're kidding, right?"

"Kidding about what?"

"I'm in 226. We've been right next door to each other all night."

Oh. My. Lawd.

This revelation hits me like a hurricane hits the coast, because, A) if he was right next to me all night, it would have been really easy to "meet up" without being detected by any fans or fellow bandmates. And B) if he was right next to me all night did he (gasp!) hear me crying? Maybe that's why he wants to see me so badly. Maybe he heard me boo-hooing and carrying on for the good forty-five minutes I did, until I finally zonked out, too tired to think anymore and too dried out to produce more tears. But wait, he just now figured out we were neighbors. That means that if he did hear me, he wouldn't even have realized it *was* me. Right?

"Still there?" he asks.

"Yes."

"You have fourteen minutes now. So hurry."

***

After ten minutes of fighting the good fight, I realize I can't do much more for myself without makeup and other necessary beauty supplies. I have at least assembled a remotely okay hairdo and erased the raccoon marks from around my eyes. I brush my teeth until my gums are raw (thank you, God, for one-time-use toothbrushes!) apply a little lip gloss to the apples of my cheeks (nod to Sara for that oldie-but-goodie beauty tip), and settle on the edge of my bed, awaiting the arrival of my guest. What's going to go down when he gets here, I have no idea. I contemplate calling Sara, but what I have to say to her will take hours, not mere moments.

Niles knocks at my door exactly fourteen minutes from when he said he would. (Punctuality for the win!) I peek at him through the peephole and swear that even after being glued to his side for most of last night, I'll never get used to seeing him up close.

I lift the handle and he pushes the door open the rest of the way with his hip. He has a cup of coffee in each hand and it smells amazing.

"Please tell me you're a coffee drinker. Because if you're not, we're done here." He cracks a wide smile and my stomach drops down to my feet. Even if I hated coffee (which I don't), I would drink it just because he wants me to. Seriously.

After sneaking a look, I decide he's even cuter right now than he was at the after-party. He has clearly taken a shower, and he's got product in his hair that he didn't have last night (pretty much confirming my suspicions that he stuck his head under a faucet on his way backstage). He must not be interested in shaving today, though, because his stubble is growing in pretty thick. He's got his trademark black jeans on and, from what I can tell, three separate shirts. This guy is an excellent layerer.

Even though he's peppy, he's sporting some dark circles. I can't tell if it's because he had stage makeup covering them up last night or if they're due to his lack of Zs. He sets the coffees on the table and slips his hands into his pockets.

"Coffee? Yes or no?" He nods at the table.

"If I could marry coffee, I would."

He beams and grabs one of the cups, folds back the plastic flap covering the mouth hole, and hands it to me. "French Vanilla creamer."

"Divine." I smile and take the cup from him. Our hands touch (yes, I probably did that on purpose this time. Or did he?) and the electricity between us flows all over again.

"You look pretty darn cute for having only fourteen minutes to get ready," he says. I'd be inclined to think he was joking, but there is no trace of a smile on his face. Niles Russell just said I'm cute.

"You look pretty hot yourself."

God, did I just say that? I take a sip of coffee to hide my mortification.

Unlike stupid me, Niles is completely unfazed. "My sister's name is Kallie," he says, walking around to the unrumpled side of the bed. "But you already knew that, didn't you?"

He kicks off his shoes (he has no socks on, as always) and props the pillows up against the headboard. He sits on the bed, leaning his back into the pillows, and pats the spot right next to him. Oh. My. God.

I try to move toward the bed, but I'm paralyzed. He stretches his legs out and buries just his feet under the covers. He wedges his coffee cup between his legs and starts poking at his phone.

"Remember this?" He angles the device until I can see one of the pictures we took last night. The one where Austin was pushing our foreheads together and the tips of our tongues were touching. I remember the moment vividly (obvs!) but didn't know it was his phone we were using. I assumed most of the pics were taken with mine.

"Of course." I nod.

He pats the bed again. "You coming? I promise I'm not a biter."

Shiver.

I slip into the spot beside him, unsure of how close to get. You could fit a full person between us right now. This must be unacceptable to Niles, since he pulls over my pillows and props them up right next to his. I scoot over, but we're still not touching. Last night, I probably would've wiggled right onto his lap, but without the drinks flowing, my inhibitions are in full effect.

"This pic is particularly interesting to me," he says, shimmying even closer. His shoulder touches mine, sending a jolt all the way through my fingertips. "I'm a bit of a germophobe, so the fact that you got me to touch your tongue is kinda crazy." I squeak out a laugh. "Seriously. I make a really shitty boyfriend because making out with tongues is not my thing."

Is he serious? There's no way he doesn't kiss with tongues. Although, not gonna lie, the thought of him not playing tonsil hockey with other girls makes me very, very happy.

"I drank off your bottle last night, too." I'm surprised at the smugness that laced through my voice.

"Yeah, I know. And that was before either of us even had a good jag going. What did you do to me last night, Kallie?"

Those words send a firestorm of excitement screaming through my body. I am sweaty hot right now, despite still wearing shorts and my sleeveless shirt. My hands feel so wet, I swear I'm going to drop my coffee. If I were thinking straight, I'd pull the covers over my legs to try to hide the goosebumps. But, I don't. I just sit and stare straight ahead.

"Do you run?" he asks. "Like outside? For fun or exercise or whatever?"

Hellllloooo, left field!

"No," I say. Or try to say. My nervous system is not yet back to functioning and the word is barely audible.

"Well, do you have any decent trails near your house? You know, that you know of?"

Sara is a runner and has been trying to get me to run with her for years. I have no interest, partly because I always end up with shin splints, and partly because I had asthma as a kid and am terrified of a relapse. Sara begs me almost weekly, though, especially since we have some exceptional trails in town. So yes, I guess I do know of some.

"Yeah, we actually have some great trails."

"Will you take me?"

I've been looking straight ahead this entire time, but his question yanks me back. I lift my left hip and turn toward him. "Huh?"

"Will you take me home with you for the day? We're wide open since Austin's visiting family. We always build an extra day or two in when we stop here. No rehearsals or anything. I don't feel like wandering the streets and I could use a good run." He looks at me hopefully, eyebrows raised.

I assume by the smile on his face that I say yes, but I don't even remember the words coming out.

"Awesome! Thank you! But let's take a quick nap first. We'll leave at ten. That okay?"

Without waiting for an answer, he sets his coffee on the nightstand, scoots our pillows down until they're flush against the bed, and nestles right in. After I do the same, he pulls the covers over us and almost instantly falls asleep on his back. I slowly ease myself onto my side until I am facing him. I sneak a few glances at first, but once I am sure he's totally out, I give my eyes permission to stare. Like really, really stare. At my rock star crush. Who is in bed with me, just inches away, sleeping as though it's the most natural thing for us to be doing right here, right at this moment.

Oh my God. This is so unreal.

CHAPTER EIGHT
Home-Field Advantage?

An hour and a half into our nap, Niles starts wiggling around, causing my eyes to pop open. I am shocked to find that I had actually fallen asleep, and even more shocked to discover that my forehead is wedged against the outside of his shoulder. I lift my head to see him staring up at the ceiling, lost in thought.

"Hey," I say. "Feel better?"

He doesn't answer. Instead, he grabs his phone and starts pecking away. After a few moments, he turns to me.

"Sorry. Lyrics. When inspiration strikes, I gotta go with it."

I know exactly what he means. While writing my book, hopping out of the shower or stopping in the middle of the grocery store aisle to capture random thoughts or dialogue ideas was status quo. I am super intrigued by what exactly inspired him right now and what lyrics he came up with, but as much as I want to ask, I keep mum. I know the creative process can be very personal.

"You ready?" He pops up and takes a sip of his coffee.

"You know it!"

I wish I felt about one speck as confident as I sound. As cool as this is, how weird will it be having him in my house? Jeez, is it even clean? I'm usually pretty tidy, but I was so flustered before I left yesterday, I probably have makeup all over the vanity and toothpaste splashes on the bathroom mirror. What if he wants a snack and I have nothing he likes? What if he sees the pile of laundry sitting on my dresser? You know, the one with my not-so-sexy undies situated right on top. What if he's disgusted that I live in an apartment instead of a house? What if we have nothing to talk about and we're trapped with each other all day and things get weird and awkward and we should have just left it all as is?

What it, what if, what if?

After packing up and discreetly getting a cab ride to my car, which is now one of only five left in the concert venue's field, we stare at each other with "what's next" looks all over our faces.

"Can I drive?" he finally asks.

I consider his question. Do I let someone who hasn't driven a car in an entire year take the wheel, or do I take it myself and die of embarrassment as I granny my way down the highway? Decisions, decisions.

"You want to drive my Mom Car?" We've yet to broach the subject of my children, but I suspect he's figured out I have them. And if he hasn't, he knows now.

"It's a nice little ride. I haven't driven in a while, though."

"In over a year. Yeah, I know." I wink at him.

"Of course you do." He moves toward me and swipes at my hair. "Bug."

I catch his wrist as it's still on its return back to his side and hold it a second. I can feel his bones and the warmth of his skin. I want to pull him toward me and kiss him right here, right at this moment, but instead, I let go and rummage around in my purse for the keys.

"Here you go." I put the keys in his palm. "I trust you."

He breaks into a huge smile and unlocks the doors. We get

situated and he shifts into gear, navigates through town, and merges onto the highway like a pro. He's doing way better than I would have been.

"Like riding a bike," he says with a wink.

An hour later, our conversation is lively (yay!) and things are going great (double yay!). Until a cold sweat breaks out across my forehead and my stomach turns . . . and not in a good way.

"Oh, man," I groan. "I'm starting to feel like crap." Memories of last night's beers and shots come flooding back. I bite my tongue to keep from throwing up. "Aren't you hung over?"

"Ha, no. I'm a 'rock star,' Kallie, remember?" he says with air quotes. "I don't get hangovers anymore." He gives me a sideways glance, then squeezes my knee. "Whoa. You're white as an Irish ghost. Want me to pull over?"

I shake my head, even though I want to say yes. All closed up like this, I can really smell his awesome scent, but the air is stifling. I crack a window, which of course breaks the sound barrier as the wind whips in.

"Have some water," he instructs, pointing to the mini-cooler he brought. I want to reach back and grab a bottle, I really do, but I'm afraid doing so will jar my cookies loose. Instead, I lean against the headrest and close my eyes.

"Just relax," he says gently, his fingers brushing against my cheek. "We probably have another fifteen miles on this stretch, then I'll need you to watch for our exit. Can you do that?" I nod. "Okay, good. You're going to be fine."

And I am. I focus on the fact that I am sitting next to Niles Russell. He is driving my car. We took a nap together in a hotel bed. I partied with him last night. He grasped my hand during his incredible, amazing live performance. He's coming to my house, for chrissake. Thinking of those things diverts my attention, and before

I know it, he's wheeling into my assigned parking space, looking up at my Melrose Place-wannabe apartment building.

"My ex got the house."

He nods and shuts off the car.

"Uh, do you have, like, a lot of people who walk around here?" he asks.

This is an excellent question because the logistics of smuggling a Grammy-winning front man into my house isn't exactly something I've had to give a lot of thought to. Sure, he's no Paul McCartney, but it's likely *someone* will recognize him, and showing up at a random fan's house could do a number on his reputation. I'm guessing there are no paparazzi hiding in the bushes, but still. I check the clock and see that it's not quite noon. It's a hot Saturday and we have to walk by the community pool to get to my unit. There are bound to be a lot of people there.

"I'd grab your hat and sunglasses, for sure." I know he has them because I saw them poking out of his running bag before he zipped it up. "Also, maybe take off a couple of your shirts. People around here don't wear so many clothes. Your mad layering skills scream, 'rock star!'" He laughs and awkwardly peels off two of his shirts, bumping the steering wheel and narrowly avoiding cuffing me in the jaw. When I look over at the finished product, he looks like a normal guy—albeit a very cute normal guy.

Satisfied, we hop out of the car and make our way to my apartment. He hangs back behind me a bit, his head down and his fingers flying across the screen of his phone. He's probably missed a thousand calls on the way here. I wonder how often he has to communicate with his "people" and about what. I get my answer when we burst through my apartment door and he plops down on the couch without so much as looking around.

"Never a day off," he says. He shows me stats of missed texts, an email inbox with seventeen new messages (he says he just cleaned them out this morning during his insomniac moments) and four voicemails. All within two hours. One of the texts, I see, is from Robbyn Forderly. Yes, *the* Robbyn Forderly. Jase's sister . . . and Niles's ex.

Oh, man. This opportunity is too prime. I cannot let this go.

"Soooo, Robbyn," I say, nodding toward his phone. I know I shouldn't go there. I really shouldn't go there. But I really, *really* can't help myself.

"Jase's sister? Yeah?" He makes it sound like she's just some girl.

"You guys dated for quite a while, right?"

Niles looks at me a moment, then straightens his lips and casts his eyes up to my ceiling. He stares up there for ages, as though magical instructions for answering a crazed fan's question about your ex-girlfriend might be hiding amongst the terrible popcorn patterns. After an eternity, he drags his eyes back to me and says, "My and Robbyn's relationship—or should I say *dynamic*—is pretty complex."

Complex, huh? What does that mean? Since his eyes immediately settle back onto his phone, it doesn't seem like he's going to offer much more information than that. All righty then. Strike a nerve, much?

I walk to the kitchen to pour a glass of iced tea and, for the millionth time this morning, think about my desperate need for a shower. But will I actually hop in while he's sitting in my living room? I would die if he saw me *sans* makeup. I already look like a wreck enough as it is.

I gotta get him out of here and onto the trails so I can pull myself together. When I ask him if he plans to go running soon, he perks right up, asking if I'm sure I don't want to go with him. Of course I do, but I don't want to keel over in his presence, so I remind him of my hangover status and he nods in understanding. We agree to grab a quick bagel on the way to the trails, and I'll drop him off and come back for him in an hour and a half. It's impossible to get lost on the trails, and I pledge to take him to a more remote spot that will better ensure his anonymity. Good. This is all good.

He heads to my bathroom to change (OMG, Niles Russell is taking his clothes off in my bathroom!) and saunters out wearing gym shorts that look like they'll fall off and a tank top you could fit three more people into.

"Dude." I yank at the hem of his shirt. "You're making the big bucks now. You should probably spring for some sleeker running clothes."

"Meh, clothes just get all sweaty. Who cares? These shoes, though? *These* sons of bitches cost me a mint." He kicks his right foot out for my inspection, and it's true. His shoes are terribly kickass.

We walk past the girls' bedroom on the way to the kitchen and even though the door is partially closed, he stops to peek in. I cringe, knowing what's coming next.

"Girls, huh? How old?"

And there it is. The "kid" conversation. I knew it was bound to come up, even though I was totally hoping to avoid it. It seems weird admitting I have young kids with someone else when the book I wrote was so clearly not written from the Kallie the Mom side of my personality. But something about the wistful look on his face and the genuinely interested tone in his voice makes me feel like it's okay. He's not judging me. He's legitimately curious. About me. About my life.

"Um, Jillian's seven and Alana is nine." Before the words are even fully out of my mouth, my mind goes to them, picturing their little bodies bouncing on their beds, singing goofy songs and giggling loudly. I see Jilly's blond hair wave past her shoulders, while Alana's brown ringlets stop at her chin. They look nothing alike, yet they each favor their parents (Jillian, me; Alana, Brad.) I wonder how they're doing. What they're up to. If everyone is getting along.

"Ah, you're missing them hard," Niles says. My eyes fill up as I nod my agreement. "Yeah, you just got that 'mom' look. My mom *still* gets that look whenever I leave after a visit home, and I'm thirty-freaking-one." He pulls their door closed. "Where are they? At your ex's for the week?"

"Try the whole summer. Brad took them to his parents' in North Carolina. They usually go for a few weeks at a time—Brad is a teacher—but this summer, they're staying longer."

"Whoa. That's gotta be rough. I can't imagine." He rubs my back for a second, then takes my shoulders and turns me toward him. "Hey, I have an idea. I'm not sure if you'd even be down for this but how about . . ." he inches closer, "how about I do what I can to keep you distracted this summer?" His funky eyes search mine, turning my knees into mush.

Well, this is unexpected. I don't know what he means by that, but it sure does sound intriguing. And if it means I'll see and talk to him again, I am all in. Like, *all* in.

"How about," I breathe, "that sounds amazing!"

CHAPTER NINE
Friendly Fire

It takes longer than I remember to get to and from the trails, so by the time I drop Niles off, I have only forty-five minutes to shower and apply makeup. A nearly impossible feat. So, I'm thrilled when he texts to tell me he needs another hour. Apparently, his run has gotten his juices flowing and he wants to spend a little time thinking through some lyrics. I hate thinking about him sitting alone in the woods, but I'm thankful for the extra time to spruce up. And maybe call Sara!

Upon phone inspection, it appears Sara has called me six times since midnight. She's probably pissed I haven't called her back yet, but what I have to say is well worth the wait. I also see there is a quick text from the girls, saying simply, "Love you and miss you, Mom. Talk to you soon."

I close my messages and scroll through my photos from last night. There are tons, though I don't see the now nearly famous (between Niles and me) Tongue photo. I'm sad. I really, really wish I had that one on my phone. If nothing else, for proof that we came *thisclose* to intimacy. Okay, that's a total lie, but still. I flip through them one by one, remembering each moment and the way it felt to be so close to him. Last night was wild and fun. Today feels different, though it's still very exciting and actually rather comfortable.

My stomach squeezes when I think again about his promise to "distract" me this summer. We didn't get into details (I was rendered positively speechless after I eked out my "sounds amazing," and he didn't say anything more either). But "summer," to me, means more than one day, right? As in, we'll see each other again after he leaves today? Where? When? How? My mind goes crazy, considering all the options.

I finally call Sara while my hair dries and I start the laborious process of putting on my face. (I am so not a natural beauty. To look even "natural" takes a lot of work. Sigh.) She answers after a millisecond of a ring, her voice a raspy, scolding whisper.

"Did you have sex with him?!"

"What? No!" Sara was never one for extreme tact.

"Then what the fuck took you so long to call me back?" I envision her hand cupped around her mouth and phone, shielding her kids from the by-products of her sailor mouth.

"You won't even believe me when I tell you." I seriously don't know where to start. I rehearsed a bit while in the shower, but now not one word I planned to say actually comes out.

"Swear you didn't have sex with him?"

"Yes, I swear. I wish, but no, we didn't. Promise."

"Did he try?"

"No." I suddenly feel weirdly bummed about this. Why *didn't* he try? "He's been a perfect gentleman." That's why.

"Did he kiss you?"

"No. Well, yes."

"Yes?? Kallie, I told you not to kiss him! But holy shit, that's kind of amazing!"

"Relax. It was just on the cheek. Insert sad face here."

49

"No sad faces needed. Cheeks are enough right now. Did you flirt? Did you get along? What's he like? Is he an ass in real life?"

I suck in a breath. He is the opposite of an ass. I tell Sara that. I tell her all sorts of stuff, but keep some of the good stuff to myself. Namely, the tongue touch and our hotel nap. I figure those details will come out eventually, but for now, I hold them close.

"Where is he now? Back on the bus?"

"Uh, not even." I pause for dramatic effect. "Let's just say that if you went for one of your beloved runs on the Greensbury Trail right now, you'd see someone interesting."

There's a long silence on her end. I can pretty much hear the hamster wheels turning in her head.

"Kallie, what the hell? Are you even saying Niles Russell is here? In town? Running on our freaking trails? While I'm here listening to my kids fight and damn near kill each other?"

"That is what I'm saying."

"My God! How did he get here?"

"He drove. My car."

"Jesus. You are such a liar."

Before she can accuse me further, I tell her the whole story of how and why he's here. I tell her how he changed in my bathroom and how he dresses like a bum, aside from some pretty spectacular running shoes. (This impresses Sara. She has more running shoes than anyone should.) I tell her how I almost barfed during the car ride home and how we walked through my courtyard without a single raised eyebrow from onlookers. She begs me to take her with me when I go to pick him up, but I tell her no way. I want to squeeze every second I can out of our time together before he takes off for their next stop. Besides, that'd be kinda creepy.

After listening to her pout profusely, I shut Sara up by telling her about Niles's promise to distract me this summer. I can tell she's hovering on the diving board of the Squee Pool, but she won't quite jump in.

"Dear, sweet Kallie," she tsks. "From what you say, Niles does sound like a pretty cool guy. But, again, I think it's worth reminding you who he is and where he's been. He could probably have any girl he wants. He maybe *does* have any girl he wants. Not that you're not gorgeous and wonderful, honey, but I'd keep your guard up. With a guy like that, you have to wonder what he really wants with little old you. You know?"

I know it's in the Best Friend Doctrine to keep watch over your favorite girl, but I'm still a little miffed by this statement. *Of course* I've wondered the same thing. But then I remind myself that I *wrote a book* about him. That's kind of a big deal. Who wouldn't want to meet the person who wrote a book about you? That's why he called, and we've connected on a hundred levels since. Less than eighteen hours after actually meeting, we're easy friends. And there is no denying there's some super-hot sexual tension there. She can be as skeptical as she wants, but I'm taking it as it comes.

And as of right now, everything's coming along pretty darn well.

CHAPTER TEN
You Can Run, But You Can't Hide

"Thanks for meeting me," Niles says. He spreads out the blanket he asked me to bring and settles onto his back. "Seems pretty quiet out here. Nobody but me is stupid enough to run on a hot day like this."

I almost didn't find him. We're on the furthest trail from the park entry and the terrain to get here was a little rough. He'd found a clearing and settled in for an impromptu inspiration break. When he texted me to join him, my own creative fire was stoked and I couldn't imagine a single thing better than hanging out in the woods with my muse. I mean, please. Maybe I'd get some great ideas for Nash and Emily #2.

"I fucking despise writing lyrics sometimes," he whines, looking up through a canopy of leaves.

I shake my head in an attempt to dislodge the words I just heard.

"Seriously? Your lyrics are amazing." There is no way my muse struggles with lyrics. No way. They're too perfect. Too him. Too—seemingly—effortless.

"You write," he says, turning to look up at me. "Sometimes it flows, sometimes it doesn't. Right?" Just like at the hotel, he pats the spot to the left of him. "C'mere."

I plop down, but again, not too close.

"Somebody's shy today," he says with a smile. Of course, my face catches fire once again. And, of course, he notices it. "That's okay. It's cute."

He props himself up on his elbows, his chest and stomach creating a nice, hard, straight line. His shirt is so big, the back of it droops toward the blanket and through the oversized armholes I get a nice eyeful of his sides and back. His skin is smooth and flawless. Not a single freckle in sight. Ohmagaw.

"So, Nash was a pretty romantic guy," he says. "Did Emily ever get freaked out by that?"

Freaked out? By a romantic guy? Uh, no.

"Not once they got to know each other." I shoot him a knowing look.

"Do you think he ever felt like a pussy? You know, for being so soft?"

A pussy? My Nash? Not a chance!

"No, Niles, he didn't. Not ever. Nash is a guy's guy, all the way. But, shit, when you fall for someone, you tend to lose your mind a little, right? Emily had already lost it for Nash before she even met him. When they finally did meet, there was heat. No denying it. No tour or ex-lover or real-life situation could thwart that. He was touched that she dug him so much and that she could feel something so raw for him from afar. In real life, when they met, it was even better. So he turned to mush a little." I raise my eyebrows to punctuate my passionate little impromptu monologue. "It happens."

"Yeah. It does." Niles takes my right wrist, which I have all my weight on, and pulls it out from under me. There's nowhere for me to go but down. In an instant, I am inches from his face, my right elbow on the ground and my left arm draped across his chest.

"Do you think something like that is happening right now, Kallie?" he whispers.

I don't even have a chance to answer; it all happens so fast. One second, his head is rising, his lips definitely traveling straight toward mine. The next second, the rhythmic stomp of running shoes and a far-too-excited, "Kallie?!" halts everything.

I fling myself off him and stare up at our intruder. Once my eyes focus, I see it's Katherine Koch, the mom of Alana's best friend. We've gotten to be friendly over the past couple years ourselves, and like nearly every mom in our circle, she is very aware of my book.

"Katherine, hey!" I try my hardest to be casual, but there is definitely a very, very big elephant in this room. "Gorgeous day, right?"

"Yeaaaahhh," she says. Her eyes are no longer on me. At all. There's no hiding this. She's staring straight at Niles. Niles without a hat or sunglasses to hide behind because they're sitting on the blanket next to him. Oh my God, we are so busted.

"Um . . ." What do I do now? I guess I have no choice. "Katherine, this is . . ."

"Wow, *yeah*," she says, flinging her hand out toward Niles. "Huge fan!" Niles takes her hand and shakes it gently. He's in rock star mode, just like that. He's sitting up straighter and has that "look." It occurs to me just how natural and normal he is when it's just the two of us. I get a chill thinking about how I've gotten to see the "other" side of him.

"Thank you. Really nice to meet you. Sorry, I'm a kinda gross." He smiles his gorgeous smile and I'm pretty sure Katherine melts just like I do.

"You're fine, really," she gushes. "Can't wait for the new album. Hope it's soon." I think Niles nods, but this is all so surreal, I'm not really sure.

"I'll, um, leave you two alone. Great to meet you. And Kallie, give me a call sometime soon, okay?" Her eyebrows lift so high that for a second I think they're going to meet her hairline.

"Sure. And Katherine?" I gaze at her pleadingly. "Could you please keep this, you know, *discreet*?"

She looks at Niles again and then back at me. "Of course. Sorry to interrupt. Take care, guys."

***

"So, I'm wondering something," Niles says. He's just gotten out of my shower (Niles was in my shower! Presumably naked!) and is standing in front of me wearing yet another set of clothes, his hair damp and messy.

I know it's rude to blow him off when he's talking, but I finally cannot resist a second longer. Against my better adulting judgment, my hand makes a beeline toward his head and hovers by his ear. "May I?"

"May you what?"

"I'm obsessed with your hair. Where do you think Emily got *her* obsession for *Nash's* hair?"

He shakes his head and laughs. "You girls and your hair fetishes." He takes my hand and steers it the rest of the way. My fingers plunge in and are happier than any fingers have ever been. I shiver, completely embarrassed that touching someone's strands could make me so crazy.

"Is it everything you dreamed it would be?" he laughs.

"And more." My fingers don't want to stop, but keeping them in there much longer would border on awkward, so I reluctantly pull them out and swear never to wash my hands again. "Now, what is it you were wondering?"

"Yeah . . . so . . . I was at this hotel once," he says, walking toward the living room. I follow. "Not too long ago, actually." He pulls me onto the couch and sits very close. "It was pretty late, after the after-

55

party. I was settling in and before I turned on the TV, I heard something." He fixes his gaze on something across the room, though I can't tell what.

"Some hotels are more soundproof than others," he continues. "This one apparently was not. At first, I thought it was someone, you know, getting it *onnnn.*" He turns to me and winks. "But then I realized it was someone crying."

Oh, no.

"Sounded like a sweet girl, and it went on for quite a while. I felt really bad for her. I would like to think she had a good night, like, with some new friends and all. But why would someone who was happy get that sad?"

He turns to look at me. There's no question. He totally knows.

"She wasn't sad," I whisper.

"Then what was wrong, I wonder?" He's trying to look me in the eye, but now I'm the one staring across the room.

"She was *too happy*, I bet. She probably had a big night. Her new friends—one in particular—probably brought out a lot of passion and emotion in her. Plus, she probably gets extra emotional when she drinks." I pause. "*And*, I bet she didn't get to say a proper good-night to her friend, and she was worried she'd never see him again. That's the one thing that made her sad. I bet."

"So, you don't think her new friend did anything wrong?"

"Not one thing."

"That's good to know. I'm sure he'd be really upset if he knew he somehow made her sad."

I turn to him and tilt my head. God, what a sweetie.

"He should not worry about that," I whisper, taking his hand. "Sometimes girls just need a good cry. She's sorry, I'm sure, if she made her friend worry."

"As long as she's fine, he's fine."

"Good. Then everyone's fine. And they all live happily ever after."

"Sounds like a good ending for a story."

"Or maybe a great beginning."

CHAPTER ELEVEN
Promises, Inspiration, and Sleepless Nights

"As much as I would love to, we can't just go to a restaurant together. Especially around here. You'll be recognized for sure."

Niles pulls into the parking lot at his hotel and turns off my car. "But I *waaaaant* to," he whines. He sticks out his bottom lip and my heart breaks a little right there.

"Believe me, I don't want to leave you yet, either."

My eyes bug out when I hear myself say this, because, yeah, I've been guarded—shy, as Niles said earlier—off and on all day. But now that it's ten o'clock and our day together is wrapping up, I'm feeling bolder. And, hell, I *don't* want to leave him yet.

"You don't know anywhere quiet around here?" His voice is hopeful, but when I tell him I don't know this area well at all, we both silently admit that it's time to say our good-byes. I have the two-hour (for me) trip back home (in the dark! Ack!) and he needs to get a little bit of shut-eye since they're loading up at 4:30 a.m. to get back on the road.

"Thank you for taking me home with you today. It was great to feel normal. And even better spending the day with you." His phone buzzes, but he completely ignores it. He's barely touched it all day.

"Please. It was my pleasure."

Like, *really* my pleasure.

I suck in a breath and lean toward him, my forearms resting on the console between us, my hands dangling over his thigh. How I wish this console were not even a thing, not a barrier between us. How I wish Katherine Koch was not out running today and cursed with the worst timing in the history of ever. How I wish our lips would have met out on that trail, that they will now. How I wish I was bold enough to make a move. To lean in even further. To end this bizarre, amazing, unbelievable two days with the best ending I could think of.

Instead, I lean back and settle my hands back into my lap. "Thank you for indulging my fangirl crush, Niles." I cast him a quick sideways glance. "It was very, very sweet of you, and you're off the hook now. Tell your people you held up your end of the deal." Because that's what this was, right? A PR arrangement? I have to keep my head on straight and remember that.

Even though he just told me it was "even better" spending the day with me.

He turns to me, a serious look washing across his face. "I . . ." He looks out the window behind me, then pulls his eyes back toward me. "I honestly don't know what this was at first. And especially now. But I know this new 'friendship' of ours is far from over." My chest tightens.

"I am sincere about keeping you distracted this summer," he says, his voice turning a little weird. "So, you better plan on it."

He moves toward me, leans over that goddamn console, and rests his forehead against mine. "I'll talk to you soon. Drive safe." His lips are so close, mine instinctively pucker. But he pulls away, grabs his running bag and mini-cooler out of the back, and hops out. He waves at me through the window as I remain in the passenger seat, a muddled mess.

And just like that, he's gone.

***

When I finally arrive home, it's after midnight and I am exhausted, but energized at the same time. I want to sit and think about every single thing that's happened over the last twenty-four hours, but I am very inspired to put some ideas on paper for Book Two (and maybe even come up with a title so I can stop calling it Book Two). I remind myself that Niles did not win three Grammys by sitting around thinking about it, so I grab my laptop and prepare to settle in. If I commit to an hour of focused work, I'll reward myself with some daydreaming. Then, I'll head to bed and what? Carry on like none of this ever happened? What does tomorrow hold for me? After a whirlwind like this, where do I go from here? Back to normal? Has my life changed? Have I changed?

I ponder these questions as my email gears up. I open my inbox and am completely elated when the name at the tippy top is none other than Niles Russell. When I open up the message, there is a picture of us—the Tongue picture—staring back at me.

"Here's to a great summer ahead!" the email says. "xo, Niles."

I respond with a simple "<3" and press send.

I ignore every single one of my forty-seven other emails and get to work. After two hours, my butt hurts and my eyes are droopy, but I'm still typing. Two hours after that, the clock on my computer tells me it's just about time for Niles to be packing up to head back on the road. I grab my phone and take a picture of my laptop screen.

I text Niles the picture with the message: "Almost 5,500 words in. Thanks, muse! #amwriting" and he immediately responds with,

"Atta girl. You're amazing. #amimpressed"

Eek!

"Get some sleep now," he types. "One of us should."

"No sleep last night for you either?"

"I didn't have my napping partner." Winking emoticon.

"Baby, I'll nap with you anytime." Double winking emoticons.

"That's what I'm hoping." Even more winking emoticons. I squee right out loud, my heart bursting. "P.S. Why weren't you this flirty earlier today? lol"

As I consider this question, Niles answers it for me.

"Oh yeah. You're a word girl. But remember, no need to hide behind them. Not with me. Capeesh? (How the hell do you spell capeesh?)"

I laugh because, really, I have no idea how to spell it. But I make a note to find out and use it in Book Two.

"When will I see you again?" I type. "Because it won't be soon enough."

Shit, thirty seconds from now would not be soon enough.

"Hang tight. I'm figuring that out as we speak. Any days you're totally off the grid?"

Ha. Even if there were, I'd move mountains to change my plans. I miss my girls like crazy, but they're gone and other than working on Book Two and a couple freelance copywriting projects, I have no specific obligations all summer.

"Sounds pathetic, but I'm wide open. Not a single plan."

"Good. Then be flexible and be ready. Hope you're not as scared of flying as you are of driving."

"If I could have flown instead of driven yesterday, I would have. Believe me."

"I do. I was hoping you'd text to tell me you made it home safe."

He was?

"Glad all is well. Now get some rest. I mean it."

I promise him I will, but hey, I'm not the one who will be performing in front of thousands of people tonight. I can sleep all I want when I'm dead. For now, I have a book to write . . . and a rock star to fantasize over.

A rock star who wants to know my summer plans so he can figure out when we'll see each other next.

Holy. Freaking. Bleep.

CHAPTER TWELVE
Hits and Misses

"You know, it would be swell if you picked up your damn calls once in a while, Kallie."

A guy's voice is in my ear, but it's not the guy I want it to be . . . and I have no idea how it happened. I lift my head off the back of my couch and realize I had fallen asleep while writing. I'm sure when I heard my phone ring, I snatched it without thinking. I'm impressed I was coherent enough to at least say hello, but I'm crushed that it's Brad's voice I'm hearing instead of Niles's.

"Hi, Brad," I say, sitting up. "Great to hear from you." If "sarcastic" was an animate object, it'd be sitting on the couch next to me right now.

"Yeah, well, your girls wanted to talk to their mother, but since she doesn't answer her phone, that's proving impossible. I told them I'd try one more time, then they'll have to wait until we get back to my mom's. So thanks for finally picking up. Now I don't have to repair their broken little hearts."

"Gee, Brad, dramatic much?" I sigh. "I've had my phone nearby all weekend." "Then maybe you should answer it. Check your call records. See how many times we've tried. Five, at least. Since Friday night. It's now Sunday. So, in my book, that's pretty shitty phone monitoring."

I think back to my calls and, sure, I ignored a few (Katherine Koch's, for example), but none of them were from Brad's phone.

"I would never not pick up a call from the girls, Brad. Your phone number never once showed up all weekend. So ease up, all right?" My voice rises, despite my best attempts otherwise.

"I called from my mom's phone."

And there it is. That trap where he does something stupid, inexplicable, or otherwise nonsensical, but somehow pins it back on me to make me look like the bad parent. It's my favorite of his how-dare-you-leave-us, now-I'll-make-you-pay tactics. Not.

I take a deep breath and try to calm down. I hate how riled up I get every time I talk to him these days. It's so strange to me how we've gone from barely talking at all when we lived in the same house to talking often, and rarely in a controlled state.

"Okay. That's why I didn't pick up. It was a number I didn't recognize." I want to tell him to quit being a baby and cut me some slack and use his own damn phone for crying out loud, or *at least* leave a message, but instead I say, "I'm sorry. I miss the girls terribly and if I knew it was them trying to call, I'd have picked up."

"Yeah. Well, here they are." He ignores my apology and, of course, offers none of his own.

Alana gets on first and The Black Cloud of Brad instantly dissipates. It's so good to hear my baby girl's voice. We talk about everything they've done in the mountains since Friday and all they hope to accomplish yet today. She tells me she's turning nice and tan but that Jilly's sunburned and I curse Brad out in my head for not SPFing them up enough. We talk about how much we miss each other and I tear up thinking we still have eight weeks before we'll see each other again. I must have been crazy to agree to this setup, but at the time, it seemed like a good idea to let them enjoy a summer without flopping back and forth between Brad's house and mine. Now I'm not so sure.

I've considered flying down there midsummer for a few days, and now more than ever, I feel like that might be an excellent plan. After I talk to Jillian, I can hardly regroup. What mother allows her children to go away for ten weeks at a time without it being a necessity? I consider telling Brad to bring them back early, but I don't want to start a fight. I need to create a nice, solid case for why and when before I broach the subject with him, otherwise the battle will be lost before it begins. I hold in my emotions as I tell the girls to have fun, be safe, and call me on Monday night. They agree and we hang up. Free from upsetting their little ears, I let the tears flow.

I allow myself my second good cry of the last thirty-six hours, then haul my gross self off the couch and into the shower. When I emerge, I hear a knock at my door, which I am tempted to ignore but find way too intriguing not to check out. It's Sunday, early afternoon. Who could it possibly be? Thankfully, my apartment door has a peephole, and I am quiet enough on my feet to slink over and peer out without being detected.

When I look out, I do a double take. There is a handsome young man standing outside my door with a gigantic bouquet of flowers and a large envelope. I fling the door open, scaring the life out of the poor guy.

"Ms. Reagan?" He blinks.

"Yes?"

"These are for you." He holds them out and I try to grab the vase, but it's awkward and heavy and we do a really weird fumble dance.

"Here, I got it." He laughs. "Where would you like them?"

I lead him over to my table, where he sets them down with a *thunk*. He smiles and holds out the envelope. "This is for you, too.

65

Came by courier. Today is Sunday, so someone went through a lot of trouble to get this stuff to you." He winks.

Someone?

Oh, *someone.*

I peel open the envelope and find a travel itinerary, a concert ticket, and a VIP pass. A smile worthy of the Cheshire Cat spreads across my face. Yep, it's from *that* someone, all right.

I want so badly to tell the delivery guy who exactly "went through all this trouble," what it is, and how he just made my entire day. But Niles would probably want to keep this type of thing on the down low, and plus, I'm standing here in my robe with wet hair and no makeup. This harsh reality (bad hair! no makeup!) snaps me back and I reach for my purse.

"No, ma'am," Delivery Guy says. "The sender tipped us handsomely for this. You've got quite an admirer it seems." He winks again, and I'm thinking he's taking notes in order to impress some lucky lassie of his own someday.

"These are unbelievable." I motion toward the flowers. "The colors! The scent! They're just gorgeous."

Oh my God, why am I making small talk with this guy? I need to shoo him out so I can drool over this incredible moment in private.

"Uh, sorry to keep you. Thank you so much for coming on a Sunday." I jerk my head toward the door.

"It's my pleasure. I hope you enjoy your goodies." After a third wink, I start to question if maybe he has a nervous condition, but it doesn't make a damn bit of difference to me. I just need him gone. I usher him out and as he wishes me well, I close the door in his face and make a beeline for my arrangement.

It doesn't take long for me to make one very distinct realization: This is the exact arrangement—right down to the fillers—that Nash sent to Emily after their first date. And I know this is the exact arrangement because I spent a whole Saturday at a few different flower shops, creating my dream arrangement so I could accurately portray it in my book.

I dig between the blooms to unearth the card.

Who says dreams can't become realities? -NR

I go weak.

When I finally collect myself, I paw through the envelope and see that Niles wasn't kidding when he said to be flexible and be ready . . . because I am flying into Philadelphia tomorrow morning for a show that very same evening!

I honestly don't know what to do next. Do I pack? Do I call Sara? Do I text Niles? Do I scream?

Yes. Yes, I scream!

This cannot be real. I cannot possibly have just received an enormous floral arrangement from my rock star crush, who is now my friend, who I almost kissed, who is flying me to one of his concerts, plunking me down in the front row, and giving me a VIP pass so I can see him after the show. This is the most surreal thing I've ever experienced.

This is my book coming to life.

CHAPTER THIRTEEN
It's Go Time!

Sara nearly swerves off the road as she makes her way toward the airport.

"Quit texting and driving, Sar. I'd kind of like to actually *get* to the airport, you know?" I shoot her an annoyed look, to which she responds with an equally annoyed look.

"Dude, I'm using two hours of vacation time to haul your fangirl ass to the airport. You could be a little nicer."

"Sorry. I'm just crazy nervous." And I am. I barely slept one second last night. For whatever reason, the anticipation of seeing Niles tonight is even more chest-crushing than the first time. Maybe because this time I know what to expect. I know there will be sexual tension, I know we'll flirt, I know—I hope—we'll have a great time. It's like a second date that's not really a date. And I've always hated second dates. They invite a shit ton more pressure than a first date, by far.

"Kallie, you'll be fine. Just keep your head together."

"I don't know if I can. I'm a mess."

"Well, you *look* like a mess, too. You do plan to change and spruce up, right?"

Man, you gotta love honest best friends.

"Of course I do." I sigh. "Give me a break, though, okay? I have seriously not slept since last Wednesday."

"Well, get out your super-strength makeup and paint that shit on. You need it." She throws me an apologetic smile. "Will you have time to nap at the hotel before the show?"

My stomach squeezes at the mention of hotel naps. Sara still doesn't know about Niles's and my slumber party. I smile inwardly at my juicy little secret.

"Probably not. I have to call Lucy. She emailed and asked me to call her today."

Sara waves her hand in dismissal. "Psh, agents. Such nuisances."

I laugh because I know she is totally joking. Throughout my whole book publishing process, she has been most enthralled with Lucy and the agent/author relationship. She gets an absolute kick out of the fact that I have to "take a call from my agent" and says it sounds so Hollywood. I love that she loves it. Sara can be really hard to impress.

She wheels into the short-term parking space and prepares to hop out.

"You don't have to come in, Sar. Get back to work. I'll call you later. And thank you."

"You sure you have everything? I mean, you did pack condoms, right?"

"What? No!" She is so completely ridiculous sometimes.

"Kallie, good Lord. Do I have to mother you, or what? The responsible thing would be to pack condoms. Though I'm sure Niles has a hefty stash, a proper lady brings her own."

"Niles and I are not having sex tonight." I groan. "What are we going to do, bang it out in a bathroom or something?"

Sara's eyebrows raise, intrigued. That is exactly the type of thing she would do. Frankly, though I'm normally a romantic-love-session-in-a-bed kind of girl, I have to admit that shagging Niles in a bathroom doesn't sound like a horrible idea.

"I shall not respond to that," she says, leaning back into her seat. "Okay, you have a great time. If it is indeed 'your time' tonight, enjoy yourself, but be smart. Promise?" She turns to look at me and grabs my hand.

"I really don't think it will be 'our time,' but if it is, then yes, I'll be careful. Promise." I let go of her hand and slip out of the car. She waves at me as I grab my bags. I salute her back and head toward the airport entrance.

It's go time, baby!

***

The hotel suite (yes, I said *suite*) is huge. The décor is stunning. The view is even better. And once again, I'm hit with a this-can't-be-real moment. My eyes flit around the room, taking it all in, and eventually land on an exact duplicate of the arrangement Niles sent me yesterday. I rush over to it and grab the card.

Didn't want you to miss out on the one at home, so here's another. -NR

Seriously?

On the bed is a greeting card with scribbly handwriting that can only be Niles's. I've never seen anything he's written other than his autograph, but the spastic way the letters are linked together almost perfectly reflects his stage style.

Welcome to an awesome summer. Hope you're up for living the rock star life for a little while. AND, I hope you're up for some serious napping! Save me a spot tonight—maybe I can sneak in later. After-party first, though. See you there!

If there were anyone in the room with me right now, they would no doubt find hilarity in the expression on my face. Niles Russell wants to hop in bed with me tonight. He wants to sneak in after the after-party. Oh. My. Gawd. Maybe this *will* be "our time."

If Sara knew this, she'd flip. But I can't tell her. Not yet. I have to keep my head together and calling her would most definitely *not* be conducive to that.

I should definitely call Lucy, though. But this bed is so soft and the pillows look so cozy. And I am so tired. I flop down. *Just for a minute*, I promise myself. An hour later, my phone alerts me that a driver will be here to pick me up at six. Which means I need to get a move on. Oops.

I wonder why I haven't heard from Niles. I check my phone to make sure I didn't miss any of his texts, and indeed, I haven't. I wonder what he does all day when they get to a new town. Is he here in the hotel? Where and when does he eat? Where does he get ready? How does all this happen away from the watchful eyes of the fans? I make a mental note to ask him some of these things, then head to the bathroom to get myself in order.

When I walk in, I almost faint. There, on the mirror, written in red lipstick, is a note that says, *Can't wait to see you tonight*. It's a simple message, but it's poignant nonetheless . . . because it's the exact same message Nash left for Emily on *her* hotel room bathroom mirror one night.

***

"Are you drunk?" Niles asks. As promised, he snuck into my room after the after-party and is lying on the bed next to me, to my left. Except for in my car, every other time we've been next to each other for any length of time, he's always been on my right. So, I'm enjoying this new viewpoint. It feels like I'm looking at a painting from a different angle.

"No. Maybe a little. You?"

"I don't know. I should be. We drank a lot. But my head seems kinda straight. I'm not sure I like that." He puffs out his cheeks and keeps his eyes fixed on the ceiling.

"What do you mean?"

"Because it's a whole lot easier to make a move when you're messed up." He turns over on his side to look at me. "We're in bed together, Kallie. Most people would be doing a lot more than just lying next to each other, right?"

I nod and swallow hard. "So, why aren't we?"

"I don't know. I want to. And I'm pretty sure you want to. But, it's not time yet." He rolls back over onto his back, takes my left hand with his right, and puts my hand on his chest. "Feel that?" His heart is thumping wildly, as though he's just gotten off stage.

"Yes," I whisper.

"That's not normal for me." He laces his fingers through mine and extends his arm. My hand is now resting against his right thigh and is dangerously close to *there*. All I would have to do is stretch out my fingers and scoot them over less than six inches and I'd get a handful of awesome.

"Hm. I have a hard time believing someone like little ol' me could make Niles Russell's heart go pitty pat. How many girls have you been with? Like millions?"

"Ha. Less than you think."

"Fewer."

"Huh?"

"You've been with *fewer* than I think." I smile at him when he looks at me.

"Really? You have to correct my grammar during a moment like this?" he laughs. "See? That right there is why my heart is thumping. You're like no other, Kallie Reagan."

He turns over again and smooths my hair with his left hand. I allow myself to stare at him and really take him in. He's not a traditional beefcake handsome guy at all, but he's incredibly handsome in his own quirky guy-next-door way. We are so close that, if I had any kind of balls, I'd only have to move inches to initiate a kiss. But I don't. I'm paralyzed and mesmerized. I close my eyes as he continues playing with my hair.

"You falling asleep on me?" he asks, his voice soft.

"Of course not." But his touch is so gentle and rhythmic and he has me so relaxed, I actually might be.

"You can. I know you're tired. You worked your ass off writing the other night and now I'm imparting my night owl ways on you."

"I love your night owl ways. I love pretty much everything about you."

He freezes.

Oops. Somebody just got spooked.

"Sorry. I didn't mean . . ."

"It's okay," he says, stroking my hair again. "I love your honesty. And I love when you don't hold back." He inhales deeply. "You don't feel like crying tonight, do you?"

"Absolutely not."

"Good. That's good. Because that really sucked. When I figured out it was you next door and I put the pieces together . . ."

"Shhh." I let my eyes drift open and discover he's staring right at me. "Pretend that never happened, okay? It was an emotional day, but it was nothing you did wrong. I promise."

"Someone sweet like you should never have to cry."

I don't mean to, but I shrink back from him a bit. Sure, his words are genuine and kind, but all I can do is think about all the times he's called me sweet. Or cute. He's never called me hot or sexy or any of that. What about the other girls—though "fewer than" I think—he's

73

been with? Were *they* cute? What's Robbyn like? Is she *sweet* or is she freaky? Does one turn him on more than the other? Probably so. All guys like freaky chicks, don't they? The sexier the better? I'm just sweet. And cute. I can't be Niles's type. Not at all.

I roll away from him and onto my back. I think about stripping down, right here, right now. That's not something a sweet girl would do. I think about straddling him, pressing my chest against his, covering his mouth with mine. That's probably what his other "lady friends" would do. That's probably what he likes, and what he expects.

But I can't do it.

"Do you think we'll ever kiss, Niles?" I can hardly believe the words escape my lips, but it's something I am dying to know, dying to *do*.

"Most definitely. Just not yet." He pulls me closer, burying my face in his chest. He rubs my back for what seems like a millennium, then kisses the top of my head. "There you go." He laughs. "Our first kiss. Well, second, really. Because I've already kissed your cheek."

"Hilarious," I say, nudging his arm. "But seriously, though. Thanks for tonight. This whole life of yours—it's pretty amazing."

"Sometimes it's amazing just to be normal. I feel so normal right now. You do that to me—*for* me. So, thank *you*."

"My pleasure." I yawn. "What time is it, anyway? Do you have to go?"

"I should." My heart sinks. "But I'm not going to. I'll stay with you. I have until five. Now, sleep." He nuzzles his chin into my hair, and in an instant, we are asleep.

And an instant later, it's five o'clock . . . and he's gone.

CHAPTER FOURTEEN
What Do You Want From Me?

I knew this would happen. Freaking knew it. My life is a whirlwind for five days, I see and talk to Niles almost nonstop, we get close and then closer, then bam! It's a new week and I haven't seen him at all.

"I miss you!" I whine, staring at his pic on my phone. "When am I going to see you again?" We talk daily—sometimes multiple times per day—but this stretch of their tour schedule is particularly heavy and they go from one stop to the next, leaving the stage, having a one-hour meet and greet with fans, then heading onward. No after-parties, no chance for me to hang with him. I'm a mess.

I've been trying to work on Book Two, but my inspiration has waned. I'm starting to think having Niles as a muse was easier before I knew him because I could just project characteristics onto him without knowing whether or not they were accurate. Now, whenever I try to write a line or a scene with Nash, I think more about the real Niles than Nash—whom I actually created and hence "know" a lot better than Niles. It's all kinds of confusing and it's making things pretty difficult.

To my delight, Niles is turning out to be every bit as romantic and caring as Nash. But he's also a bundle of contradictions. *Yes*, I want to have sex with you, but no, I'm not going to do it yet—even though I'm a rock star and rock stars are known for that exact type of behavior. *No*, I don't want to ever make you cry, but it's been a week since we've seen each other and now all you do is mope . . . and cry. *Yes*, we'll kiss someday, but not yet—even though I almost kissed you on the running trails when I was at your house, being "normal."

I mean, what if we *would* have kissed that day? Would that have been it? Or would we have gone back to my apartment and done more? Even if not, with that first kiss out of the way, would we kiss every time we see each other now? Would that night in Philly have been our first roll in the hay? So many questions messing with my mind I can hardly stand it.

And the irony of it all? Niles's promise to me was that he'd distract me from the girls this summer. Now, it's my conversations with the girls that distract me from Niles.

They're having a ball in North Carolina. And even though we miss each other a ton, I think being away is getting easier for them. Brad's mom has them constantly on the go, even taking summer gymnastics classes at a local dance studio and cooking classes from a friend of a friend.

Of course, they have no idea what my life is like back here and I don't dare share any of that info with them or Brad. Brad is already so bitter over my book for reasons spanning from its success (hey, it's *hard* to get a book published) to the obsessive passion and time dedication it takes to fuel a project like that, to the fact that it was about another guy. If he ever found out I actually met and hung out with Niles, oh boy! But the more I think about it, the more I know he will someday find out. After all, Katherine has already called and texted multiple times to get the scoop on how/why Niles was in town with me, how we met, and what our relationship status is ("just friends" will not fly with her—not after what she saw on those trails).

I've ignored her completely, which is probably only fueling the fire. With tongues wagging like they do in this town, I'm surprised the whole world doesn't already know.

As soon as I hang up from the girls, my phone springs right back to life with the text message I've *so* been waiting for.

"How does a trip to Beantown sound? On Wednesday? We have a little breather. Didn't think we'd be spending the night there, but now I guess we are. Flights are confirmed, concert ticket is ready, VIP pass is yours. All you have to do is say yes." *Pause.* "PLEASE say yes. I miss you."

He misses me?! Did I just read that right? As much as *I've* missed *him*, I've never actually come out and said that to him for fear of sounding like a lovesick fangirl. Even though I've been Mopey Maggie over here, he'd never know it because I always try to be full of sunshine and unicorns whenever we talk. Sure, I've told him multiple times that I can't wait to see him and hang out again, and that I'm dying to watch him kill it in front of a crowd once more, etc., but I know he's under a lot of stress and he's probably tired. He doesn't need some crazy fan whom he's befriended blathering on and on about missing him when he's out there doing his job of entertaining the masses.

In a not-so-surprise move, my stomach squeezes tight and so does my heart. "I. Miss. You. Too." I type. "And my answer is HELL, YES!"

"Awesome! I know I've been busy, but you've seriously been on my mind. A lot. I can't wait to see you. Thanks for saying yes."

Suddenly, all the time I've spent in a funk over the last week seems so insignificant. I am alive again, and Wednesday can't come soon enough. I mentally make plans to hit the gym hard over the next two days and realize a trip to the mall for a sassy new shirt is definitely in order.

"Thank you for asking me. I was wondering when I'd ever see you again. I was losing hope." Sad face.

"Ha, don't give up on me. I told you I'd keep you distracted this summer. This past week was a bit sucky, but it's always like that on the East Coast. After NYC on Friday and Saturday, things will ease up."

New York! Oh man, have I ever let myself fantasize about joining him there, too. I'd stay at some awesome hotel, meet Lucy for lunch on Friday, and swing by my publishing house with her to say hello to the very people who manage my writing career. I'd go to both concerts and after-parties, and maybe even crash at Niles's apartment for part of Saturday, since that's their home base and Niles keeps a place there. Then I realize there is no way, no how, that would ever happen so I push that idea out of my mind and focus on what I know: I'm going to Boston on Wednesday!

"I'll never give up on you," I type. "I seriously, seriously cannot wait to see you again. I really have missed you a lot."

It takes him a minute to respond, but finally, he types, "Why, Kallie? Why do you miss me? Because I'm a rock star? Because I'm a hot mess that's fun to fuck with? Because my life is a whirlwind and it gives you good inspiration for your characters? Tell me why you miss me so much. I seriously want to know."

What?!

I shake my head, stunned. I don't know what he's getting at, but this is not a conversation that can be covered over text. Without thinking at all, I hit the "call" button and hear the ringing tone before his voice.

"Sorry," he answers. "That was totally assholish of me. I'm just having a freak-out day. It happens. I'm sorry."

"Niles. Don't you dare think for one second that I like or miss you because you're a rock star. I learned of you because of your talent, yes, but there are a lot of talented people out there. You are so much more than your talent."

There's nothing but silence on Niles's end, so I race on. "You're a complicated motherfucker," I laugh, "but you are so amazing. In so many ways. I feel like when we're together, you're actually you, am I right? I mean, in addition to all the laughs we've shared and the fun we've had just hanging out, we've slept together twice. And by 'slept,' I mean we've actually *gone to sleep*. You haven't even tried to bang me yet and you definitely could, any time, any place. I would not be the one to say no. So, what gives? Why haven't you tried? What do you really want with *me*, Niles Russell?"

Not gonna lie, I'm a little shocked by what just came out of my mouth. I'm about as nonconfrontational as they come. But hey, this has been on my mind and if he's demanding answers, I'm going to, too.

"I don't fucking know, Kallie. I know that you wrote a book about me and I know that for whatever reason you find me interesting and I know that now that I'm getting to know you, I find you interesting, too. But beyond that, I don't freaking know anything. I know I want to screw your brains out—trust me—but I don't want to hurt you because, really, I'm a piece of shit and you deserve better. Yet, I can't tear myself away from you, which is stupid because throughout my whole life I've perfected the art of tearing myself away from just about everything. No promises, no regrets. So yeah, I guess this is fucked up all around and I don't know anything except that I'm going to be really damn happy when I look out into the crowd on Wednesday and see you there, front and center. Then, I'll be even happier when I can glue myself to your side at the after-party, even though the guys are wondering what the fuck my problem is and why I'm not behaving like my normal self."

"The guys are noticing?" There are so many points of this

conversation to focus on, yet I choose this one. Why? I don't know. It seems important.

"Yeah. They think I've lost my freaking mind. I kind of hate that they think that, so that should say something." He pauses. "*Plus*, I'm starting to get crap for how long it's taking me to write this next album. So I'm a bit of a head case right now. You'll have to excuse me."

Ummmm . . .

"Did you just say you're writing a new album while you're *out on the road*?"

"Yeah. I mean, we're on fire, right? Overnight success, or so they say. They have no idea how long we've been at this, but none of that matters. One great album demands another, and within quick succession. If we wait too long, we're irrelevant, just like that. We signed up for this. There's no turning back."

This is absurd. I cannot imagine writing while out on the road. I tried eking out a few paragraphs of Book Two while on the plane to Philly and I couldn't put two cohesive sentences together. How and why is he expecting to write an album while *touring*? How can his mind even go where it needs to when he's on a bus or in a hotel room or on stage in front of thousands of people? Talk about an unreasonable expectation.

"Wow. I'm sorry you're going through this, Niles. I had no idea." What comes out of my mouth next kills me, but it seems like the right thing to do and say. "Maybe it's best if I stay away. You have a job to do and I don't want to be a distraction."

"Fuck that. You just told me you wouldn't give up on me!"

"I'm not giving up. I just don't want to mess up your . . . whatever."

"Exactly. I don't even know what it is you're messing up. So, let's pretend this conversation never happened and just get your adorable little ass here on Wednesday and we'll go from there. Yes?"

There it is again. Adorable. Sweet. Cute. *That's* why he hasn't jumped me. My gears turn. I hatch a plan. I can all but bet that after Wednesday night, Niles's confusion will disappear and we will be napping partners no longer.

Nope, we'll be so much more.

CHAPTER FIFTEEN
Night Skies and Fireworks

What the heck is this place? I'm standing in some hallway that is backstage, but not. It's like some underground alley and it's dark, and quite frankly, I'm a little freaked out. But Zeke the bouncer—whom I now consider a friend—insists that this is where Niles requested I wait for him. So I wait. And wait.

I hear all the usual commotion and relax a little because I must not be too far from the action. After a bit, Zeke shows up with a six-pack of chocolate-coffee craft beer and a bottle opener and tells me to crack one open while I wait.

"Thanks, I need this. Any idea how much longer?"

"Not long. Niles is whipping through the hellos. He seems pretty anxious to see you." He looks me up and down. "And I can see why. You look extra hot tonight. But don't tell Niles I said that." He winks.

I'm thankful for that shot of confidence because I feel a little weird. I've always worn short shorts and shoulder-bearing/girls-enhancing shirts to each concert, but this time, I upped the ante a little. I have on a super short, tight gray skirt and a citrine-colored tank top that hugs the ladies oh so well. My hair is a little more rock star than I usually wear it and I have more makeup on than normal. I needed a punch of boldness today, so I figured dressing the part was in order. We'll see if it helps.

As Zeke walks away, I drain my beer and think about how awesome it was to see Niles doing his thing tonight. It's hard to imagine he's going through any stress at all. When he's up on stage, he is one thousand percent there. He owns it. There is not one glimmer of self-doubt, self-depreciation, or self-loathing (I still can't believe he called himself a piece of shit. What was *that* about?). He works that stage and he works the crowd, bantering back and forth as though he's having one giant conversation with ten thousand people at a time.

I'd run out of fingers if I tried to count how many times we made eye contact during the show tonight. We held hands for a few seconds when he reached straight for me, and his grasp was gentle at first, with a tight squeeze at the end. The girl next to me playfully nudged my shoulder with hers and mouthed, "Lucky!" before pouting and turning her attention back to the stage. Tonight, I was the only person in the crowd that he touched—the only one. That girl is right. I am lucky.

Just as I pop open another beer, which is heavy but super delicious and will probably have me drunk after just one more, I hear my favorite voice in the world.

"Have one to spare?"

It's as if it were the first time I'd seen him all over again. My heart jumps to my throat, while my stomach plummets to the ground. I can't take my eyes off that face, that smile, that slender body swimming in a vintage Van Halen concert T-shirt with a button-up haphazardly layered over top. I feel like I'm in one of those hokey commercials where the couple runs through a field of wildflowers and slams into each other in a dramatic hug, just as the music crescendos.

If I'm being honest, I'm saying that I had no idea how this would go. Ever since our little unexpected convo on Monday, I've been a bit, shall we say, on edge. On one hand, I'm kind of pissed over his outburst. How dare he accuse me of caring for him only because he's a rock star? But on the other hand, I feel sorry for him, since he probably has people (girls) doing that to him all the time.

Still, I feel like our relationship (can I call it that?) is different. I'm never, ever fake around him. Sometimes reserved, sure, but never fake. And if he's fake around me, he's putting up a good front, because I can tell instantly when he's switched from Normal Niles into Rock Star Niles. Maybe he has another layer under there I don't know about, or maybe he's a complete poseur, but I just don't think so, and I'm generally a pretty good judge of character.

I've spent the last two days thinking this through, and even though he ended our conversation Monday with a request to pretend it never happened, something like that is a little hard to ignore. So, I wonder if he's done that? Or is it still on his mind as much as it is mine? As he walks toward me, I try to read him . . . and all I see is a genuine smile and sparkly eyes that betray anything other than legit happiness.

In an instant, his body is pressing into mine and his arms are squeezing me tight. My face gets buried in his shirt and his familiar scent makes me completely weak. For a moment, I wonder how he does laundry on the road and how he gets everything to always smell the same. But when he whispers in my ear, any thoughts about anything at all completely disappear.

"You do not even know how happy I am to see you," he says. "I'm so sorry I was such a prick. You didn't deserve that."

"It's okay," I whisper. "I thought we were going to forget it even happened."

"I couldn't." Hearing him say this makes me happy. Not that I'm interested in hashing everything out right here, right now, but I'm relieved to know he hasn't just pushed it out of his head.

He pulls back from me a bit, keeping his hands on my bare shoulders. "I freaking hate that I hurt you. I said I didn't ever want to hurt you, but then that's exactly what I did. And I'll probably say it again, then I'll probably do it again. It's not on purpose. I have good intentions. Usually. It's just that I really, truly am a piece of shit."

"You are not a piece of shit," I say, looking up at him.

"You have no idea."

He hangs his head for a moment, and in move so bold I totally shock myself, I tilt his chin up so he's looking at me and I say, "Well, it just so happens I love shit." I raise my lips toward his and finally—finally!—they connect and neither of us pulls away.

I feel our electricity in every single cell of my body. My vision is nothing but white light and gold fireworks. My torso is tight and prickling with energy. Out of respect for Niles's germophobe ways, I'm careful not to use my tongue. But even without it, our kiss is the stuff dreams are made of. His hand plunges into my hair and my arms wrap tighter around his waist. This feels better than I could have ever imagined, and if it's even possible, I press myself even closer to him.

After ages of being absolutely outside of my own body, he pulls away. "So, uh, *that* happened." He shakes his head and a huge smile takes over his face.

"Yeah. It did." My brain cells are like a heap of mashed potatoes right now, each one of them good for nothing. If someone asked me my name, I don't think I'd even get it right. As cliché as it sounds, I'm completely weak. I lean into him for support.

"Let's get out of here," he says, taking my hand. "I have a driver ready for us."

Whoa, we're leaving? Holy crap, is this it?

"No after-party?"

Gah! If this is it, I'm ready. I am *so* ready. But still.

"Not tonight. Just us." He looks at me with big eyes. "Trust me."

I nod my head and follow as he pulls me along by the hand. At this point, I'd follow him anywhere. If he wants to lead me into some catacombs of death, hey, I'll go. Lead me to an airplane where we'll parachute into the darkness? Sure, why not? I'd even get behind the wheel and drive down a damn highway right now, as long as I'm with him.

When we get to the car—a black Escalade—he nods to the driver and pulls me into the seat next to him. He holds my hand with one of his and runs the fingers of his other hand up and down my arm. My tummy butterflies rage so hard I can hardly breathe, but I feel relaxed at the same time. This is blissful.

"I love Boston," he says. "You ever been here?"

"Nope." I don't want to move an inch because I don't want to disrupt our comfy little people-heap, but I also want to turn around to look at him. If I do, I'll be tempted to kiss him again, though. Is that bad? I'd feel kind of weird smooching in front of a stranger. Or would I? I try to turn just a bit, but decide I'm much more comfy as is, so I stay put.

"You okay?" he asks.

"Never better."

He squeezes my hand and settles his head against mine.

I don't dare ask where we're going, because if it's to a hotel, there will be no dancing around what's coming next. I hear him breathing next to me and can't help but think about how that breath just carried him through almost two hours of singing his brains out, running up and down the stage, jumping, bouncing, and belting out every perfect syllable. It's staggering to me that the person who just entertained thousands of people is now sitting so close I can hear his breath. Talk about bizarre.

We pull into a drive that seems to lead toward a park. Though it's beautiful, it's not quite what I expected. I don't know if I'm relieved or disappointed. Maybe a little of both.

"C'mon." He pulls me across the seat and out the door. "Over here. I hope you like it."

He brings my hand to his lips for a quick kiss, then guides me over to a blanket spread out on the bank, strewn with rose petals and lined with tea light candles. Holy swoon.

"Are you serious right now?" I breathe. On the corner of the blanket, I see a wine bucket with a bottle already chilled and opened. There are two glasses nearby, and a small cooler filled with beer. I look at him with tears in my eyes. "This seems a little familiar."

"I one-upped Nash, though." He nods toward the cooler. "Nash forgot the beer." He winks, then pulls me into him. "You like?"

"I don't like. I love." I don't mean for it to, but a tear slips out. Niles wipes it away, then kisses the spot he just wiped.

"That's not a sad tear, right?"

"No way."

"Good." He smiles at me, then looks up at the sky. "Do you ever look at the stars and think of someone you dig?"

Like probably every other lovesick teen, of course I've done this before, but not in years and years. I shake my head. "No, I guess I don't."

"You don't?" His voice is incredulous. "I figured that's totally something you would do."

"Do you do it?"

"I did. Robbyn and I used to do it all the time. Mostly during our last tour. She didn't travel with us as much then because she had so much other stuff going on." He looks out over the water. "I don't do it anymore."

He shrugs and I wonder why on God's green earth he chose *this* moment to bring up Robbyn. Seems like a bit of a buzzkill, no? I also wonder why I haven't seen her at any of the shows I've been at. It's my understanding she goes everywhere with them. She's like their traveling personal assistant or something. (Yippee.)

"Where's Robbyn been?" I ask. "I haven't seen her."

"I don't think you'd know her if you saw her. Any pics you've seen of her are probably old. She looks completely different. She's gained some weight, dyed her hair, wears tons and tons of makeup. Not the same girl, for sure."

"You do that to her?" I'm joking, of course, but the way he reacts makes me realize I hit the nail on the head.

"Told you I was a piece of shit."

Do I really want to go there? I'm not sure if I do. Here, just inches in front of us, is the Charles River. Just inches behind us is a blanket strewn with rose petals. Talking to Niles about his ex-girlfriend does not seem to fit this scene. I'd much rather be canoodling. Yet, it's starting to seem like he brought this up for a reason. Maybe there's something he wants to get off his chest.

"So . . . where *has* she been?" I guess if this question is answered sufficiently—as in, she and I can't stand to be within twenty miles of each other anymore, so she's moved to Timbuktu—I'll let it all go. The ball is in his court.

"She's around. She was there tonight. And the last time you were there, in Philly."

"She was?!" This is monumental to me. Tonight, he snuck me away, but in Philly, he was like a tumor on me the entire time. Did she see us? I think back and try to remember a cute girl that maybe was a little chubby and wore lots of makeup. No one in particular stands out. There was a girl that was with Jase a lot, but I swore she had light brown hair. Was that her?

88

"So, she's . . . seen us together?" My breath catches as this question comes out. I don't know why I feel so weird about this. If they're broken up and we're—I don't even know what we are—what's the big deal? There shouldn't be one. But yet I feel so dirty.

"She has, yes. I thought you should know that. That's kind of why I brought this up. I wanted to get it out of the way so we could, you know, move on."

Well, this isn't the most opportune time to bring it up, but okay. I guess I should be happy he's willing to share this with me. Maybe this somehow validates our "togetherness?" Maybe?

"Is she taking it okay?"

"Most definitely not. Again, that's why I brought it up. She's not, how do I say this nicely, particularly stable right now." He pauses and chews his lip for a moment. "She came up behind me when I was texting you the other day, Kallie. I didn't know she was there . . . until I heard the camera on her phone. I think she snapped a pic of my screen when I had your number up." He wrinkles his nose. "I'm super sorry, but if you get any nasty texts, consider this your fair warning. Just ignore her. Okay?" He looks at me hopefully.

I'm really not sure what to say. I obviously don't know their situation nor do I fully understand the reason behind their breakup (a couple blogs reported they split amicably because they simply "no longer fit"). I really don't love the idea of being a thirty-something woman caught in a high school jealousy-type situation, but I also would beat down any girl who stood in my way of being with Niles. And if Robbyn even tries to do that, how am I supposed to ignore her?

"Kallie? I know what you're thinking. I can tell by the look on your face." I squint my eyes. "She's harmless. And we're through. I swear."

I honestly feel like I've been transported back to the ninth grade.

I've never even been face-to-face with the girl, but the thought of her history with Niles drives me mad. "It's fine," I lie. "I won't let her get to me."

Unless she tries to get to you.

CHAPTER SIXTEEN
Let's Get It On

"Water: love it or scared of it?" Niles sets down his beer, takes my hand, and walks me toward the edge of the bank. I guess he's hoping I love it. Which, thankfully, I do, or this would get really awkward, really fast.

"Love it, for sure. I'm a Cancer, born under a water sign. You're a Pisces, so you're a water, too."

"I am?" Niles looks at me, fascinated. I never know if my obsession with astrology will freak people out or intrigue them. It's usually a mixture of both.

"Yep. Which is not terribly surprising, since many creatives are waters." Niles's eyes narrow and he shoots me a look that says, *Go on.*

"It's said that writers, actors, musicians . . . people like us . . . we help make sense of the human experience via our art." Niles blinks a big blink, then moves so he's standing behind me. He brings his arms around front and pulls me in tight. I flash back to the first night we met, when he did this very same thing. I decide this is one of my favorite ways to be around him. I feel so close.

"It makes sense, right?" I continue. "You tell stories through lyrics. I tell stories through, well, stories. It's really us trying to capture what most of mankind is feeling, but we get the added bonus of putting our own personal stamps on those stories—telling them through our viewpoint or our warped way of thinking, or whatever."

Niles shifts. "That's exactly what it is. So few people understand that." His voice turns to a whisper, his lips right outside my ear. "But you do. *You* understand." His right hand moves my hair, while his left arm pulls me even tighter against him. His breath is on my neck, then his lips land on my shoulder, soft and warm. He works his way up my neck, kissing me softly, his hand moving up and down my arm.

Just when I think my legs will give out and I'll plummet straight into the water, Niles pulls me onto the blanket and positions himself over me, half leaning on the blanket, half atop me. He smooths the hair away from my face and looks into my eyes.

"You are so beautiful," he says. "Not just your face and your body, but your soul, too." He leans in and kisses me lightly on the mouth. "Out of all the people I've met in this crazy life of mine, I dare say you know me best. Already." He leans in again and this time his lips are much stronger. Our mouths move in sync and any sweet, gentle kisses are left behind in favor of powerful, passionate ones. Before long, I feel his tongue on mine and my head and heart nearly explode. We kiss for what seems like forever, and by the time we're finally through, Niles is completely on top of me, the weight of his hips pressing against mine.

"As you can see," he says, rolling off me and onto his back, "I'm ready for a whole lot more." He takes my hand and puts it *there*, and yep, he is indeed ready for show time (which I already knew because it was pretty evident while he was on me). "But . . ."

I already know where this is going. "Not yet."

"Do you agree?" He looks at me with sincerity, but honestly, I don't know if I agree. Are we still at "not yet" because we're in a park and this is not the right place to do it? Or is it because we're not far enough into our relationship? That doesn't seem right. People have one-night stands all the time. And though I'm not one of those people, it seems kind of safe to assume that we're already well beyond one-night-stand status.

I roll my head to the side so I'm looking away from him. There's really no good way to answer this without flat-out lying, so I take a deep breath and let 'er rip.

"No, actually I don't agree. Not one bit." I think about my outfit tonight. The hair. The makeup. Every bit of that was carefully planned to give me a sense of confidence I don't always have.

So, I swallow my nerves and run with it.

"I want you *so* bad, Niles. I want to be as close to you as I possibly can. I want you on top of me, inside me, under me, whatever. I want to experience every bit of you, without abandon. I want that right now, and we've clearly got something special going here, so I don't know what's with the wait. Sorry if I sound brazen, but you asked. And that's the God's honest truth."

I drag my head back so I can see his face. His eyes are huge and his smile matches.

"I want that, too," he whispers, running his fingers along my collarbone.

"Then why aren't we running toward the car right now?"

"Because," he says slowly. "I don't want to hurt you. And if we go there, I'm afraid that's exactly what will happen."

I drop my head back on the blanket and focus on the millions of stars above us. The stars that are bearing witness to a boner-sporting, red-blooded man shooting down a very willing sexy-times participant. *I'm sorry you have to see this, stars. I don't get it either.*

"Niles," I sigh, turning back to him, "I appreciate how gentlemanly you're being right now, but let's not forget that I'm a divorced mom of two who is, you know, completely conscious of her big-girl decisions. You don't need to protect me from whatever pain you think you'll cause. I can handle you." I punch him lightly in the arm just to lighten things up.

He doesn't smile and he doesn't laugh. Instead, he sighs before he picks a fuzz off the blanket and drops it onto the grass behind him.

"I shouldn't be telling you this, but here's the deal." He looks at me quickly before dropping his eyes to search for another fuzz. "For many years, I've told myself, 'No promises, no regrets.' As in, if you don't promise anyone anything, you can't regret it when you don't fulfill those promises." He sits up straight and pulls me up with him, nestling close enough so I can drop my head onto his shoulder.

"I am in a dangerous place with you, Kallie Reagan. I feel like I want to make all kinds of promises to you, but I know I can't. And I shouldn't. I did the same thing to poor Robbyn and look at her now. I can't do that to you, too."

"I'm not Robbyn." I have no idea what point I'm trying to make with that statement, but I feel like I need to counter him somehow.

"So true. You are far from Robbyn. Night and day. But you're both good people and I know what I'm capable of and I don't want that for you." He positions himself so he can look right at me. "Listen, I totally get it if you want to tell me to take a hike. But I hope you don't. I'm already more into you than I've ever been with any other girl—Robbyn included—which is super, super weird for me. I hate it kind of, but I love it, too. You're bringing out some weird shit in me. Part of me wants to go all-in, but the other part of me—the part that knows myself too well—says to hang tight. So, I hope you can hang tight a little longer, too."

"Till when?" I'm sure this sounds childish, but seriously, is this something he'll ever overcome? Or will he always hold me at arm's length? If it's going to take some act of God to get him to open his heart—or at least his zipper—then what's the point of all this?

"I think we'll both know. Until then, can we just keep having fun? I mean . . . for fuck's sake, I have something big to ask you. This really is big for me, so maybe this is a sign, I don't know."

"*Ohh-kay?*"

"Will you come to New York this weekend? You can fly in Thursday night or Friday morning. Maybe you can make arrangements to meet up with your agent or your people or whatever. Maybe do a last-minute book signing or something. Then, come to the show on Friday. We'll party hard after. I'll go home to my apartment that night. You can get a hotel . . . or you can come with me." He pauses. "I'd love for you to stay with me. But, no promises." He tilts his head and looks at me sheepishly.

"Niles, I would freaking love that." In thirty seconds, he's just changed my whole tune. He's describing my every fantasy about going to New York and made it even better by wanting me to stay with him. I decide that I need to let go of any pressure I'm putting on him, me, or our "relationship." I am living a fucking dream right now. There is no need to mess things up with expectations maybe neither of us can uphold.

"And also? You got it. From here forth, I vow to just let things be. Let them unfold. Whatever happens, happens. No expectations, no promises. Just two awesome people who dig each other pretty hard having a really great time. That's it."

If I could bottle the energy and sincerity behind his smile right now, I'd be a zillionaire. "You are amazing. Seriously. We don't shove out again until late Monday night, so bring lots of clothes. Or not. Your choice." He winks at me and I wink back.

He draws me close and we kiss again until we lose our breath.

CHAPTER SEVENTEEN
Wagging Tongues and Mad Hornets

I don't know how Niles does it. I don't. It's Thursday at 11:42 a.m. and I've been up since five, preparing for my flight home. Niles and I left the park at one in the morning and went to an all-night diner where we talked and ate grease-heaped plates of terribleness until nearly three. We went back to our hotel, brushed our teeth in our respective rooms, and found our way back into each other's arms (his room), falling asleep all snuggled up together until my phone screamed my wake-up at five.

Niles awoke long enough to call the driver back to get me, then with a grateful smile, rolled over and passed out again after I told him to get some rest. The guys don't have a show tonight, so they don't need to leave until mid-afternoon.

I, on the other hand, had to catch my flight home only to shower, pack, and fly back out again tonight. After whipping off an email to Lucy to see if she's available for lunch tomorrow and a confirmation that she is (timing is great, she says, since she has something she wants to talk to me about), I fly into the Big Apple for only the second time in my life at 9:50 tonight. Ack. I'm exhausted (but exhilarated!) just thinking about it.

Sara took an early lunch so she could come pick me up. Naturally, she wants every single detail of what went down in Boston, but I am very selective about what I tell her. I'm feeling fiercely protective of Niles's privacy, and since our relationship status is a confusing jumble of question marks, trying to define or pin things down for her benefit proves difficult.

"So, you still haven't had sex with him? *Still?*"

"That's correct." I knew this was coming, so I'd already decided to save us all some heartache and keep things simple and matter-of-fact. "And we probably won't for a while, so you can just get it out of your head."

"And what exactly is the reason for the delay? I mean, am I missing something? You've been around him privately enough times. There are bathroom stalls everywhere." She clucks her cheek.

"I dunno. It just hasn't happened yet." *Now, leave it alone.*

"But he's a good kisser?'

"Ugh. He's *amazing.*" I know I sound gushy, but my insides fire up again just thinking about it. It can't be tomorrow night soon enough.

"And now you're going to New York? For the whole damn weekend?"

"Yes!" This comes out as a squee, which gets Sara even more excited. I throw her another bone: "I'm having lunch with Lucy tomorrow, too!"

"Stop it! Aw, can I come, Kallie? I promise I'll just peer out from your purse. You won't even know I'm there."

"I wish." Of course, this is only half true. It would be a hoot to hit the city with her—Lord knows we fantasized about it enough during our *Sex and the City* marathon days—but I also love the idea of conquering New York by myself for a weekend. I'm not exactly sure how much time Niles and I will spend together, but if he has rehearsals and sound checks and we're careful to avoid the public eye, then I may end up on my own quite a bit. And I'm perfectly okay with that. Seems like a Girl Power-type moment. Hear me roar!

"Okay," Sara says, her voice turning serious. "This kind of blows, but I have to bring you off your cloud for a sec."

"Uh-oh. What's wrong?"

"Brad called me." She says this with a sigh, sending a pang through my stomach like a tidal wave.

"What? Why?" This is not the first time Brad has called Sara. The calls always start out being about the kids or me, but quickly turn friendly and chatty and could easily be misconstrued as an excuse for him to talk to Sara. I know he thinks she's hot (he's told me as much, and really, she is very pretty) so we're trying to figure out if he's coming on to her or what exactly his motives are. The idea of those two dating sends Sara and I both into hysterics, but Brad is just full of himself enough to think it could happen.

"He was sleuthing on you. Truly. There is no way this call could have been an 'excuse' for him to talk to me."

"Go on." My cheeks turn hot, which means my blood is pretty much starting to boil. This is not going to be good. I can feel it.

"Turns out your pal Katherine squawked to a friend or six about what she saw that day on the running trails. Namely, you and Niles about to suck face."

Sara hates Katherine. She absolutely cannot understand why I would want anything to do with those yip-yappy, gossipy school moms, and she stays far, far away. I've always given them the benefit of the doubt, thinking it would be fun to suck down Momtails at each other's houses while the kids hang out. Now I can see—and appreciate—the reasoning behind Sara's aversion.

"*Shiiiit.*" I slam my head back against the headrest.

"You didn't really believe people would never find out about you and Niles, right? I mean, you've had him here in town, and now you're about to fly to your third city to be with him. Like, are you guys a real thing now? Because tongues are wagging, Kal . . . and not just yours and Niles's. You're probably going to need to set the record straight. Espesh with Braddy-boy."

"No, we're not a thing." This, of course, is a big, fat lie. But we're not a *defined* thing, so I guess it's true. Right?

"Well, Brad thinks you are and he's madder than a hornet. You don't have to defend yourself to him, but maybe you should clue him in. Out of respect for the girls, mostly."

Respect? For the girls? So, it's *respectful* to admit that I'm flying up and down the East Coast so I can make out with a rock star and drink more than I have since college? What am I missing here?

"Brad does not need to know what I'm up to, and neither do the girls. As far as they're concerned, it's business as usual." I'm so mad, I can hardly speak. "This is bullshit. Brad could be banging some chick in North Carolina for all I know and I'm not calling his best friend asking about it."

"Well, this is maybe a little different, Kal. Niles is a celebrity. And, he just happens to be the celebrity that broke the camel's back."

I look at her in disbelief. "Niles did *not* ruin my freaking marriage, Sara. It was already dead. You of all people should know that." I swear if I could punch her without making her crash this car, I so totally would.

"Sorry, I'm just saying . . ."

"Just saying what? And what did you tell Brad? Jesus, I can't trust anyone anymore!"

"Easy, Kallie," she says, eyes flashing. "I didn't confirm or deny anything. That's your job, not mine. I never did *anything* to break your trust." She sighs and grips the steering wheel tighter. "And for the record, you're the one who chose to share your heart with the whole damn world. What did you think might happen?"

Oh my God, she's right. I made the bed I'm now in. This crazy, wacky, seriously awesome, but totally uncomfortable bed.

"I'm sorry. You're right." My breath catches. "What am I going to do?"

"Face the music," she says, her stature softening. "No pun intended. Well, kinda." She reaches her hand over and squeezes my knee. "But seriously, what's the big deal? You and Niles are dating. Hanging out. Whatever. If people find out, so what? It's your fucking dream coming true. You should be shouting this shit from the rooftops."

She's right. My dream *is* coming true. I *should* be shouting it from the rooftops. But I can't. It's all so complicated. Between not knowing where we stand, knowing the summer will eventually come to an end, and having my baggage of an ex and two children, this all sounds so ridiculous and implausible. So why admit to anything?

I mean, really, what am I even doing?

CHAPTER EIGHTEEN
Stars in Our Eyes

"This is amazing. I am so excited to finally meet you." Not sure how, but Lucy's in-person voice is even more bubbly and sincere than her phone voice. This is so fun . . . and so cool.

After a big hug, she settles into the chair across from me and I size her up. She is absolutely precious. A tiny little thing with big, round brown eyes and kinky-curly dark brown hair. Her smile is wide and contagious, just like in the photo on the agency's website.

Many—most, even—authors fire off multiple query letters (and by multiple, I mean dozens and sometimes hundreds) in hopes that at least one agent finds their work intriguing enough to request pages or even (gasp!) the full manuscript, which they promptly devour. They then change your life by offering representation and the whirlwind process of publishing commences. (Except it's not a whirlwind at all. It's more like one notch above glacier speed.)

As I prepared to send Nash and Emily out into the big, bad literary world, I vowed to avoid that same hundred-agent process. I wanted to score The One after courting but a few. It only seemed right, given how devoted Emily was to Nash right from the get-go. The instant I saw Lucy's picture and read her bio, I knew she was my dream agent. She just looked like someone I could be friends with, as well as build a career with. I had to have her. Thankfully, she felt the same about me and my work. And now, here she is, right in front of me.

"Kallie, I can't tell you how happy I am that you're here," she gushes. "I love meeting my authors, but don't often get to do so. I'm so glad you made the trip." She leans in and whispers, "Are you here because of Niles?" I nod a little too enthusiastically as a crazed-fangirl smile breaks across of my face. "Knew it! See, writing a book about someone is the ultimate form of flattery. Maybe I should write one about George Clooney." She laughs and I fall in love with her a little bit more.

The waitress comes over to take our order, and as she turns to leave, Lucy says, "Oh, and could you please bring two small glasses of champagne? Before the food?" She tilts her head and flashes me a smile. My eyebrows shoot up in response. I've always wondered if publishing people drink during business lunches. I don't know if this is commonplace or not, but I'm not going to turn down a nice midday glass of champagne. In New York. With my agent. On a Friday.

We chat a little more, mostly about the city and food and shopping, and I can tell she'd love more details about what's going on with Niles and me, but is behaving too professionally to ask. I contemplate offering a little tease of info, but then the waitress arrives with our champagne and Lucy sits up straight, her white teeth gleaming through her back-again giant smile.

"So, Kallie, I have some pretty incredible news." I wonder how the words are even coming out of her mouth, she is smiling so wide. As a reflex more than anything else, I realize I'm smiling now, too.

"Yes?"

"We are starting to get a lot of interest in . . . wait for it . . . are you ready . . . ?"

"Yes!"

". . . film rights for your book! Is that not amazing?"

There is no way she just said what I think she just said. There's just no way. For the love of God, I dare say every author's dream, after having their book published, is to have a movie made about said book. A movie! Where your story unfolds right there on the big screen and your characters come to life via some A-list actor or a no-namer who becomes the next big thing because your character takes them there. I am seriously not sure if I am breathing right now.

"Honestly, I don't think it will be long before we have a deal. I'm not saying you're going to be a millionaire next week or anything, but I'd be prepared for some pretty awesome news in the next month or so." She's looking right into my eyes and even still, this does not seem real. She holds her glass out. "Cheers?"

My mind rewinds to when Niles and I first met and he held out his beer, presenting "cheers" as a question, just like Lucy is now. This, all of this, is because of him. My muse. If my book becomes a movie, I owe every bit of it to him. In a Grinch-like fashion, my heart swells about three times its normal size. I cannot wait to tell him, see him, hug him, *thank* him.

I hold my glass out until it clinks against Lucy's. "Cheers!"

***

"Man, don't you ever get tired?" I hand Niles a towel to mop up the sweat that covers every visible inch of him. He worked his ass off on stage once again, this performance as powerful, or even more so, than any other I've seen. It's his home crowd, and he brought it. How he doesn't collapse the minute he leaves the stage, I'll never know.

I've never seen him so soon after a show, but Zeke snuck me back and I even got to watch the last song of the encore from back here. Once again, I'm floored by the fact that one-third of the trio that captivated a venue full of people is standing just inches away from me. And I get to spend the rest of the night with him.

"I stayed motivated because I knew I'd get to see *you* afterwards." He leans in for a quick kiss. "I've missed the hell out of you."

The original plan was for him to meet me at the airport last night, but they ended up doing a radio show interview super early this morning, then had sound check in the afternoon. We decided to just meet up after the show, which totally sucked because even though it's been only a day, it seems like we've been apart forever. But now that we're inches away from each other, all seems right with the world again.

"I'm gross," he says. "Come on." He leads me through a hallway to a dressing room. There are clothes and accessories everywhere. (How many guitar straps does one band need?) It's kind of understood that I shouldn't follow him in, so I just lurk in the hallway, waiting for him to clean up. A few random people walk past, but then I'm alone.

I lean against the cool wall, the enormity of this day taking over my mind. Any conflict I had in the car with Sara yesterday has at least temporarily melted away. There's something about New York City magic—oh, and a rock star love interest and a possible movie deal—to break a girl from her bout of self-doubt and confusion.

Until my phone vibrates, that is.

Because there they are, in all their glory. Seven texts from Brad, each one incorporating more four-letter words than its predecessor. Phrases like, "What the *bleep*?" "How could you betray your family by bringing that *bleep* to town?" and, "You should be *bleeping* ashamed of yourself!" assault my eyes. Guess Sara was right. Brad is definitely in the know.

I look at the ceiling, imagining all the choice words I could fire back at him. "Mind your own business, dickhead," comes to mind first. I seriously have no idea how I'm going to address this, but if there's one thing I've learned since our separation, it's to not respond to him right away. Let him fester. Engaging him when he's in the throes of pissed-offness leads to nowhere but more pissed-offness, so it's best to let him hang for a bit. Besides, I need a plan. Somehow I need to temper this down before his head explodes or the world bursts into flames or whatever.

"Oh, hey," someone says. I hear the words and feel someone walk up, but I'm so lost in thought, I'm nearly startled out of my skin. Once I get a grip, I focus on the person standing in front of me. She's a couple inches taller than me, with light brown hair, gorgeous skin, and a tell-tale long, straight nose.

Oh. My. God. It's Robbyn.

I try to respond but nothing comes out. I continue staring at her. She really is pretty, and yes, though she may have put on a few pounds, she's still quite small and her full lips are pink and shiny. I can't help it. My mind immediately acknowledges that those lips have been on Niles's. Many times over.

She's wearing a loose pink tank top and a funky boho skirt. I notice how flat her chest seems and silently applaud myself for one-upping her in that department. But she totally has me when it comes to skin. For someone who is supposedly so heartbroken and unstable, her skin is seriously not tattling on her. Yeah, I'm jealous.

"I'm guessing you're Kallie Reagan, famous author." Her voice is flat.

"I'm guessing you're Robbyn, Jase's sister." I work hard to make my voice equally as flat.

"Yes, and *Niles's girlfriend.*"

"Ex-girlfriend."

"Right. Okay." She laughs and rolls her eyes. "Naïve people make me smile."

"Whoa, hey, ladies," Niles says, bursting through the bathroom door. It's hard not to notice the look of horror on his face as he races toward us.

"Kallie and I were just getting to know each other," Robbyn says. She moves away from Niles as though she's afraid to touch him.

"I bet you were." I've never heard Niles be rude to anyone, but that comment, and the way he said it, most definitely qualifies as rude. "Probably best we keep some space, Rob. Kallie's here all weekend. Things don't need to be . . . awkward. Right?" He moves in front of me, acting as a shield. I wish I could see the look on his face.

"Nothing awkward about getting to know the girl who wrote a book about your boyfriend," she deadpans. "This kind of thing happens every day."

"Right, well, Kallie and I need to get going. Later."

"No after-party tonight? The three of us can hang out." She shoots him a sugar-sweet fake smile.

"Sounds like a blast, but we'll pass." Niles scooches past her to grab the rest of his stuff from the dressing room. While his back is turned, Robbyn glares at me. And I mean *glares*. I know somewhere in there must be a decent girl or Niles wouldn't have stayed with her as long as he did, but if this chick could kill with her icy gaze, I'd be a dead woman right now.

"I read your little book," she says quietly. "Someday I'll tell you about the real Niles. He's pretty much the exact opposite of Nash. You'd be shocked."

"Oh, thanks, but I think I'll figure that out for myself." I tilt my head and toss her a wink because, dammit, I am so not interested in getting into a pissing match with this girl right now. Or ever. Yes, they have a history, but Niles isn't hers anymore. And, frankly, this conversation has already lasted long enough.

"Ready?" Niles emerges from the dressing room and takes my hand. He's not one bit tentative. It's like Robbyn isn't even there. I'm impressed by his calmness and wish I could mimic it. But I can't.

When I'm sure Niles is at an angle where he can't see me, I issue Robbyn an icy glare of my own. She looks hurt, and though I feel a quick flash of sympathy, I also feel totally and completely satisfied. Like, hopefully our handholding is clue enough that there's no need for further interactions between her and me. Let's see if she takes the hint.

With that drama out of the way, Niles leads us down a hallway and out to a car. *Is* there an after-party tonight? If there is and we're not going to it, where are we going?

We slide into the back seat and Niles pulls me close to him. "I should have seen that coming a mile away. I'm sorry. I shouldn't have left you alone out there."

"It's fine. I can handle her." I squeeze his hand as if to reinforce my half-truth. I mean, I *can* handle her. I'd just sure as hell prefer not to.

"So . . . um." I take a deep breath and turn toward him. I know I probably shouldn't do this right now, but really, when *is* a good time? "Why *did* you guys break up, anyway? Was it me? 'Cause if it was, I'm sorry. But not really." I try to lighten the moment by jabbing his leg with my knee. Niles responds with a half-laugh, but he seems so far away.

"Complicated," he says. "Was then, is now, probably always will be. I really don't know what else to say. Our dynamic is just pretty fuckin' weird."

I bristle. *Probably always will be* is not something I want to hear. Does this mean she'll be in the picture forever? Because that will get old really fast.

"How long?" I ask.

"How long, what?"

"How long have you been broken up? And how long before your ties are broken, like, forever?"

"Will they ever be? I don't know. She travels with us. We see each other almost every day. She's Jase's sister and he's integral to our success—and in a weird way, she is, too. So, it's not like I can just make them go away. We just balance it out the best we can."

He's quiet as he stares out the window for at least a minute, then he sighs and angles himself to look at me. "This right here, Kallie? This is exactly why I hold so tight to my 'no promises, no regrets' mantra. Because the one time I let that slip, I created a monster. And now I'm full of some serious regrets."

CHAPTER NINETEEN
Night Moves

We burst through the door of Niles's apartment, arms laden with takeout food, beer, bottled water, and some of my luggage. When we stopped at my hotel, I grabbed enough stuff to stay here for one night, mostly as a way to give us both an out in case this doesn't turn out as awesome as we hope. Ever since Niles's confession about being under pressure for the new album, I've become acutely aware that my presence could be impeding whatever it is he needs to accomplish. So I'm trying to give him some space, but, damn, I hope he doesn't kick me out. I really want to stay here all three nights.

I also want to further explore the Robbyn situation, since we pretty much let things drop in the car. It was not my idea; I would have kept talking. But after Niles's statement about creating a monster, he pulled out his phone and started pecking away. He almost never does that around me, so I took it as a sign the conversation was over . . . for the time being. This is obviously a touchy topic for him, but it's also one I'm not crazy excited about sweeping away. I feel like there's more to the story than just a random old breakup and I really want to get to the bottom of it. Maybe the timing just needs to be right. Or maybe I'll never know.

I set my armload of goodies on a nearby counter, push all the Robbyn thoughts out of my mind, and look around. This is Niles's home. Where he lives on breaks and when he's off tour. Where he walks around in his comfiest clothes and messed-up hair, not needing to impress a single soul. The fact that he invited me here, into such a personal place, is pretty astounding. I don't mean for them to, but my eyes immediately get foggy, which, of course, does not go unnoticed.

"What's wrong?" he asks, setting down his bags. "If it's Robbyn . . ."

"It's not. I'm just . . . I'm just kind of floored I'm here."

Niles relaxes and a smile spreads across his face. He looks so endearing, so normal. Just a really cute guy hanging out in his NYC apartment on a random Friday night.

"It's a big deal for me, too." He wraps his arms around my waist and pulls me into him. "I'm happy you're here."

"This is so crazy, Niles. Being here with you. I mean, what the hell?"

"It's what you wanted, right? Like, Emily really wanted Nash to invite her over. It was a big deal to her." He backs up so he's looking into my eyes.

"I can't imagine anything I'd want more right now. Well, maybe *one* thing." I playfully bump my hip into his.

Even though I'm speaking the truth, that comment lightens the moment and we break apart, sifting through the food and drinks until we claim what we want. As we settle onto his couch to eat, I take it all in. Either he's a super tidy guy, or it's simply because he's mostly gone, but the apartment is very clean and orderly. It's pretty minimalist—not much in the way of knickknacks or artwork—but his color palette rocks (gray tones with deep blue accents) and his furniture is ultra sleek. There's an exposed brick wall that screams quintessential NYC charm, and gleaming hardwood floors that look like they've recently been redone. I can dig it.

I spot his TV and, next to it, multiple gaming systems and components. I wonder how often he plays. He's mentioned in interviews that he's a die-hard gamer, but I suspect his schedule doesn't allow for that much now. Maybe I should challenge him to a game later. That could be fun. Unless he's super intense and competitive, of course. Then maybe not so much.

"Not a bad pile of bricks, right?" He shovels a forkful of rice into his mouth.

"Not at all. But where's the bedroom?"

"Easy, girl. I'll show you later."

I die right there on the spot. "Oh my God, I seriously didn't mean for it to come out that way. I was just taking a mental tour of the place and that was something I didn't see, so . . ." I give up, knowing I'm only digging my hole deeper—a hole I can heave my dead self into to hide my outrageous embarrassment. He must think I'm the horniest son of a bitch this side of the Great Lakes.

"Kallie, it's fine. I'm just joking." He sets down his fork and reaches for my hand. "No need to get embarrassed. Okay?" I shake my head because I really don't know what else to do. He pulls my chin until I'm looking at him. Into those gorgeous, crazy eyes of his.

"The other night in the park? That was totally badass. You told me what you wanted and you did not make one single excuse for yourself. It was the real you coming through, unfiltered. And it was terribly hot."

"Thank you."

Thank you? Did I really just say *thank you*? What kind of ridiculous response was that? But still, hearing those words come out of my mouth reminds me of something just a little bit huge. Amidst Brad tearing me up one side and down the other over text and the whole Robbyn drama from earlier—and now my awe of sitting in Niles Russell's apartment—I forgot to tell him my big news!

"Oh my God, Niles! Speaking of thanking people . . . I have the most amazing news!" I set my food down on the coffee table and bounce and clap my hands like a little kid.

"What?"

"When I met with Lucy earlier, she told me . . ." I pause because I can hardly catch my breath.

"She told you what?" Niles is on the very edge of the couch, his takeout container barely balancing on his knee. I envision it crashing to the floor and staining the super cool area rug that's right beneath us. He waves his hand in front of me, pulling me back to the present.

"She told me that interest in my book—for movie rights—is getting hot. Movie rights, Niles! My book—the one you inspired—is probably going to become a movie!"

Although it's generally inappropriate to squee around a guy, I totally let 'er rip. I'm smiling so big, my cheeks hurt and my teeth are dry. I think there is more bouncing, but I'm not completely sure, because the next thing I know, I'm moving the takeout box from Niles's lap to the coffee table and tackling him in a horizontal bear hug that flattens us both out on the couch.

As I balance on top of him, I look him in the eye again and prepare to say what my heart really wants to say, what it's wanted to say for ages now. If he gets off on Unfiltered Kallie, that's good. Because he's about to get a whole lot of it.

"Thank you, Niles," I breathe. "Thank you so much for being my muse and for leading my heart. Because of you, some of my wildest dreams are coming true." I smooth the hair off his forehead, then lean down and kiss him gently. He tastes like chicken tikka masala. I lower my mouth near his ear and whisper, "I owe this all to you."

Instead of kissing me back, Niles gently rolls me off to the side and sits up. "That's amazing, Kallie. But I didn't do any of this." His words are soft and laced with sadness. "You did this all yourself. It's your talent, your dedication, and your hard work. Not me. I'm just a schmuck."

A schmuck? Really? Man, what is it with this guy? Why can't he just accept his awesomeness? Seriously, he must have missed the memo proclaiming all rock stars to be egomaniacs. Or if he did get it, he didn't read through the whole thing. Because he is the complete damn opposite. And it's kind of infuriating.

"Niles," I sigh, "do you not remember what I told you the very first day we met? When you blew my mind with your whole 'why me' question? What I said was true. Was then and is now. You inspire the hell out of me. Whether you want to believe it or not."

"Well, Kallie," he looks me dead in the eye, "I hope you know the feeling is mutual."

Thud.

Did he just say I inspire him, too? Little old small-town-girl me?

Honestly, it's been so hard for me to envision myself as anything other than a lovesick fangirl that he's just indulging and maybe having a little fun with that it never occurred to me I could have an impact on him, too. We artists . . . sometimes so full of ourselves, but most of the time, so very, very humble. And blind.

"Thank you," I reply. And this time *thank you* feels like a completely appropriate response. Because you know what? I'm not going to question or challenge his statement. I'm not going to try to negate it or blow it off or anything else. I'm going to accept it because that is exactly what I would want from him. And it feels good to let myself feel good. Especially with someone from whom that compliment means so very, very much.

"Done eating?" he asks.

I'm not really, but my mind is on everything but food, and I can tell he's done, so I nod.

"Good, because I have a surprise." He throws our containers away, cleaning up any rice that's wiggled its way loose.

"A surprise, you say? Care to elaborate?" I'm generally not a big fan of surprises, but methinks this has potential to be a good 'un. I shiver with anticipation.

"Oh, you'll see soon enough, dear girl. But first, this . . ."

He sets down the washrag he'd been wiping the counters with (a guy who cleans up after a meal? Yes, please!) and walks toward me quickly. He wraps his arms around my waist and pushes against me, walking me backward until I'm up against a wall. Once we stop moving, he kisses me hard, and I nearly lose my mind. His hands are all over me, so I let mine explore him, too. I wiggle them up the back of his shirt so they're touching his smooth skin. They find their way into his hair, back around his waist, and finally onto his bum. I am so breathless I'm not sure how I'm still standing.

His kisses get softer, until his lips leave mine and find their way onto my neck. He unbuttons the shirt I had thrown over my tank top due to the cool night, and kisses my chest. His hand comes to rest on one of my boobs, and after a moment, he pulls away and smiles. "Very nice."

I laugh, and put his hand back on my chest. "I don't want to stop."

"I don't either, but we need to go."

Huh?

"Go where?"

He pushes me against the wall again, flattening himself against me so hard he almost knocks my wind out. From what I feel in his, ahem, central region, there is no way we should be going anywhere other than to his bedroom. He kisses me again, then backs away completely, leaving me a jumbled mess against the wall.

"Grab your laptop. Follow me."

"My laptop? You light me on fire so bad I can't even function, but you want me to grab my laptop? What are we doing? Making a sex tape?"

He smiles, clearly amused. "No. We're gonna write."

***

I've always dreamed of seeing New York from a rooftop, and now here I am. Though we're not a zillion stories high at some swanky condo tower, it's still ridiculously cool to sit in the summer night on the rooftop deck of Niles's apartment building.

"It's been quite a day," Niles says. "I'm feeling extra inspired because of you. We should put that inspiration to good use."

"I can think of something else I'd rather put to good use," I say, playfully grabbing at his business.

He catches my hand as it's on its way back to my side and puts it back on his groin. "Still half-mast. See what you do to me?"

"But you'd rather come up here and write?" I seriously don't get this guy. Either he has a passion for running around with blue balls or he has the self-restraint of a saint. I haven't decided which yet.

"Shhh. I had this all worked out in my head. Don't distract me." He smiles a shy smile and points behind me. "See? Look over there." I turn around to see a tiny table set for two, just like in the movies. There's a bottle of chilled white wine, two glasses, and the best part . . . dessert! "Please say you like cheesecake. I got three different kinds. They're chilling in the cooler."

"I freaking love cheesecake."

"I thought you might." He takes my hand and walks me over to the table. "Madame." He pulls out my chair and kisses my hand as he guides me down. As he settles into the seat across from me, my breath catches over how completely amazing this moment is. "We'll write after dessert. And wine. You want wine?"

"Is guacamole made from avocados?"

He stops pouring long enough to look up at me. "Beauty, talent, smarts, *and* funny as hell. You're quite the package, aren't you?"

"I try."

"I don't think you have to."

I take a sip of my wine, which is delicious, and point to the chocolate cheesecake when Niles opens the cooler and instructs me to choose one. He takes the cherry and we sample a bite from each other's plates.

"I still can't believe I'm sharing a fork with you," he says. "That goes against my every germophobic conviction, you know?"

"I feel privileged."

"You should. And tongue kisses, too? My God, I'm a wrecked man."

"Glad I was the one to break you." *Was I* really the one to break him? Did he seriously date Robbyn for over a year (reportedly) without ever tongue kissing her? I find that truly hard to believe.

"It took a special girl. And if we keep talking about it, I'm going to get all riled up and we're going to do it all over again."

"Hmm, well let's keep talking about it then."

That's all it takes. In an instant, Niles is at my side, pulling me up out of my seat, kissing me fiercely. I open my eyes a bit and take in as much as I can. Niles's face, the stars, the wine, the table, the skyline. I cannot believe this is my life at this moment.

After a few very steamy minutes, I slowly pull away. I catch Niles at that magical moment when his eyes are still closed and his lips are swollen and shiny; it's a sight I'll remember forever. Those lips—the lips that sing to millions of people across the world—were just on mine. And the person who owns them was just vulnerable putty at my hands. *My* hands.

Talk about inspiration.

"You're a freaking awesome kisser," I say, straightening my hair. "Now, let's get to work. Let's write."

CHAPTER TWENTY
Raise the Roof

"It's getting chilly," Niles says. "You can either come keep me warm or we can go in."

I glance at my watch. It's one fifty in the morning, and I am on an absolute creative bender. I'm sitting at the little table where we had dessert and Niles is sitting in a lounge chair he pulled up next to the table. I wave my hand at him in dismissal.

"Whatcha working on?" he asks, trying to peek at my screen.

"As if you don't know." I flash him a quick smile. He looks cute as hell right now. And definitely chilly. He's huddled up on the chair, with his arms pulled into the body of his shirt so the sleeves hang limp. His laptop is resting in his lap, his phone balancing on his knee. I've hardly looked down at him since our writing sesh began, but I've heard him tap at the keys a few times and record stuff with his phone. I hoped he would sing a few verses, but all he did was speak. And maybe hum a little. It was hard to tell without completely staring.

"You're certainly being productive over there," he says. "I see lots of words on your screen. You're beating me."

Ugh. As much as I love hearing his voice, I'd *so* love for him to be quiet for just a second more. I'm seriously in the middle of a huge scene, and am really feeling my groove. I keep typing, without looking up.

"So dedicated," he says. "I like that." He chomps his teeth, as if he's a tiger or something. "*So hot.*" He's totally taunting me, but I refuse to let him derail my streak.

I put my finger to my lips. "Shushy a minute. I need to get this out."

My scolding must work because he falls quiet, aside from the bang his laptop makes when he closes the lid and the creaking of the chair as he wiggles around. He sneezes and I realize that's the first time I've ever heard him do so. Of course, I find it totally precious, because even his sneezes have a beautiful "voice" to them. I bless him and keep right on typing.

He's quiet again, but starts the wiggle process all over after another few minutes. I feel kind of bad. Just a few more paragraphs, though, then this scene will be done and he can have all of my attention he wants.

"*Kal-lie,*" he finally says, in a super-loud whisper.

Ugh, hang on. I'm so close. So close.

"Kallie? You with me?"

"One sec, Niles," I whisper back, still typing.

"Why did you get divorced, Kallie? What went wrong between you and Bub?"

Well, dang. *Now* he has my attention.

I reluctantly press Save and spin around in my seat until I'm facing him.

"Bub? You mean Brad?"

"I don't care to say his name." He says this with childish flair. I can see *someone* sure gets goofy late at night. And I like it.

"Oh, right. Bub. Gotcha."

"So?" he asks. He sits up straight and throws one leg over each side of the chair. He sets his laptop on the floor and motions for me to come sit between his legs. When I do, he guides my shoulders until my back is against his chest and my temple is against his chin. He rubs both of my arms, which eliminates the goosebumps I had from the chill, but sparks new ones just because of his touch.

"So, what? What do you want to know?"

"What happened? Marriage is a huge commitment and you two bailed. There must be some pretty big reasons."

I think about this. Almost every single person in my circle—family, friends, acquaintances, former coworkers, *everyone*—wanted to know "what happened." So, I've been asked this many, many times, but have yet to come up with a good answer that doesn't either trivialize our reasons, or invite further discussion.

"It was a combination of things, I guess. But nothing huge like cheating or spousal abuse or anything." Niles spins a section of my hair around his finger, lets it go, then does it all over again.

"That's good. So, you just, what? Fell out of love?"

"I suppose so. Of course it's not that simple. It didn't happen overnight. It was just a great big storm of boredom and disconnect and being in two very different places. I mean, he's complacent and I'm not. He's into simplicity and I like a little excitement. We never did anything fun together and we stopped taking the time to learn about each other. Over time, we—I—fell out of love. And by then, we were at the point of no return. In my opinion, anyway." I wish I could see behind me so I could read Niles's expression.

"So, was Bub on board? Or did you break his heart?"

I sigh. "I broke his heart. But now that we've split, he's being a total ass, so I'm pretty sure he's over me."

"No, he's not. He just doesn't know how else to treat you right now."

Since we're on the topic of home stuff, I remember that I'd better let Niles know just how much the hive is buzzing over his recent trip home with me. A heads-up mostly, in case Brad's rage and Katherine's big mouth prompts *US Weekly* to call him and say, "Hey, we heard you're kissing fans on running trails in Smalltown, USA. Care to comment?"

I drop the bomb, fully expecting Niles to wig out, but he barely seems to care. Instead, he shrugs and says with conviction, "So, Bub is calling your best friend, asking about you? Yeah, he is so not over you."

"Okay, whatever, but didn't you hear me? Aren't you worried about being 'caught' with a fan?"

"Not as much as I'm worried about you ending up back in the arms of your ex-husband."

Wait, what? He's worried? That I'll go back to Brad? Huh. That seems like something only people who are a real "thing" worry about. I don't know what he has planned for us, but I do know one thing for sure . . .

"I have no interest in going back to Brad, Niles. That chapter is closed."

"You have two kids. That chapter will never be closed. You'll be seeing each other at functions and events forever, really. It's not just a divorce, and you both move on. This is a totally different ball game."

Hm. This is some pretty insightful reasoning for someone who has no kids. "True. But let me put it this way: the *book* that we created by having kids together will never be closed. But the chapters focused around the marriage between Brad and me have been written . . . and read. Trust me."

Niles goes quiet, and while I further contemplate his supremely obvious insecurity about my reuniting with Brad, he starts kissing my neck.

"Have you ever thought about moving to New York, Kallie?" he whispers.

His kisses are seriously messing with my mind, but I'm pretty sure he just asked me if I've ever considered moving to New York. Which I haven't. Ever.

"No, never have."

"Sounds like maybe a great place for you to be, what with a successful author career and now most likely a movie. Plus, it would make sleepovers a whole lot easier."

My stomach drops through the roof and straight down to the basement. Is he seriously saying that he wants me to move to New York? And have sleepovers with him? Like *sleep*-overs or let's-finally-get-it-on-overs? Either way, it's kind of sounding like he wants to spend a bunch of time with me. Beyond this summer.

"The girls," I breathe. The way his warm mouth moves all over my neck and ear, I hardly remember I even have a pulse, let alone children.

"We have good private schools here."

"Brad."

"Bub can fend for himself."

"He'd never let me take the girls away from him."

By this point, Niles has wiggled around so he can easily reach my lips with his. His tongue wastes no time plunging into my mouth and his hands are groping everything that's in reach.

When he pulls away, my head is spinning. "You seriously confuse me," I say.

"You *make* me confused."

"I'm not trying to."

"I know." He launches himself off the lounger and stands up to collect his computer and cooler and whatever else he can carry. I watch the way he moves, the way his hair blows in the wind, the way his watch peeks out from his sleeve every time he extends his arm. I want to be that watch, close to his pulse, feeling the warmth of his skin. I want to be the one keeping him on track, guiding him through his day.

I also want to pull him back down next to me and get him to open up. Tell me about Robbyn and what happened to split them up. Was he sad? Is he now? He doesn't seem to be, but maybe he's just rude to her, as he said, because he doesn't know how else to treat her. Maybe he still loves her, or maybe he's starting to fall pretty hard for me and he doesn't know how to handle such conflicting emotions. But then why is he suggesting I move to New York, for crying out loud? Does he see a future for us? *Could* there be a future for us? The thought of it makes me shiver right down to my core.

"You gonna help me, lazybones? Early morning tomorrow. We should get some rest." He hands me a chair and we make our way toward the elevator. He looks so tired and it really dawns on me how much exertion it must take to be up on stage in front of people most nights. Even though the adrenaline surely kicks in, it has to be draining to be "on" all the time. Then, there's the physicality and emotional aspect of it. I know how drained *I* feel when I write a scene that has a lot of emotion in it—I can't even imagine how he feels singing emotional songs while running around on a stage. I feel awful for keeping him up so late.

We share an elevator with five other people on the way down to his floor. If any of them know who he is, they're either totally over the fact that they live in the same building with him or they're giving him some space, because no one does anything other than nod in our direction. And Niles does nothing to hide the fact that we're together. He must not think these people run the risk of "exposing" us.

Or maybe he's just too tired to care.

After another trip to the roof for the table, it's almost two thirty in the morning and neither of us has showered or brushed our teeth in what seems like days.

"Okay if I shower?" I ask. "I know it's super late, so I can wait 'til morning, if you want."

"Of course." He motions toward the bathroom. "Make yourself at home."

I venture into his bathroom, which is as tidy as everywhere else in the apartment. He's got a stack of fluffy towels and washcloths on a little cabinet, so I help myself, wondering again about his laundry. How does he have time? Where does he go? I somehow don't see him sitting in the laundry room in the basement of his building, sorting through baskets of lights and whites and darks. He must have a "person" who does this stuff for him. Lucky person.

I pull back his shower curtain and feel oddly jealous of the walls that get to see him naked all the time, when I have yet to. I marvel how one minute he feels like a normal guy, and the next minute I remember he's an international performer. And I'm about to get in his shower.

Once the water's warm, I hop in and check out his products. He has one shampoo, one bar of soap, and one drugstore facial wash. That's it. I so wish I were a guy. Totally unfair that he can look that awesome with such little help.

I make every effort to speed through my shower since I'm usually a twenty-minute-plus type of girl. Poor guy is out there waiting his turn, and he has a day like today to do all over again tomorrow. I catch a glimpse of myself in the mirror post-shower and panic, wondering how I'm going to face him with wet hair, blotchy skin, and no makeup. I decide that I, at least, need to put on mascara, then I take a deep breath and burst out into the hallway, a plume of steam trailing behind.

I peer across the hallway into his bedroom (which, for the record, he never did show me). The small lamp next to his bed is pretty dim, but I can make out his light gray walls, steel gray comforter, and a long dresser with a TV on top. I also see Niles, lying on his bed, on his stomach, with his face buried in his pillows and hair scattered across his forehead. He's totally passed out.

Should I wake him or let him rest? He's got to be totally gross, but maybe guys don't care about that as much as girls. Every night we've spent together, I've felt completely guilty about not properly washing my face and putting on eye cream. Sounds vain, maybe, but not taking care of your face is like sending breakouts and wrinkles a personal invitation to wreck your life. I decide that if it was that important to him, he'd have turned on the TV or found a way to stay up, so I let him sleep.

Since he's lying on top of the comforter, I go in search of a blanket. My eyes travel to his closet. It's wide open, so it's fair game for a look, right? I run my fingers along all his clothes, most of them hanging neatly, but a few wadded up and stuffed onto the built-in shelves. I spy several pieces of his band merch, and make a mental note to ask if I can "permanently borrow" one for my collection. He has *a lot* of clothes, which explains and/or supports his layering fetish.

I find a fuzzy, cozy blanket and smell it to make sure it's fresh and not musty or dusty (cue the mother in me). It smells just fine, so I open it up and drape it across Niles. He looks so peaceful and he's breathing so quietly, I lean in to make sure he's okay. Of course he is, so I smooth his hair away and kiss his forehead gently. "Night, sleepyhead."

I look around, wondering what to do next. I assume we both assumed I'd sleep in here with him, so I peel back the comforter on the other side and wiggle into the sheets. His bed is super comfy. I arrange the million pillows just so, and prepare to totally crash. But my mind has other ideas. It's reminding me that, although Niles and

I have already slept in a bed together, this is different. This is his place. His bed. His sheets. His stuff. Everywhere, all around me.

When I started penning Nash and Emily, there is no freaking way in the world I could have ever imagined I'd be living this for real. Emily was freaked out the first time she slept at Nash's, too, but they had just made love. I wonder what that will be like with Niles. Will it be sweet or hot? Or both? Will it be slow and deliberate or fast and efficient? Will we roll over and fall asleep, or will we snuggle up and hold each other tight? I've wondered this many times, but being in his bed, I know now that I want it to happen here, not in a hotel room.

I sit up and glance at the clock on the nightstand next to Niles. It's 3:05. I allow my fingers to gently pull through his hair, glide across his blanket-covered shoulders, and rub a circle on his back. Then, I lie down and force my mind to quiet. I guess it works, because the next time my eyes open, it's 5:05 and I shoot straight up . . . dripping in sweat.

CHAPTER TWENTY-ONE
Bedtime Stories

"Kallie! What's wrong?"

My eyes see only black, but the voice I hear is instantly recognizable. Am I dreaming? Is this real? My hand swipes across my forehead that's covered in sweat. My T-shirt clings to me so tightly I feel like I need to rip it off in order to breathe. I fling back some covers and stand up on a floor that doesn't feel like my own. What is going on?

"Hey, are you okay?" In an instant, I'm wrapped into a warm hug. I don't know if it's welcomed or smothering. My eyes finally focus and I make out Niles's shape. I look around and remember I'm in his room. I'm here with him in New York City and we spent the evening together on the roof, writing and eating cheesecake and kissing until our lips hurt. It was real. *This* is real. This is not a dream.

Then why do I feel so empty?

I pull away from him, my heart still racing. Words flood my brain. *Our dynamic is fucked up. I'm a piece of shit. I know what I'm capable of. Sometime I'll tell you about the real Niles—you'd be shocked.*

I walk backward away from him until I am against his closet door. He walks around to his side of the bed and turns on the lamp. When the light shines on him, I feel two very conflicting emotions: happy and scared.

"Kallie, are you sleepwalking? You look like you've seen a ghost." His voice is low, yet palpably concerned.

I take a deep breath, remembering now what woke me up so suddenly. "I have," I whisper. "I've seen *your* ghosts."

Niles stares at me, his expression both confused and concerned. "What?!"

"Tell me about Robbyn, Niles!" I feel so out of it, yet I hear myself shouting. "Tell me about your relationship with her then and now. Why did you break up? I asked you, but you never answered. *When* did you break up? I asked you that, too, and you never answered. Shit, for all I know you two could still be together." I lean over so my palms rest on my thighs. I'm totally out of breath.

"Kallie, it's, like, five o'clock in the morning. You obviously had a bad dream. Let's lie back down. I'll hold you close." He walks toward me with his arms outstretched.

"Stop!" I shoot out my hand. "I want to get in that bed with you more than I want almost anything else, but I need to hear this from you first. Why are you avoiding these questions, Niles? I was straight with you about Brad, yet every question I ask about Robbyn gets the brush-off. What the fuck went on between you two that you won't tell me anything? Why is your 'dynamic' so 'fucked up'? Why did she try to tell me you're the opposite of Nash, but yet she's obviously still so obsessed with you?" I catch my breath, pulling up my eyes to meet his. "And, most importantly, why are you so freaking hard on yourself?"

Niles straightens and looks up toward the ceiling. When his eyes meet mine again, they're flashing. "You want to know what happened? Do you really? Because when I tell you, I promise it will change the way you think about me!" His voice has risen, his face awash with pain. "I'm *not* fucking *Nash*, Kallie. I'm a fucking wreck. Have been for years and probably always will be."

"We're all fucked up, Niles."

"Not like me." He shakes his head and breathes a heavy breath out of his nose. He looks back at me, narrowing his eyes. "You ever think about offing yourself, Kallie? Like, really think about it? To the point where you're there, in the moment, ready to say 'Go!' until someone comes and saves your ass? Like, literally saves your ass?"

My heart stops. I shake my head no.

"That was Robbyn, Kallie. She saved my ass. I was one step away from jumping off a bridge. No kidding. I'd been at this shit-game of entertainment for so long, never making a name for myself. I'd had it. My voice was my life and if it wasn't good enough to get me where I wanted to be, then what was the point? I said, 'Fuck it,' went to the bridge and prepared to dive off."

"Oh my God, Niles." Though I'm willing him to look at me, he's staring at the wall. Tears flood my eyes.

"Oh wait, there's more." He runs his hands through his hair. "So, Robbyn comes up and talks me down. Followed me there because she knew something was up. Tells me she believes in me and that there are good things to come. Tells me she loves me, has for ages, and was so glad Jase was part of the band so she could get close to me. She's a cute girl, right, and we were always friendly, and hell, she just saved my fucking life. So, what do I do? I fucking make love to her in her car. Right in her fucking car. Two minutes before, I was about to die; now I'm busting a nut and using a poor girl who had genuine feelings for me to make myself feel better. Great guy, huh?"

I'm stone silent.

"Thank God she did what she did, though, because the very next day, we got "the call." The one where some big shot tells you they can blow up your career with the stroke of a pen. You got the call, too, so you know, right? Yours was a publisher, mine was a record label." He looks at me through tears in his eyes. "Then, the whirlwind began. Oh, and it was everything we dreamed. In my mind, at that time, I had no one to thank but Robbyn. Without her, I'd have missed out on my dream. I'd have been shoveling lava down in the deep, hot south for a guy named Luci who would take such crazy pleasure in my pain." Heat pricks the back of my neck.

He turns to look out the window, then faces me again. "I allowed myself to make Robbyn promises I knew I couldn't and shouldn't keep. And, of course, we were stupid and foolish, so there was the whole quintessential pregnancy scare. I promised her that if we had a kid together I'd be a great dad and I'd make her my wife, blah, blah, blah. Well, guess what? Sure as fuck, she *did* get pregnant, and what did I do? Started fantasizing about her getting an abortion! Because God forbid a kid screw up the budding career that I worked so fucking hard for." He punches the bed and looks up at me. "She ended up miscarrying very early anyway, but by then she was convinced we'd someday be married. Even though I cared for her, I knew that'd never, ever happen. I don't even think I was ever completely in love with her. And not only that, marriage is sure the fuck not in my cards."

He's breathing hard. Anger for himself spreads all over his face. "Shall I go on?" I don't know what else to do, so I nod.

"I stayed with her out of comfort and convenience, and because I realized what a piece of shit I was. This sweet girl saved me and I owed it to her to treat her well. So, we carried on as a couple for a year." He raises his eyes and walks toward me. "But then I read your book. Someone on my team was a big fan of it and saw a lot of very obvious similarities between Nash and me. She was absolutely certain it must have been inspired by me. I remember laughing my fool head off because I couldn't imagine who could find me interesting enough to model an entire character after. And a good guy, at that. I read it anyway, and even though you made Nash a hell of a lot more awesome than I am, I was really touched by how much of the real me showed up in that character. The me I haven't seen in a long, long while. It's like you knew me. All the stuff you projected onto Nash was either the real me, or the guy I wished I could be. And because of that, I felt like I knew you in return."

He inches toward me until he's finally close enough to put his hands on my shoulders. "I was already starting to pull away from Robbyn. And she was pulling away from me, too, though she'll never admit it. Toward the end, I know she was talking to other guys, doing her own thing, even while she was out touring with us. But she likes being part of our group because it makes her feel important and special and it helps her career in promotions, so she thinks. So, she stays around. And likely always will."

I breathe for the first time since he started his monologue. "So, if she was already talking to other guys, why is she so upset that you split?"

"Because no one likes to be dumped, Kallie. And no one likes to be replaced as quickly as she was. Especially when at one time you thought you'd marry that person someday."

Replaced? Wow. If I'm her "replacement" and he's talking about me moving to New York, I guess I really am more than just a fun-time fangirl. Right? The moment I get this question answered for good is the moment I'll be happier than a pig in shit. Now's not the time to press it, though. We're still not done with the Robbyn conversation.

"How come Jase doesn't hate you?" I ask. I mean, most brothers are fiercely protective of their sisters, and if Jase knew any of this, how could he not hate Niles?

"He knows almost none of this story. The bridge, the pregnancy, none of it. As far as he's concerned, we just hit it off one night, dated for a while, decided we weren't right for each other after all, and that's that. He sees how wrecked she is now, but he knows she can be a bit dramatic at times."

I'm not sure "dramatic" is the word I'd use here. Their history is way more intense than I could've imagined. And given how hard I've fallen for Niles in the short time I've known him, I can definitely see where she'd get a little screwy. This is so weird. All of it. I stare at the side of his face, imagining myself burrowing into his ear, sifting through the folds of his brain until I get him figured out. It's probably so messy in there. Just like he said. Just like he warned.

"So, now that you know the extent of my shit-ness," he says, sitting on the bed, "are you going to pack up and head home? Can't say I'd blame you."

"Of course not, Niles."

The words come out before I've given myself a chance to think about them. Why *shouldn't* I pack up and go home? Do I really want to put myself in a position to be crushed by him, too? I have two kids. This is complicated. He is probably the last person I should be letting into my life.

But just tell that to my heart.

"This is why I've been so careful around you, Kallie." He takes my hand and pulls me onto the bed next to him. "I told you back in Boston that I don't want to hurt you like I hurt her. Not just because I don't want to earn another asshole card, but also because I have some serious feelings for you. Already. And that freaks me out a whole lot. But you already know that because I've told you that, too." He turns to look at me, giving me puppy dog eyes and a cheesy smile. "See? I'm trying to be upfront and honest."

He's right. He *has* told me all those things. He's been honest and now he's let me in. He's shown me his dark side and shared something that must have been very hard to share. That's big in a relationship, right? For the first time, I feel like we're finally on even playing ground.

"I'm not going anywhere." I lean forward and kiss him gently. "And I appreciate your honesty." I bite my lip hard then because what I really want to say next is, *And I love you even more for it.*

CHAPTER TWENTY-TWO
Out of Control

After our little (okay, huge) moment, poor Niles decided to hit the shower. The clock says 5:45 a.m., but it feels like it's been an entire day. Maybe even a week. I am so tired, but my mind continues to race. I absolutely cannot believe the conversation we just had. I play it over and over in my head as I shimmy beneath the covers and put the comforter up to my nose. I breathe in, wondering if Niles ever migrates to this side of the bed, or if he always stays on the left. What time does he go to sleep when he's alone and not on tour? Does he read in bed? I look around and don't see any books, so probably not. He must watch TV, though, since the remote is perched on the nightstand between the lamp and the clock. Or maybe he doesn't do anything in here but sleep. And, well, some of that *other* stuff. There's so much I don't know about him, but I want to know everything. All of it. From the big stuff he just told me to the completely mundane.

The shower is still going and my mind is ablaze, so I decide to snoop a little. I know it's wrong, but tell me what girl hasn't snooped her love interest's bedroom, even if casually? I ease out of the bed and peer under it. It's as barren as a desert. Not a dust bunny, discarded paper, or matchless sock to be seen. The top of his dresser is clean, too, aside from a small pile of change and his wallet. I suppose this makes sense, given his self-proclaimed germophobia.

I look into his closet again and open one of the built-in drawers. There are two stacks of running shorts, all black, and from what I can gather, all Nike. I wonder if they're all as huge as the ones he wore when he was at my house. I close the drawer and pull out the sleeve of one of his shirts. I hold it up to my nose and breathe in, wishing I could bottle his scent for all those times I can't be with him. I close my eyes and envision lazy Sunday mornings in bed together, the two of us pecking away at our laptops, fully engrossed in writing and sharing each other's space. Our knees would touch as we both sit cross-legged on his bed, then we'd scoot a little closer until the magnets that seem to reside in both of us pull us together and our laptops get tossed aside in favor of pawing and smooching.

I must be more immersed in my daydream than I realize, because when my eyes snap open, he's standing in front of me with wet hair, no shirt, and a towel wrapped around his waist. I literally gasp.

"Want to borrow that shirt?" He nods toward the sleeve I still hold in my hand. I drop it, embarrassed, and shake my head.

"I'm good," I say, stupidly, when what I really want to say is, *Want to take off that towel?*

"We technically don't have to get up for another couple hours." He slips on an oversized white V-neck that seemed to materialize from out of nowhere. "Wanna lie back down?"

I do. I really, really do. But I *do not* trust myself in bed with him right now. Not even for an innocent nap. After his soul-bearing monologue, I feel closer to him than ever, and I can just imagine how amazing his skin would feel, all fresh and out of the shower. If he thinks he's getting under the sheets with nothing on but that T-shirt and towel—and making it out alive—he's so very wrong. Unless that's what he's hoping for. A good bone-jumping. But that can't be, right? He's made it very (very!) clear; he's being careful. He couldn't have possibly changed his mind in the last twenty minutes. Or could he? He *is* a guy, after all.

Nope, it's best to play it safe. "You rest. I'm going to squeeze out a few more paragraphs." I step toward him, because that's what the magnets within me demand, and wrap my arms around his neck. "You look so tired. I am so sorry I kept you up so late and for waking you up when you finally slept. Forgive me?" I make a puppy-dog face of my own, and stick out my bottom lip for good measure.

"Of course." He drops his chin so his lips sail toward me, but I intercept by catching his forehead against mine. I know what will happen if I let him kiss me.

"Thank you. Now, sleep."

"Okay," he says, looking almost relieved. "But are you really going to write?"

"Yup. You've inspired me yet again, my muse."

"I'm seriously impressed with your dedication, Kallie. Truly. I quite think *you* are the inspiring one, my dear." I could be wrong, but I think I see a genuine look of adoration in his eyes.

"If some lyrics come to you, come join me. I'll be on the couch . . . snuggled up with this." I pull the fuzzy blanket I covered him with earlier across the bed and bunch it up in my arms. "Night."

I blow him a kiss and walk out of his room, closing the door behind me. I lean against it, just like they do in the movies, and swear I hear him say, "Jesus. That girl makes me fucking crazy."

I feel a smile break across my face, while my stomach does a little flip. "You make me crazy, too, my muse," I whisper. "Sweet dreams."

***

When I open my eyes, I'm greeted with an upside-down Niles hanging over me. "How did I know you'd fall asleep? You should've just hopped back in bed with me."

It takes me a minute to figure out that my back is against the arm of his couch, my legs are stretched out across the cushions, and my head is tipped back, barely clinging to the corner of the backrest for support. Niles stands behind me, bent at the waist until his face is above mine. He gives my forehead a quick peck, then walks around to the front of the couch, feeling for my legs under the blanket. He lifts them up and plops down in the middle of the couch, repositioning my legs and the blanket on his lap. I die a little.

"Get any writing done?" He peeks at my laptop screen, which has gone black. Evidently, I've been snoozing for a bit.

"What time is it?"

"Eight thirty. I finally feel rested. You?"

I nod and hit the space bar on my laptop, waking it up. The clock in the corner tells me that the computer went to sleep at 7:11, which means I got a good hour of writing done, plus an hour-or-so nap.

"I got a lot done," I say, remembering some of my words. I wasn't kidding when I told him I was feeling inspired. I am 99.99% sure that I wrote some of my best, most heartfelt stuff *ever* during that hour. An excellent scene (if I do say so myself) where Nash tells Emily something he'd never shared with anybody (ahem) and how amazing she felt that he trusted her enough to share it. I look at Niles and my insides warm, knowing I have him to thank for that creative burst.

"That's great," he says. "I'm a little jealous. I could really use a hot streak like that right about now."

He somehow bends far enough to wiggle his arm and shoulder alongside my hip, and he rests his head by my left boob. My free hand doesn't even try to stop itself; it immediately races toward his head, where it fiddles with his hair, runs the backs of its fingers across his forehead, and even allows its thumb to trace the perimeter of his eyebrows. I hope he doesn't hate this because I could go on like this forever.

"You're making progress, though, right?" I seriously can't even imagine the pressure this poor guy must be feeling right now. Again, I feel a pang in my gut, worried that I've become a hindrance to his creative flow. I know how hard it is to get your groove. But I also know how awesome it is to run with it when you *do* hit your groove. That's where I am right now. But obviously he's not.

"Some. Showers are always good for thinking. A few things came to me in there this morning." He turns his head and nuzzles closer, if that's even possible.

"I've had some seriously incredible dialogue chunks come to me in the shower." I laugh. "Many times, actually. I came up with some awesome one-liners for you, er, *Nash* in there, back in the day." I lift my left elbow in an effort to playfully jab him, but all I do is make his head bounce.

"I had a direction," he says quietly. "For the whole album, kinda. But I can't go there now. So I started from scratch."

I look down at him the best I can from my angle and see that he's looking across the room. I can't read the expression on his face, and he doesn't give me time to follow up.

"Why didn't you get back in bed with me this morning, Kallie? Did my dirty secrets scare you away?"

"Not at all, Niles," I whisper.

"Then why?"

Unfiltered Kallie takes a deep breath. "The truth? It's because I feel closer to you than ever right now . . . and I didn't trust myself to give you the space you needed. So I left."

It's quiet for a minute as I try to stay cool. Things got very real a couple hours ago and I realized that I need to strive for a place of respect, for us both. He wiggles around, then a big breath leaves his nostrils.

"Do you know that what I told you this morning, I didn't think

I would ever tell another living soul, ever? Not *ever.*" I pull my hand out of his hair and instead run it up and down the arm that's draped across me.

"I know it was hard for you. And I thank you, again, for being so honest."

"You weren't supposed to get to me like that, Kallie. I'm supposed to be in control here. But for whatever reason, with you, I lose it." I can't tell if he sounds sad or defeated or frustrated or surprised. But if he thinks he's not in control—of himself, or even our relationship—I beg to differ.

"Niles, please. As you well know, if it were up to me, we'd have done the horizontal tango long ago. I'd venture to say you still have plenty of control over this . . . whatever this is."

"That's just one chunk of it, Kallie. I promised myself that after the whole Robbyn ordeal I would never lose my cool ever again. But guess who became a blobby mess this morning? My own mother doesn't even know that shit, and you know from some of my lyrics and interviews how close I am to her." He peeks up at me from his awkward angle. "How is it that *you* pulled it all out of me?"

I shrug as though he can see me. He sounds so vulnerable, and in as many words, I suppose that's exactly what he's telling me. Does he get like this with all the girls he's involved with? If he surrendered to Robbyn, and now he says he's lost control with me? Jeez, maybe this is his M.O. I made Nash pretty vulnerable, too, but I always thought that was a character-reach and never imagined it'd be a real characteristic of Niles. Maybe I was more right than I knew.

"Maybe it's the girls I end up with or because I've become a spoiled brat rock star, but I'm pretty much used to calling the shots," he continues, completely overturning my suspicions. "I stay guarded. Easier that way. Even with Robbyn, the only real personal side of me she ever saw was that bridge episode. I didn't really share anything else." He pauses and lets out another breath. "She would've ended the pregnancy for me, even though I know she wanted the baby. She would've done anything I asked her to, and that's pretty much the way my relationships work. If you can even call them relationships." He lifts his head again to look at me. "I'm not proud of that. It's just kind of the way things always shake out."

He laces his fingers through mine and kisses my hand. "But I think you might not be like that. I feel like you would—you *will*—give me a run for my money. Challenge me a bit. Make me forget about myself, even just a little . . . for once."

I feel his warmth against me. I hear his voice and digest his words. I see his face smashed against my shirt. I feel his slender arm digging slightly into my rib cage and his fingers grasping mine for dear life. This is my celebrity crush . . . who has turned into my real-life crush. At this moment, I would throw a boulder off the top of a mountain for him. I'd bait a hook with live bees if that's how he told me was the best way to fish. I'd eat venison jerky, which I despise, and read a book about paint drying if he wanted me to. I know *exactly* how Robbyn and all of his other girls must've felt.

"I'm not so sure," I say, pulling his hand up and resting it on my cheek. "You make me a whole lot like putty. Right now, I'd do just about anything for you, too."

"The thing is . . . for once, I feel exactly the same way."

I swear if my stomach squeezed any tighter I'd need smaller pants. I cannot believe I am hearing this. He is totally falling—or *has fallen*—for me. It's *not* a one-sided fangirl fantasy anymore. At all. My big question has been answered. We're truly becoming a thing.

He lifts himself up and rests his weight on top of me. I study his face, just inches from mine. He is so beautiful, he melts my soul into a million tiny pools. I need him. He needs me. We need to figure this out. We need to be a "we."

"I'll tell you what," I say. "Since we're both used to calling the shots, maybe this is our big chance to ease back. No one's in control, no one's the submissive. We'll just take it easy and . . . challenge each other. One day at a time."

He squeezes his eyes shut, knitting his brows together so tightly that his forehead looks like sand ripples on the shore. "No promises, Kallie. I can't promise you anything."

I want to tell him I know. Tell him I understand that he's scared of screwing up again and hurting me and hurting himself and committing to something he doesn't yet know he's strong enough to commit to. But I don't. Because, in truth, I have no idea where we're going or, given all of our baggage, how we're even going to get there. I've already gone way out of my comfort zone with him and know that pretty much anything is up for grabs right now. I'd be a fool to promise anything, too.

So instead, I lean my head against his and say, "I don't need any promises, Niles. I just need for us both to let go a little. And just be."

CHAPTER TWENTY-THREE
For Realz, Yo!

"Sara, holy shit!" Within seven seconds (well, give or take) of Niles leaving the apartment, my phone is already glued to my ear. I settle in, anxious to bend my best friend's ear—and what a bending it will be.

"Kallie, for real! Can you not take eight seconds to shoot me a quick text to let me know you're alive? Jesus, I've been worried sick."

"I'm fine. We've been super busy."

"Oh, I bet you've been *busy*." This statement is laced with such innuendo I can pretty much hear her winking right through the phone. I am seriously not going there with her right now. I have a much bigger fish to fry.

"Sara, what am I going to *do*?" Yeah, my voice may have just morphed into a little-kid whine, but I don't care. This is some serious shiz.

"What are you going to do about what? What's wrong?"

I suck in a breath and let 'er rip. "I am in love with him, Sar. I am really, truly, seriously, completely in love with him. Holy crap. This is insane." I bounce up off the couch and pace the floor. I have so much energy right now, I could single-handedly tackle the offensive line of any football team on the planet.

"Easy, killer," she says. "Fucking someone does not mean you're in love with them. What are you, a teenager? Relax a little and take it for what it is, okay?"

"Sara, I'm not kidding. Things are getting real up in here. We are in a very serious place. We've had some big old conversations in the last couple days and we are really and truly becoming a thing. This is not what I expected. In my wildest freakin' dreams, maybe, but surely not for real."

"Okay," she sighs, "I'll bite. What is it that's got you so bent? He's a great piece of ass, I get it. He's a rock star, I get it. He's everything you dreamed of and more, I get it. But that doesn't mean you're in love with him. You're infatuated. Dr. Phil says so. Don't you ever watch that show? Dr. Phil freaking knows, Kallie."

"Dr. Phil would keel the fuck over if he saw what was going on over here." I stop myself because as much as I want to tell Sara absolutely everything, I refuse to betray Niles's trust. If he never even told his mother about what went down with Robbyn, I surely have no right telling my best friend.

"Such as?"

"Let's just say we've had some very deep convos. He's told me stuff and I've told him stuff. We've bonded in huge ways, and no, we have not had sex. And I am not lying, so you can save your breath and stop calling me a liar before you even start."

"You have not had sex yet, you say? Mmm-kay. Well, you know what I say to that?"

"No, Sara, what?" I sigh.

"You. Are. Such. A. Liar."

"Ugh, you *just* couldn't help yourself, could you?"

"Kallie, please. I may not be the most astute person on the planet, but I was not born last week. There is no freaking way you two have been alone together as much as you have without sealing the deal. There's no way. Especially since you've wanted to jump his bones since before you even put pen to paper. Are you two zombies and forgot to tell me or something?"

"We're just not going there yet. It's a calculated decision. It'll happen in time, God willing, but just not yet."

"A *calculated decision*, hey? Sounds a little scientific for my tastes. Have you at least kissed again? Or is that off limits, too?"

"That is most certainly not off limits. We do plenty of that, believe me." Sara breathes a relieved sigh, which is both ridiculous and amusing. She's over there caring so much about my impending roll in the hay, while I'm over here struggling with the fact that even though I swore off men after the divorce, and even though I knew I *wanted* to fall in love with Niles but never, ever, *ever* thought it would happen, I am now really truly in love with him and it feels so very amazing and crazy and messed up all at once.

"Sara, please, let's focus. This is not about sex. This is much bigger. And I'm being serious here. This is a big deal to me, you know?"

"Okay, yes, I get it. You think you're in love with him. So, what's the problem? Does he dig you, too?"

"After our chat just now, I would say that is a big, old, massively-fat yes."

"Really?!" Sara squeals this, as though she's totally shocked. I suppose I would be shocked, too, if she called me from some rock star's apartment and told me that he was in love with her.

"Obviously, neither of us will go near the L-word with a ten-foot pole at this point, but it's clear this is much more than a little fangirl fun. I seriously can't believe it."

"So . . . if that's what you wanted, why are you freaking out?"

"Because that's what I wanted in my dream world. How the hell am I going to deal with this in real life?"

"Well, that's a good question. Because when you get home, you've got some problems waiting for you on your doorstep. Fair warning, honey. I'm sorry." It's hard not to notice that her voice made a major transition from jovial to oh-shit.

"Wait, what? What happened?"

"What hasn't happened?" She sighs, making it painfully obvious she's about to bust my happy little bubble into zillions of jagged fragments. "People around here are talking. Don't be surprised if the media starts reaching out. Surprised they haven't already, actually."

I've thought about this a lot since I revealed Katherine's bean-spilling incident to Niles last night. And the reality of it is, I am a no one. And Niles isn't exactly Brad Pitt. Nobody is going to give a shit whether we're seeing each other or not. I tell this to Sara.

"Oh, people care, Kallie. The local news will be all over this. Think about it. Hometown-girl-turned-author making her dream into a reality by taking up with the celebrity she wrote her book about? That's huge. I know they can't prove that Niles is the guy who inspired Nash, but between your pal Katherine's big mouth and the rest of the world's assumptions, that's kind of an accepted theory right now."

I exhale. Journalism 101 says that if a local news station's story is juicy enough, larger markets pick it up. If it's a slow news day, Niles and I might look a lot more interesting than a giant rare squash or a cat with twelve toes. This is not good.

"Okay, what else?"

"Brad is livid, of course. Even halfway across the country, he's totally clued in, Kal. He's a mess. He's pissed, he's sad, he feels betrayed, he's annoyed that you're flying all over the country to be with Niles, when you barely talk to your girls. This is what he said, not me."

"I know. He texted me." As soon as I say this, a thought snaps in my head. "Wait. You talked to him? Again?"

"A couple times."

"A *couple times*? Why didn't you tell me?"

"You never called!"

"Sara, when shit like this goes down, leave me a fucking voicemail. That's what they're for!" I nearly drop the phone when I throw my head back. I can't believe she didn't call to fill me in.

"I didn't want to ruin your experience, Kal. I mean, it's not like this is going to last or anything. So I figured I'd let you enjoy it while you can."

Her words hit me like a WWE star took a table to my head. Not going to last? Who says it's not going to last? Did she not just hear me say I'm in love with him? So, what does that mean to her? That I'm going to pack up and fly home on Monday and this will all be over? It won't be. He's into me, too. A few weeks ago, I may have agreed with her. But as of now, I know this is far from over—this is just the beginning.

"I can handle all that."

Of course, I'm not sure how much I believe the very words I just said. When Niles and I are together, the rest of my life, except for my writing, falls away. I'm in another dimension and, admittedly, my at-home reality isn't really part of that. Once the whole world knows what's going on, that separation will disappear.

Being in love with a rock star is proving to be very hard work.

"Yeah? You can handle the media? And a pissed-off Brad? And your girls who miss you? And your best friend who does, too? You can handle that while you're wrestling with thoughts of being *in love* with some celebrity that's showing you a little attention back?" She says "in love" in such a completely mocking voice, my stomach lurches with hurt. "Well, more power to ya, girl. You've got bigger britches than me."

I'm stunned. I've stopped pacing and plop back on the couch where I started. I can hardly catch my breath. It sounds an awful lot like my friend is challenging me. And not in a good way.

"Sara, what the . . . ?"

"You have lost hold of reality, Kallie," she snaps. "You're caught up in a dream world that is fine and dandy on paper, but is not going to transfer well into real life. Have you forgotten that you have two children? I mean, I'm no saint and I sometimes count down the minutes until Ben gets the kids for the week or weekend, but I still always put them first."

"You were just squeeing with me."

"I squeed with you when I thought you were under the same impression normal people would be. That this is a temporary summer romance with all the trimmings. An innocent notch on your bedpost, and a brag-worthy one at that. But now you're talking about love and it sounds like you have the two of you walking down the freaking aisle. That seems a little out of touch."

I'm so glad when she pauses; I don't want to hear much more.

"Niles is a rock star, Kallie. He doesn't have a normal job or a normal life or a normal anything. How, seriously, do you see that fitting into your future? I mean, really?"

"I don't know yet. But I do know I'm not stopping something before it starts."

"Okay, well, that's fine. You called me wondering what to do and how your new love for Niles would fit into your life. You had the same doubts I'm putting out to you right now. So why am I the bad guy?"

"Because you're telling me all the reasons it won't work. When what I wanted you to tell me is how it would and should and could work. I wanted you to be excited for me, and instead you're essentially calling me a fool. Fuck that, we'll chat later."

As my finger hovers over the End Call button, I hear her yell my name.

"Yeah?" I huff.

"Kallie, I'm sorry. I just don't want you to end up a crumpled heap on his floor someday. And I really don't want you to lose yourself in the process."

"I'm not going to lose myself, Sara. And I know it's hard to believe, and it sounds outrageous, but Niles truly cares for me. I don't know what's going to happen or how, but I was hoping for your support."

Aside from a few deep breaths, Sara's quiet. "Kal, I love you," she finally says. "And I'm glad you're getting to experience this. Everyone should have at least one dream come true, and yours is a biggie. I just wish you wouldn't have let it get so deep. Your life is here. And you have a whole shitstorm waiting for you when you get back. That's all."

"I get it. But you don't see what I see with him. I guess if it all falls apart at the end of the summer, you win. But from where I'm standing, that's not going to happen. And I'll figure out whatever needs to get figured out. I hope you're with me when I do, but if not, I understand."

"Well, just keep your guard up. Especially there in New York. If you two are going to get exposed for real, it's probably going to happen there. And if *that* happens, you can be sure there will be even more backlash here. It's just the reality of it."

"Yep, I get it." And I am *so* over this conversation. "If anything else crazy comes up, please call, okay? I don't like surprises."

I hang up the phone without waiting for her response. That is not at all how I expected our convo to go. I need to regroup. I'm rattled, yes, but I'm not rocked. And I am not letting one word of that conversation ruin my time here. No way.

Niles and I are meeting back here for lunch in two hours (he's bringing surprise takeout! Yay!), then he's off to do interviews and sound checks. That gives me a few hours to shop and wander. Clear my head. Maybe grab a new outfit for tonight. A little possible-movie-deal treat. And a consolation prize for spatting with my best friend during one of the most awesome times of my life. Yes, a little retail therapy is most certainly in order here. And I shall indulge.

I head into the bathroom to poke and prod at my hair in an effort to whip it into some sort of glam style. Because what if Sara's right? What if the paparazzi really do care about Niles and me? What if they snap some pictures tonight? I'd better look good. But not too good. I don't want to be "that girl" who looks like she tried too hard. Nope, Effortless Chic (which is not at all effortless) is totally where it's at. Now, if only I could create it.

The more I tease and twist, the more Sara's comment about the girls weighs on me. I'll be the first to admit that if ever there was a good time for them to be away, this is it. And I'm a big fan of signs, so maybe this is a sign that things are supposed to go down like this between Niles and me. If this would've been two months ago, when school was still in session, no way could this be taking place. Me traveling all over? Never. This has got to be happening for a reason. I am sure of it.

Still, I hate when I doubt myself as a mom—and having my best friend be the one to make me feel that way is a huge bummer. I've sacrificed plenty over the years so the girls could come first. That's what being a parent is. I'm not neglecting them in any way, shape, or form right now. They're away at their grandparents. With their dad. They're not at home alone, eating cold SpaghettiOs straight from the can and drinking water from the bathroom faucet. They're having a fun summer adventure and so am I. What's wrong with that?

You know what's wrong with that?

Nothing. Absolutely nothing at all.

CHAPTER TWENTY-FOUR
The Crazy Truth

"To us," Niles says, holding out his shot glass of whiskey. I clink his with mine and slam it, expecting my throat to catch fire. It doesn't.

"This must be some fancy-pants whiskey, because it's delicious." My general rule is that if it's consumed in a shot glass and doesn't have the word "Pucker" behind it, I hate it. So this is a pretty big win. I'm impressed.

"Only the best for you. For us." He takes my shot glass and his and sets them on the table next to us before nuzzling my neck and nibbling my ear. "You look fricking amazing tonight," he whispers. I forget to breathe for a moment, then repay him the same compliment. He does, after all, look incredible right now, too. He's still wearing his stage clothes because tonight we went straight from the venue to this little dive club that has been the guys' favorite haunt for years. No showers, no time to change, no nothing. Off the stage and into the car. And totally sexy.

"Remember, things might get a little wild tonight. So, if you want to leave at any time for any reason, just tell me."

He warned me of the potential wildness over our takeout lunch earlier (which was the absolute best steak I have ever had in my life.

And who gets takeout steak, right? Only in New York.). Truthfully, I'm a little nervous. But as long as he's with me, it can't be that bad. Right?

"Oh, and there will most certainly be a girl here who shows me her tits. Does it every single time we're here. She tells me she's in love with me, wants me to run away to Aruba with her and sing her to sleep on the beach." I stare at him, every jealous nerve in my body on overdrive. "We can't kick her out, though . . . she's the owner." He squeezes my hand. "And she's about sixty years old."

I relax a little as the shot starts to do its job. I suddenly don't care about sixty-year-old titty-flashers, or the roomful of people around us, or any of the shit going on at home. I wrap my arms around Niles's waist and pull him into me. "You know I love this jacket, but you need to lose it. It's keeping you too far away from me."

"I'm a sweaty mess underneath. It was fucking hot up there tonight. More than usual." He moves my hair behind my shoulder. "Unless it's just because I saw your sweet face in the audience and I couldn't calm down."

Aww, swoon.

"Yeah, I'm sure that's exactly what it was." I giggle and tug at his sleeve. I don't care how sweaty he is, I want to feel every inch of him I can, and this big ass leather jacket is totally hindering that.

"Slow down, young lady. I'll take it off in a second. But first, I need to grab something out of the pocket."

He jams his hand into one of the inside pockets and pulls out a velvet box, which he nervously holds out to me. "I guess I'm not totally sure what your jewelry style is yet, but since Nash got something like this for Emily, I figured it'd be a safe bet." He smiles a shy smile and pops the top open, revealing the most gorgeous diamond stud earrings I have ever seen. What the what?

"Oh my God," I whisper. "Are these for me?"

I am *so* good at asking stupid questions.

"Of course they are, goofball. Do you like them? Are they too big? Too small?" He cocks his eyebrows and looks so damn cute I can't decide if I want to stare at him, or the earrings.

"They are so perfect, I can't even believe it. I just . . . these are . . . this is totally amazing. Thank you so much."

I know my eyes are sprouting pools and I am trying hard to prevent that from happening, but damn, this is seriously crazy. Watching my book—my dream—come to life is way more emotional than I could've imagined.

"Want to put them in?"

Of course I do. I am just too frozen to do so. I must nod, though, because he wiggles one out of its slot in the box and holds it out. "Don't drop it." He pretends to hand it to me, then snatches it away quick, so my hand totally airballs.

"Ha, you're funny. Now, gimme it, before it really does fall."

I take out my cheapo hoop earrings and gaze at him adoringly (and probably ridiculously) as I wiggle the stud into my left ear. He presses the other earring against his lips, then holds it out. "Promise you'll think of me every time you wear these?"

Is he serious right now?

"I promise. And plus, I think of you all the time anyway." I know it sounds hokey and completely sappy, but it's true. After so many years with Brad, I've forgotten how absolutely intoxicating new love is. Niles is on my mind nearly every single second, whether he's a foot in front of me like he is now, or miles away. I haven't felt like this in ages—maybe ever, really. My stomach is in a constant tangle of good knots, and at any given moment, my heart is one millisecond away from bursting.

"They're gorgeous on you. You're gorgeous on them. Really. You're stunning."

"Thank you," I say, because really, it's all I can manage. If he keeps this up, I'm going to need a respirator.

"Are you ready to have some fun tonight?"

"Yeah. For sure."

"Good, because there are a couple of beers over there, calling our names. Let's hit it." He grabs my hand and tries to pull me toward the bar, but I dig my feet into the floor, pull him back, and kiss him hard.

"Thank you so much, Niles. *So* much. I really . . . *adore* you."

He smiles his cute little close-lipped smile and raises my hand along with his, up to his heart. "You're welcome, Kallie. And I really . . . *adore* you, too."

The way his heart pounds through his chest, which I feel as strongly as I feel my own, I know there is no question.

What he just said to me is true.

***

Sure, Niles and I have gotten tipsy together before, but this is insane. While he's using the restroom, I stand alone in the hallway that leads to it, with my face flat against the wall, trying to cool my burning cheeks.

"Hello, wall," I say, giggling at my own ridiculousness. "Thanks for holding me up. You're so . . . cool!" I turn my head so that my opposite cheek is against it and laugh some more because it's super hilarious. To me, anyway.

Niles bursts out of the restroom and grabs me from behind. "Ooh, lucky wall." He nuzzles his chin into the crook of my neck. I laugh again. This wall is completely entertaining and I am *so* ticklish right now.

"I have to step out back to take a call," Niles says. "My mom left me a voicemail about my sister, but I couldn't really understand her."

152

"Everything okay?" I attempt to pull myself together amidst my incessant urge to giggle. He shrugs and leads me to a high table near a window. There are no chairs, so I am forced to remain erect. This should be interesting.

"I'll be right out there," he says, motioning toward to window. "Don't move, okay?" He looks worried and I'm not sure if it's because of what's going on with Sister Kallie or because Girlfriend Kallie (ack! Did I just say *girlfriend*?) is a hot, drunken mess.

I nod and stand straight, showing him I can be trusted to not fall on my face. He hands me a bottle of water that seemed to appear from the heavens and stoops down to look me in the eye. "Here, drink this. Can you do that for me?"

If anyone else spoke to me like I was a child, I'd probably have something snarky to say in return. But hearing it from Niles, and seeing the expression on his face, makes it all alright. "I can do that for you." *I can do anything for you.*

"Good. Be right back."

He kisses my forehead and disappears out a side door. I glance around the room and see lots of people looking my way. Oh man, what are they thinking? We've had tons of people come up and talk to us tonight and each time Niles introduced me to someone, he'd say, "This is Kallie." Not "my friend, Kallie" or "my girlfriend, Kallie." Just plain "Kallie." But each time we met someone, he was either holding my hand or had his arm wrapped around my waist, so I suppose they could draw some pretty accurate conclusions without him giving me any formal title.

There have been lots of pictures snapped, too, but hardly anyone straight up asked for pics of Niles. Unless they were doing it on the sly, the only pics I've seen anyone take of him—aside from a few photos with fans—were when all the band members were together and they actually posed.

I look around for paparazzi or journalists and don't see anything conspicuous. There probably aren't any here. I'm sure the guys and the owner filter attendees so that those who are here respect everyone's space and privacy. Besides, Niles was right. There are people here doing some crazy-ass things. Couples making out in every nook and cranny of the room, pills being handed back and forth, smoke coming from a phone booth-sized room back near the stockroom. Clearly, these people are engaged in far more interesting activities than watching Niles and me. Still, I smooth my hair and slick on some lip gloss, just in case.

As I put my gloss away, I fiddle around in my purse, attempting to look busy. I really should take this time to text the girls or check messages, but my head is far too foggy to do anything that requires concentration or coordination, and plus, I'll probably just find more nastiness from Brad anyway.

Though my head is down, I sense a presence on the other side of the table. "You look lonely," someone says. Ah, hell. I don't even have to look up because I know the voice the second I hear it.

Robbyn.

I drag my eyes up and sure enough, there she is. Just seeing her makes my arm hair stand on end. "Where's your boyfriend?" She leans forward and smirks, punctuating the amused look that was already on her face.

"Taking a call." My hand starts motioning toward the window, but I don't want her to know anything about his whereabouts—or that he's currently out there alone—so I poke at a grain of salt on the table instead.

"Nice earrings. Those from Niles?" I'm not sure what would make her even ask that; for all she knows, I could've had these for years. But there is no sense in denying it, so I nod. "I got a gold bracelet once," she says, holding out her wrist. "Still wear it every day. Never got any bling like that, though."

Yep, I'm pretty much done here. This convo seriously needs to shut down before it even gets going. "Um, I need to hit the restroom, so . . ."

"*Heeey*," she interrupts, "didn't Nash get Emily earrings like that in your book? That's what Niles did, right? He recreated the whole Nash thing, didn't he?" She smiles and shakes her head. "Huh. How romantic. He can be pretty good when he wants to be."

I try to read her face, but there's really nothing to read. Is she being sarcastic? Serious? I have no idea how to respond to this, so I let my gaze wander over her right shoulder and around the room. Where the heck is Niles?

"Nothing beats how mushy he gets right after he screws your brains out, though, am I right?"

I stare back at her in horror. Did she really just say that to me? Is she really trying to compare notes? Not that I have any notes to compare, but she doesn't know that. Man, this girl really is whacked.

I don't say a word and she doesn't seem to notice. She looks wistful, not instigative. Oddly enough, I don't think she's trying to start something. But still, her comment is like a blow to my innards. I smash my lips together and let a breath puff out of my nose. If I clench my lips any tighter, my teeth will slice through. I hate how jealous I feel right now, and I really hate that I don't know if it's because she's been on the receiving end of his love-making or because she's been the recipient of his after-sex mushiness. Probably both. But mostly, it's probably because she has a year's worth of experiences with him where I've had just a few weeks. She knows him so well. Or not. He did say that he hardly shared anything with her, right? But if that's true, why did he get mushy with her? What did he say? Will he get mushy with me when—if—that day ever comes? He's told me that I "already" know him so well, but I don't know that side of him at all. I want to know that side of him. So very, very badly.

155

"I really didn't think things would go so far with you two." She turns her gaze back toward me. "I almost feel threatened. But I know that once he's gotten all that he needs from you, he'll be back." She smiles and pulls her ponytail forward over her shoulder.

I want so badly to ignore her. Wave a wand and make her go away. Have Niles pop up at that very second and interrupt this completely bizarre conversation. But none of that happens. And because of the drinks, my filter's switch is positioned to off.

"Sorry, Robbyn. But I'm pretty sure he won't be back. We're together now." I state this as matter-of-factly as I can. I'm not trying to start anything either, but this chick needs to back the fuck off.

"Honey, you are not *together*." She smashes her own lips together and raises her eyebrows as though she feels sorry for me. She studies me for a second and when I don't say a word, she says, "Kallie, wow. Are you really that naïve? You seem smarter than that to me."

Okay, now I'm hot. Whatever button she just pushed sends me into overdrive. I stand up straight and square my shoulders. She's taller than me, so I'm sure I'm not at all threatening, but still. I refuse to back down.

"Robbyn, I don't know what you're trying to say, but don't bother. Niles and I very much understand each other. Things are great. Getting more awesome by the day. I know it's hard to hear, but if I were you, I'd move the hell on. He won't be coming back to you. It's that simple."

She tosses her head back and laughs. I size up her exposed neck, thinking about how many times Niles has kissed it. Same with her collarbones and her chest. I look at her nose and forehead and chin, knowing he must've smothered those with kisses, too. My heart aches and I want to run away.

"Okay, Kallie," she says, "I shouldn't tell you this because it's kind of like betraying the only man I've ever loved, but maybe this will move things along quicker, so here we go: Niles does not like you in that way. Sure, he's really falling into character here, but the long and short of it . . ." she tips her head toward me and widens her eyes ". . . you wanna know?" I instinctively nod in return. "He's using you. Get it? *Using. You.* He was bone-dry coming up with ideas for the new album and needed some inspiration. He finds out some random chick in Anytown, USA, wrote a book about him, so he says, 'Hey, let me see what makes this girl tick. What would make a married woman think that way? How is she so obsessed with someone she doesn't even know? Why would she risk so much to write a book like that?' He thought there was a story there, Kallie, something he could build the new album around. Heartache and obsession and voyeurism and all that. So he called your ass up. Befriended you. Got you to trust him and spill your heart. That was his plan, anyway. And it looks to me like it's working."

She looks at me expectantly, but my heart has stopped and I'm pretty sure I'm going to black out. I hold on to the table for stability and let my head drop against my will.

"So, see what I mean? It sucks for me to watch him buy you bling and hold your hand and shit, but I know it's for the greater good. He'll write his next blockbuster album, kick your skinny butt to the curb, and come back to me. I just gotta be patient."

From the corner of my eye, I see her fiddle with her bracelet. My brain has no idea what to do with this information. She's either completely delusional or totally telling the truth. Really, what she's saying is plausible. Why else would a rock star text me out of nowhere and then proceed to spend so much time with me? I think back on our time together and try to make sense of it all. If he's "in character," then he deserves a damn Oscar, to be truthful. I mean, he's all but told me he loves me, he's gifted me with diamond earrings, and he spends nearly every available second either with me or talking to me.

If he's just acting, he's really doing it up.

But, maybe *that's* why we've never had sex. Maybe he won't go there because this is all a fraud. He'll kiss me and mess around with me and tell me all the stuff I want to hear, but he won't betray Robbyn or step into full-on bad-guy territory by making love to me.

Oh my God. Maybe it's all true.

"Here he comes," she says. "Listen, as a fellow sistah, I'm sorry to bust your bubble like that. But you gotta know the boy is mine. Always will be. Don't forget it."

She excuses herself and touches Niles's shoulder as she walks by him. I drop my eyes and pretend to dig around in my purse again, but really I'm hiding the tears that are threatening their spill.

"Aw, shit. Again?" He thumps his hand on the table. "I knew I should've had you come out there with me. Whatever she said, I apologize in advance. I'm sure it was nothing good."

I don't answer him because I can't. I'm still digging and the tears are still threatening.

"Kallie? You okay?" I shake my head, still looking down. "Dammit! What the fuck did she say?" He steps around the table so he's right in front of me. He lifts my chin, but my eyes stay fixed on his shoulder. I cannot look at his face.

"Tell me what she said." He's calmer now, and he positions his face directly in front of mine so there is no way I can't look at him.

I take a deep breath, battling with the corners of my mouth, which insist on turning downward. "Remember when you said that if I was uncomfortable tonight, we could leave?"

"Yeah. Of course."

"You can stay, but I gotta go."

"You are not leaving without me. Let's go." He takes my hand and leads me toward the door. I allow it, but what I really want to do is run in the opposite direction. What's going to happen next? Do I tell him what Robbyn just told me? Do I hold out and see if he exposes himself for the fraud Robbyn says he is? Do I pretend none of the last ten minutes ever happened and go on like all is well?

We crash through the door to the outside and I dash to the side of the building. In an instant, my stomach unleashes all the doubt and jealousy and alcohol it's held all night. Niles is at my side, holding my hair away from my face, rubbing my back. He tells me it's okay and that he's here with me, and that everything will be fine.

Everything will be fine.

My head goes fuzzy and my body shakes . . . because as much as I want to believe him—as much as I really, really want to believe him—I seriously doubt that any of this is going to end up being "fine."

CHAPTER TWENTY-FIVE
He Loves Me, He Loves Me Not

The city streaks by through the cab window as Niles rubs his thumb across the top of my hand. He hasn't let go of me since the second we walked out of the club. Even as we slid into the cab seat, he held my hand. Seeing the concern on his face and watching the tender way he's treating me, my heart refuses to believe that what Robbyn accused him of is true.

I lift my forehead away from the cold glass of the window for a brief second, then let it crash down all over again. I simply don't have the energy to keep my neck straight. My skin crawls thinking about how many germs are on this glass (Niles must be completely beside himself), but I don't care. It feels good and it gives my eyes somewhere to look, other than at him.

"So, are you ever going to tell me what happened?" he asks. His voice is soft and caring, but also has an edge to it. Not knowing what went on in there is obviously killing him.

My mind goes wild. How can this sweet, sweet person—the guy who will not peel himself away from me, who told me how hot I make him, who told me how inspiring I am, who told me things he's allegedly never told another person—how can he really be a fraud?

Can all this really be an act? Is he that good of a liar? I simply cannot believe it. But why would Robbyn have lied?

Get it together, Kallie. She's jealous of you. A jealous ex-girlfriend who is not particularly stable. She's heartbroken. She wants him back. She can't accept that he's moving on. And she really can't accept that he's moving on right under her nose, where she can see him gifting you with diamonds and canoodling every chance he gets.

It would be torturous to witness someone you still love taking up with another person, I'm sure. I mean, we've all been there, right? We've seen our ex-high school crush or ex-lover or ex-whatever moving on with someone hotter, uglier, skinnier, fatter. It all hurts, no matter how much time we have invested or whether or not we thought we'd have a future together. In their case, she'd been pregnant with his baby, was with him for a year, thought they'd get married. Of course she'd be teetering on the deep end of desperation. I'm sure I would be, too.

But then why am I still so haunted by her words?

"Whatever she said obviously really upset you, and I hate that so much," Niles says, bringing me back to the here and now. His thumb stops moving before he sucks in a breath. "I also hate that you're not saying anything. Does that mean you think you can't talk to me? Because, if so, that's a huge bummer. I really thought we were . . . I thought we were much bigger than that."

I snap my head to look at him. With those few words, my heart just broke. He's right. He's absolutely right. We *are* bigger than that. I have no business letting an insecure, jealous ex-girlfriend put doubts in my head when the person I should be putting all my faith in has never given me any indication he's not one hundred percent genuine. I turn in my seat until we are knee to knee and throw my inhibitions out the window. Cabbie be damned, I don't care who sees me right now. This is something that must be done.

I boost myself up until I am straddling Niles's lap. At first, he looks shocked, but then he settles right in and clutches my waist. I hold his face and kiss him hard. He kisses me back with such fire, it's hard to catch my breath. This goes on for ages, until I finally try to speak, in between kisses.

"She . . . she talked a bunch of shit . . . said some things . . . tried to make me doubt you . . . but I don't care . . ." I pull away, my heart absolutely racing. I look at him, stare at that beautiful face, and smooth his eyebrow with my thumb. "I don't care what she says. I know what I know." I kiss him again. "And what I know is that this is good. This is very, very good."

Even though Niles kisses me back, his posture suddenly stiffens. I pull back again and drop my hands to his shoulders. "What's wrong?"

"Nothing, I just . . . what do you mean she said stuff to make you doubt me? What did she say?"

"It doesn't matter, Niles. I *don't* doubt you. At all."

His brows scrunch up and he shakes his head so slightly it's barely noticeable. "She's jealous, Kallie."

"I know."

"She can't stand to see us together."

"I know. I get it."

"She calls and texts me all the time. I should have told you, but I didn't want you to worry. Because it really is over between us. Really." He looks at me, his eyes speaking volumes. "I didn't not tell you to be sneaky. I promise."

I tip my head, smiling a small smile to let him know it's all right. "I know, Niles. Really."

"Kallie," he whispers, pulling my head down so my ear is near his mouth. "Let me make love to you tonight. Let me show you that you have nothing to doubt. That I'm, *we're*, for real."

I am absolutely sure I just lost consciousness. Niles Russell just told me he wants to make love to me. This is what I want most in this world right now and all I have to do is say yes and it will happen. Finally. Just like that. After all the thinking and wishing and dreaming and hoping, it's here. The time is finally here.

All I have to do is say yes.

***

Niles stepped out quick (to get condoms? I assume so, but I didn't ask.) and I am so thankful for this time to freshen up. My hair is disgusting and my eyes are screaming red from puking my fool head off earlier. I need to make myself hot—or at least presentable—before our big moment.

My stomach is in so many knots I can barely function. I want to be calm and cool, but I can hardly stand up. I can't remember the last time I was so nervous. I don't think I ever have been . . . well, except maybe right before the first (and second) time I met him.

What is this going to be like? It seems weird knowing it's about to happen. Like, I kind of just thought it would go down naturally, without thought. I expected that we'd be in a "moment" and be so hot for each other that doing anything other than *that* would be impossible. Lord knows we've come close a bunch of times. I just assumed that's how it would be.

I fluff my hair, brush my teeth, spray on some dry shampoo, and do a quick shave of my pits. I spruce up "down there" and dust everywhere I can reach with shimmering powder. I'm feeling as good as I can under the circumstances and squee at myself in the mirror.

This is it, Kal. This is your moment. The guy you've dreamed about for years is about to get as close to you as humanly possible. In just a short while, you two will become one. Keep it cool, this is what you want. Don't freak out. Don't blow it.

Despite my best efforts, all the pep talks in the world can't stop my mind from going batshit crazy. What's he going to look like naked? What will he think about how I look? Will he be, ahem, big? Small? Average? I don't have a lot to compare him to, but I don't think it will matter anyway. Even with my nerves turned up to full blast, I'm already so hot all it will take is for him to put a hand on my boob and I'll lose my mind, I just know it. This is so bizarre. I kind of wish I didn't have time to think about it. I'm freaking myself out and nothing has even happened yet.

I've done all I can do, so now I just wait. I put all my toiletries away and take one last look in the mirror. As I fix a clump of wayward hair, my phone bloops and I grab it, expecting it to be a text from Niles. When I see a number I don't recognize, I almost ignore it, but open the text instead.

"In case you didn't believe me," it says, "I have some proof. Stay tuned. Sending it through."

I wait a second, scrolling through all of my recent contacts, looking for a number that matches. It must be Lucy, texting from her personal phone. Maybe she's about to send me a copy of a movie rights bid or something. Oh man, that is quite possibly the only thing that could make this moment even more amazing.

"Feast your eyes," comes the next text.

Feast is not the word. Because when I open the attached photo, I see a snap of a notebook page, scribbled on with handwritten notes. Notes that say, "Figure out where she was coming from. Where was her head? Why me? Why now? What does she see in me? What is she expecting? What does she want? Why a book? Why a story about someone she doesn't know? Why take such a risk? Build album around these answers."

For at least the tenth time tonight (and for so many reasons) my heart stops. I scrutinize the writing. I've only seen Niles's handwriting on the card he left me in the hotel room back in Philly, but I've drooled over that card so many times I can see the writing as though it were right before me. And, as much I can't stomach admitting it, the writing in this photo matches it precisely. Oh my God.

I scrunch my eyes shut as I set down my phone. These are the things Niles wanted to learn about me so he could write his next album. These, right here, are the reasons Niles reached out to me. Why he keeps me around, keeps asking questions, keeps winning my trust, keeps convincing me he cares.

This is picture proof. What Robbyn said was true.

Niles is fucking using me.

CHAPTER TWENTY-SIX
Tough Love

Kallie, get a grip, I tell myself. Think this through. Don't jump to conclusions. Maybe it's not what you think.

But how can it not be?

It really does make sense. Niles reached out to me because he was creatively dry. That's why he keeps telling me how impressed he is with my progress on Book Two. He must find that intriguing because he's coming up so empty. I'm sure I'd feel the same way.

But if he needed me for inspiration, yet he's still not making much progress, what does that mean? He's obviously not getting what he needs from me. Or maybe his feelings for me really *are* real and I'm distracting him. But even if that's the case, does that excuse the fact that he used me?

Ugh, what the hell, what the hell, what the hell?

"Kallie? Hey, I'm back."

Oh my God, he's here. What am I going to do? I can't just jump into the sack with him. Not now. Not knowing what I might know. But, I *want* to jump in the sack with him. Whatever it is that's going on here, I have genuinely fallen in love with him. Well, the him I thought he was. But even if he's not that guy, he's still my rock star crush, and who wouldn't want to get it on with their rock star crush when the opportunity arises?

I mean, right?

"You fall asleep on me?"

Oh, his voice is so playful. He's so charming and seemingly genuine, there is no way that what is going on between us is not real. I've heard his heart thump, I've felt his body react to my touch, I've seen him cry as he admitted all his wrongdoings, then plead with his eyes for me not to hate him because of them. His kisses are too deep to be fake, the way he looks at me and touches me and acts so protective of me—those are not the behaviors of a con artist. And now, he's asked to make love to me to prove he's for real. He said it himself. This is proof he cares.

But what about the picture?

He knocks on the bathroom door. "Are you okay in there? Come on out. I miss you."

Oh, I miss you, too.

I open the door slowly and see that quirky face I just can't get enough of. I could stare at him forever.

"You are so beautiful," he says, stepping toward me. Even though part of me wants to punch him, I remind myself that I don't know the whole story yet. I let myself fall into his arms and bury my face in his chest. I love how he feels against me. I can't help it. We fit.

Man, I just want this night to go as perfectly as it was supposed to. I want to take him by the hand and lead him to his bedroom. I want to strip us both naked, where we'll kiss every square inch of each other and finally maneuver ourselves so that instead of two people, we are one.

I want to take it slow and easy, feeling every feeling that needs to be felt and going to every place we're ready to go. When it's over, I want to look him in the eye and tell him straight up, without reservations, that I love him. That there is almost nothing he could do wrong and no reason I could ever stop loving him. That whatever brought us together doesn't matter, and that the only thing that does matter is where we are now.

But I don't know how true that is. Call it cynicism or the skittishness of enduring another failed relationship, but I'm not sure if I can move forward with something that's already laced with doubts and hidden agendas. If the reason I am melting into his chest right now is because he needed my pathetic fangirl story to inspire his new album, maybe I shouldn't go any further at all.

I seriously have to find out what he was thinking. Right now.

"Niles? Do you really, like *really*, care about me?"

"More than I want to admit."

There was no hesitation. No pause, no nothing. He didn't miss a beat. His arms tighten around me, bringing us even closer together.

"But I'm a head case, right?" I lift my head just a touch, then plop it right back down again. I can't look at him. It'll be much easier speaking to his shirt than into those beautiful eyes.

"I mean, I wrote a book about some guy I didn't even know. Celeb-stalker. Who does that? Who risks the judgment of pretty much everyone just to tell a fangirl story like mine? There must be a reason behind that madness, right?"

I pause, then with my heart up in my throat, I just plain old put it out there. "Shit, I bet you could write a whole album about that."

And with that, he stiffens. Like really, really stiffens.

Bingo, I got him.

Damn it, damn it, damn it, I got him.

"I can't get in bed with you tonight," I say, stepping back as my chest tightens. I glance at him just long enough to see the pained look on his face.

"Why not?" he whispers.

"Maybe this is all too fast after all."

"It's not, Kallie. Come on. We're there now. We have been. I was just too scared to let it happen."

"Why? Afraid of *hurting someone*?" My cheeks flush and I clench my hands together, mostly because I don't know what else to do.

"Yeah," he says, his voice rising to match mine. "You!"

"Me? Really? Are you sure you don't mean *Robbyn*?"

He throws his hands up and looks back at me with flashing eyes. "Kallie, what the *hell*? I thought I've been perfectly clear about all that!"

"I can't have sex with you tonight, Niles," I say again, turning my gaze to the floor.

"Yeah, okay, I get it. But will you please be straight with me about why? This is not about Robbyn. It better not be. We're done. I've told you that. A million fucking times."

"Well, that's not what she says," I spit. "But that's also not the real issue here."

"Then what *is* the real issue?"

I think fast, because I'm really not sure where I'm going with this next. I suddenly feel panicky about tackling this head on. I've forgotten how hard new relationships are, and I certainly couldn't have predicted the effort it takes to be in love with someone you idolize, but obviously barely know. I'm not ready to completely walk away from us, but I know that I can't go even the tiniest bit further without thinking this through.

I take a deep breath and say the only thing I can think of. The thing that will buy me some time. The quintessential statement that almost every person who has been in a relationship throws out before getting in too deep. The biggest cop out of all, really.

"I need some space, okay? This is just . . . too fast. It was a fangirl infatuation that went really far, really fast. And maybe we need to step back."

"Oh, come on, Kallie. You are so full of shit," he says, rolling his eyes. "There is no way you really believe that."

"Yeah, well, there are a lot of things I've been forced to believe that I really don't want to!"

I walk into his room to gather up my stuff. "I'm going to stay at the hotel tonight. And I think I should fly home tomorrow instead of Monday."

"What? You're walking away? You're really not going to tell me where all of this is coming from?"

I glance up at him; he looks so sad. How can I do this to him? Oh yeah, because of what he did to me.

"I just need some time. I think we still have a lot to learn about each other."

"Well, we can't really learn about each other if *one of us* refuses to talk." He gives me a pointed look, which makes me feel both guilty and mad. He must read this on my face because he walks up and tries to put his hands on my shoulders. I shrug them away.

"Okay, here's the deal," he says, crossing his arms over his chest instead. "There is no way I am buying what you're selling. No way. There is something shitty going on here and you need to speak up or else there is not a damn thing I can do about it."

Ugh, why does he have to be such an intuitive son of a gun? He is making this so difficult. I really just want to spill everything, but my line has been drawn. I need to stick this out. I need to remember who I am and what I need. I need to let him know that I can call some shots, too. I need to figure out how I feel about this and decide what I'm going to do next. And he'll just have to be okay with that.

"What you can do," I say with a very measured voice, "is give me some space."

"Fine." He walks toward his door. "I kinda thought we were at a place where you could tell me anything, but sure, okay, if you need space, by all means." He holds open the door, his face full of hurt and confusion and annoyance and sadness. I pick up my bag and as I walk past him, he gives me a rough peck on the cheek. "Call me when you're ready. I hope it's soon."

CHAPTER TWENTY-SEVEN
Worth a Thousand Words

"Kallie? It's two o'clock in the morning. Are you okay?"

Oh God, how I needed to hear this voice. There is nothing in the world quite like a friend who answers your excessively off-hours calls.

"You were right, Sara. You called it and you nailed it. I am so naïve."

With those few words, with that short little admission, my emotions fall out. The tears I held in as I left Niles's apartment, the tears I held in throughout the cab ride here, and the tears I held in as I rode the elevator to my room, burst through the door, then flung myself onto the bed . . . they're all loose now. They're cascading down my cheeks and onto my shirt and onto the pillow and right to the sheets and the blankets. They're everywhere, dampening everything, making my vision blurry and my head and my heart absolutely ache.

"I called what? Oh my God, what happened?"

"He isn't what I thought," I wail. "What I hoped. He was . . . using me."

I don't even try to pull myself together, and because Sara has seen me at my worst many times over, I know she doesn't expect me to.

"Girl, slow down," she says, compassion dripping from her voice. "What do you mean, he was using you? Using you for what? Did he hurt you?"

"No, he didn't hurt me." I sniff. "He wouldn't do that. But he couldn't come up with any ideas for the new record," *sniff,* "so he befriended me to get into my head. He was gonna write his new album with my stupid fangirl obsession as the focal point. Can you believe that?" I pick up a pillow from the bed and whip it across the room.

"He *told* you that?"

"No," I blubber. "Robbyn, his ex. She told me. At a party tonight."

Sara clucks her tongue, then laughs more loudly than she should at 2:00 a.m. "So his *ex* told you this? And you believed her? Kallie, *that* is naïve."

"She sent me a picture, Sar. It was right there in front of my eyes. A notebook page filled with notes in his handwriting, with all the questions he needed to ask in order to build the new album around my sorry obsession. I feel like such a fool. You questioned what a rock star would want with little old me, and I didn't listen. Why didn't I listen?"

"Oh, honey, it's okay." Her voice is like a hug through the phone. "You fell hard for him and were blinded. That's what love does. Don't be so hard on yourself. This is not your fault."

"Why did it have to be this way?" I cry. "I really thought, in some weird way, we actually had a chance." I swipe at the tears trailing down my cheeks and try to sit up. My body doesn't cooperate, so I flop back down and stare up at the ceiling instead.

"I know you did, love." She pauses a second, clearly trying to assemble the right words. "But, you know, this is probably for the best. I'm sorry you are hurting, I really am. And it's awesome that you had so much fun while you did. But hidden agenda or not, your chances of being a real thing? I mean . . . it probably wasn't going to happen. It was a dream, not a reality."

Of course she's right. I didn't listen to her before, but I obviously should now. I was crazy to think a small-town girl like me could ever attract an international rock star on her own merits. Of course there was something behind it. And yeah, things may have gotten real between us, but how sustainable is something like this? I'm a dreamer—always have been—but sometimes a little kick in the reality pants is all I need to come to my senses.

I scrunch my eyes shut, pushing even more tears down my face. "I just want to come home."

"Can you fly out tomorrow? You probably should. Can I help call someone for you? Are you okay where you're at?"

"Yeah, I'm at the hotel. I'm fine here. I'll try to get my flights changed, but for now, I just need to finish my cry and sleep this off." My voice shakes as I paw through my bags in search of pajamas. "Thanks for listening, my friend. I'll call you tomorrow."

I don't wait for her response, and I couldn't hear her if she said anything else anyway. I cry and cry and cry some more, thinking about my entire journey with Niles, from the moment I conceptualized my book to less than an hour ago. The feelings I developed for him before even meeting him, the knots in my stomach the first time we came face-to-face, the pangs of emptiness I felt every time we were away from each other for even the shortest of moments. I think about the realization that he isn't who I dreamt he was, who I made him be in my mind and on the page, or who I wanted him to be more than anything.

Oh, why couldn't he have just read my book, thought I was cool, and called me up just because he wanted to get to know me better? Because I was someone with whom he connected? Because I was someone worth knowing, not because I provided fodder for his next artistic foray? I feel like such a joke, such a moron, such a fool for handing him my heart on a platter, only for him to take the butt of his microphone and grind it right in.

What am I going to do next? Do I tell him this is it? That we're done just as fast as we started? Do I ask to remain friends? Do I say, "Hey, maybe our paths will cross again someday, so farewell for now?"

Ugh, I'm not ready for this change yet. I've become far too accustomed to how things have gotten and that's how I still want them to be. I want to see his face and hear his voice and smell his smell. I want a zillion texts a day and more pictures on my phone than it can viably hold. I don't want to imagine what life will look like now. Already. Without warning.

Somehow, some way, between all the tears and questions and muddled thoughts and sadness, I fall asleep. He's in my dreams, of course, and all is well. But I must remember it was a dream. All of it was only a dream.

***

I wake up to Niles's voice, singing inches from my head. I have one of his songs as my general ringtone and hearing it call to me first thing this morning breaks my heart all over again. I make a mental note to change it as soon as I can.

Lucy's name flashes on my screen, so with a froggy voice and mush for a brain, I answer as cheerfully as I can.

"Good morning, Lucy! Happy Sunday!"

"Kallie, hiiiiiiii," she drawls. "Have fun last night?"

I puff a breath through my nose and feel the corners of my mouth turn down. If I won't be seeing Niles anymore, I'm sure I'll need to come clean to her eventually. But now is not the time.

175

"Yeah," I say, my heart tightening all over again. "It was nice."

"I see that. You looked great. And you two are fabulous together. Nice work."

Wait, what? I guess my stunned silence clues her in, because her voice bubbles as she says, "You haven't seen *Page Six* yet today, have you? You guys are in there. And you look incredible. This is huge. Congratulations!"

I am stunned. Absolutely stunned. *Page Six*? I'm in *Page Six*? With Niles?

"Do you know who Niles's publicist is? I can find out, but if you already know, that's cool. We've been talking about doing that for you, but now it looks like the sooner the better. I'll get with the team first thing tomorrow."

I can't even believe what I am hearing. The world is opening *Page Six* this morning and seeing my face in it? And now my agent is talking to me about getting a publicist? This is all part of that unbelievable dream I was living, just hours ago. And now it's crashed and burned. Just like that.

"You there?" she asks. "You're so quiet."

"Sorry, yes, I'm here. Just the first time I've ever been, you know, internationally exposed."

"Ha, well, enjoy it. Looks like this is just the beginning. You guys will probably be the next media darlings."

I fall back on the bed, stretching my arm so it reaches into the bag next to me. I dig through until I find the sweatshirt I took from Niles's apartment last night. I put it up to my nose and breathe in. Hoo boy.

"Do you think we can announce on your fan page that you're dating? Your readers will go absolutely crazy."

No! Oh my God, no!

"Um, we're not really *dating*."

"Well . . . you obviously spend a lot of time together."

"Yeah, as friends."

Lucy laughs politely. "Kallie, I know it's weird talking about your personal life, but when we get off this call, look up the picture. It pretty much screams that you two are way more than just friends."

Holy cow, what the hell? What are we doing in the picture? I run my mind back through last night—the stuff I can remember, anyway. I assume the snap was taken at the after-party. If that's the case, then yes, anyone there would not have had a hard time catching us in an embrace of some sort. Wow, this is huge. I wonder what Niles will think. I wonder what his publicist is thinking. I wonder what this means for us going forth.

"Listen, Kallie, you've been seen at a lot of his shows. People are making the connection between him and your book. I know Niles is super private, but he's not so private that he hid his obvious affection for you while you were at a huge party where he had to know there'd be cameras. This could be really big for your career, especially as we shop your movie rights. I think it'd be smart for you to make an announcement on your fan pages. Or at least say something cheeky about the photo. It doesn't have to be weird. We can make it fun, but it's still an admission by default. What do you think? This could be great. For both of you."

More silence on my end. I truly don't know what to say. I envision myself announcing to my fans that Niles and I are a couple. That dreams really do come true. That being true to your heart can get you everything you want in life and more. I envision my fans going crazy, my books flying off the shelves, my royalties climbing to the sky. I envision congratulatory comments on my fan page, messages of hope and encouragement, fans reveling in the fact that true love always wins. It could've been that way. This could have been just the beginning. This could have been my life.

But, as of last night, that's no more.

"Uh, I have to think about this, Lucy."

"Sure. Take your time. Talk to Niles and see what they're doing on his end. I just think that if you're going to make a move, sometime today would be your best timing."

"Right. Okay." What do I do? Do I tell her that Niles and I are no more? That the pic from last night is the last one she'll ever see like that? That this was just a fun little fluke and my luck has run out and I'm back to being that small-town girl with big dreams who will probably end up dating someone from high school, just like her best friend? Or do I say nothing and hope all the hype dies down and Niles and I can just fade into the sunset with no one wondering or questioning or getting giddy about what they see in the tabloids?

"I'm genuinely excited for you two," Lucy says. "I know how much you care for him. What a dream, right?"

Well, shit.

"A dream. Exactly." My voice is flat, so I wonder if she can read me. I really shouldn't say anything more. "I'll be in touch, okay? Thanks so much for letting me know. I'll talk to Niles and see what's up from here."

We hang up and my fingers fly across my keypad. *Page Six*. There it is. I scroll past A-listers, a few has-beens, and gaggles of reality stars until I see the photo in question. Holy cow, there we are. And the picture is gorgeous. Oh, it's so gorgeous. We're facing each other, our hips so close a piece of paper couldn't fit through. His arms are around my waist, my hands are on his upper arms, and we're looking into each other's eyes, smiling the biggest, most genuine smiles we could possibly be. My hair is flowing perfectly over my shoulder and my skin has just the right amount of sheen. And the earrings! You can see my new diamond earrings just as plain as day. We look relaxed, happy, perfect together . . . and in love. We look totally, completely, unmistakably in love.

And everyone who reads *Page Six* is seeing it.

CHAPTER TWENTY-EIGHT
Word to Yo Mutha

I send the link to Sara with instructions to "Check this quick" and wait for my phone to blow up. And thirty seconds later, that's exactly what it does

"Kallie! Holy crap! Is this from last night? Before you found out?" Her voice is so high I'm not sure how she doesn't have a line of dogs outside her window. "It's clear you've only given me part of the story here. So spill it. Now. This is *Page* Freaking *Six*! And you're in it!"

I stare at the screen of my laptop. I have to admit the photo looks even better on a larger scale. "Yeah, that's from last night. At the after-party. There's just so much to tell, I can't even. I don't want to. But yes, at that moment, life was amazing. Then the shit hit the fan."

"Listen," she says, her voice dropping several octaves. "I know what I said last night, and I know what I've said before, but I am looking at this photo now and do you know what I see?"

"Lies?"

"No. I see a gorgeous rock star who probably had a million people in that room fighting for his attention, and his eyes—and hands— are squarely on you. *You*, Kallie."

Oh, how those words sting.

"Seriously, did you look at yourselves? I know I basically called you two a pipe dream, but this picture is worth the proverbial thousand words. This dude is into you. It's written all over his face."

"Maybe he is now. But that's not where we started." My stomach tightens again. Oh man, I am so confused.

"Okay, this is ridiculous. I need the whole story here, and you've obviously been holding back. Tell me what he said when you asked him about the notes. Did he deny it? Come clean?"

I swallow hard. "I didn't ask him. He doesn't know I know."

"Wait, *what*? If you didn't confront him, then what did you two fight about last night?"

I glance at the photo again and decide there's no good in holding back. Maybe I'm missing something. Maybe Sara can help set me straight. Or maybe she'll agree that he fucked me over big time and then I can move on in peace.

"We were finally going to have sex last night, Sara. He was ready. I've *been* ready. It was time. But then Robbyn sent that picture. She had told me about it at the after-party, but I chose not to believe her. But then when I saw it for myself, how could I not?"

"So you just walked out on him? Did he not see the picture, too?"

"He was gone when it came through, so he never knew I got it. When he came back, I didn't know how to bring it up, so I just acted normal and we just kind of, you know, held each other for freaking ever and it was amazing. But then I decided that I couldn't go further with him unless I knew the truth, so I said something to trip him up. And the way his body posture responded? I totally busted him. It was a dead giveaway that Robbyn was actually telling the truth."

"Um, okay. So to recap . . . you're telling me that he never saw the photo Robbyn sent you. At all?"

"No."

"No, that's not what you're telling me, or no, he never saw it?"

"No, he never saw it."

"And you never told him you received it?"

"No."

"And you never told him what Robbyn said to you at the party?"

"No."

"So, essentially," she says, in her best psychiatrist voice, "you tricked him into nonverbally admitting something he didn't know he was admitting to?"

Well, when she puts it that way.

"Good gravy, Kallie, listen to me. You need to talk to him about this. You are totally not being fair. He needs to know what you're thinking so he can explain himself. Maybe it's not what you think."

I close my eyes, more conflicted now than ever.

"Sweetie, I know you're confused, but here's what I want you to do. Do not leave New York City today. Stay there. Take a long shower, get some coffee, clear your head. When you're ready, invite him somewhere neutral. Don't go to his place, don't make him come to you. Meet somewhere out. Wherever you can go where you won't get spotted. Then talk to him. Tell him what you know, how you found out, and what your concerns are. Let him tell his side of the story. You owe that to him, and if he really did what you think, he owes you an explanation, too."

I sigh. She's totally right.

"Honestly, Kallie? I can't take my eyes off this picture. You look like you're in your own little world. It seems so weird seeing my best friend in a photo with a celebrity and frankly, I am totally, totally jealous. But there is something there between you two, it's so super-duper obvious." I lick my lips and feel a smile spread across my face. "Give him a chance, Kal. If he doesn't tell you what you need and want to hear, you can pull the plug then. But don't give him the boot until you figure this thing out. Okay? Do you promise?"

"Yeah. I promise."

"Keep your guard up. He's still not off the hook. But you gotta let him speak. You have to get the whole truth and then decide how big of an issue it really is."

I'm about to tell her I hear her loud and clear, but my call waiting beeps and I see that it's him.

Oh my God, it's him!

"Holy shit, Sara, it's Niles! He's buzzing in. I'm gonna do it. I'm gonna talk to him. Thanks for everything, honey. I love you soooo much! Later!"

Before she responds I click over, which automatically turns my tongue into a jumble-up, tangly heap. Big surprise.

"Hi," I squeak.

"Hi. How are you doing this morning?"

I want to say what I would normally say: *better now that I'm talking to you.* But I keep it cool instead. "I'm okay. How are you?"

"I think you know."

I answer with silence.

"I know you said you need some space, and I'll respect that if it's still true. But I really want to see you. Can I see you this morning? Please?" His voice teeters on begging, and against my better judgment, my heart melts all over the place.

"Give me 'til ten? I look a wreck."

"Really? Ten? Okay, yeah, you got it." His voice is suddenly smiling. "See you then."

"Hey, Niles?"

"Yeah?"

"Have you seen *Page Six* this morning?"

"No. I don't read that crap."

"Well . . . you might want to today."

***

"I brought coffee," Niles says, his outstretched hand clenching a Starbucks cup with my name scrawled across the side.

I close my text messages—from a fuming Brad ("Nice to see you partying it up with your boy toy while I take good care of your daughters"), Katherine ("OMG, you two are hotter than hot! I need the scoop!"), my cousin ("Does your mom know you're dating a rock star?!") and a handful of others. I had no idea so many people were clued in to celeb sightings. I can't believe I *qualify* as a celeb sighting.

"I had a feeling you would." I make sure my fingers don't brush his as I take my cup. Avoiding our white-hot electricity is probably a good idea right now.

Despite Sara's urging to meet him somewhere neutral, it looks like we'll be powwowing at my hotel. But having him in the room with me is not nearly as awkward as I thought it would be. What's awkward is the inner battle I'm having with myself to keep from plunging into his arms like I really want to. My heart is telling me to go for it, my head is telling me no way. Not yet.

"So, *Page Six*, huh?" he says. "That was a surprise, right?"

"Uh, yeah. A little."

"Did you like the picture, Kallie? Did you get a good look at it?" He sets his coffee down and slowly walks toward me.

"Yeah. I did."

"I think it speaks volumes, don't you?" His voice is low as he inches even closer, takes my coffee, and sets it on the table next to his. He takes my hands and wraps them around his waist, pulling me closer to him with a careful and deliberate touch. In a breath, I'm leaning into him, which pisses off my head, but is exactly where my heart wants me to be. My entire body catches on fire while my eyes close tight.

"I'm still really, super pissed that you wouldn't open up to me," he says. "But I'm also sorry for whatever I did. Something obviously happened last night and if I hurt you, I never meant to." He kisses me on the forehead, then tilts my chin up and looks into my eyes. "You don't really believe this is too much, too fast, do you?"

"No."

"I didn't think so." His shoulders visibly relax, as though someone just removed a piano from them. "So then tell me what really happened so we know how to fix this. Don't close up. I've always told you not to hide with me."

I know what I need to say, but the words won't come out. How do you tell someone they were busted red-handed? I mean, if I hated him, it would be easy. But I am out-of-control in love with him. Still. No matter what.

"What are you going to do about the *Page Six* picture? I bet your publicist is flipping out."

He steps back to look at me again and laughs. "Seriously? You're going to try to change the subject?" He shakes his head and glares at me with a mock annoyed look. "Kelsey is thrilled. She'd love to see a million of those pictures out there. A gorgeous mystery girl who captured the heart of a very in-the-shadows front man. She just about orgasmed when she saw it. But that's beside the point, isn't it?"

"What do you mean?" I ask, secretly giddy that his publicist approves.

"I mean, this picture will be a one-off if we don't get whatever's bugging you fixed. So, let's do that. Let's talk."

He backs away to grab his coffee, and I look at him long and hard. He looks tired. So tired. He usually always has some faint dark circles under his eyes, but today they seem extra pronounced. And it looks like he's taken a shower and haphazardly thrown some gel in his hair. It's crazier than normal, but I love it just as much.

It's probably a good seventy-five degrees outside already this morning, but he's wearing a cream-colored, baggy long-sleeved tee over top of another, presumably (hopefully!) short-sleeved, navy blue tee. The blue brings out the little bit of blue in his eyes even more. He's wearing jeans and his ever-present Sperry's with no socks. He is captivating.

"I'm guessing that whatever happened had to do with Robbyn. I'm not sure how or when because in the cab, everything seemed fine. *More than* fine." He takes a sip of his drink and turns back to look at me. "I've tried to explain myself so many times when it comes to her, but clearly I've done a shitty job. So the only way I'll know how to fix this is hearing it straight from you. So let's go. Gimme whatcha got."

Just as I'm about to start talking, his phone rings and, surprisingly, he picks up. I honestly can't remember a time he's ever done this around me, so this must be something big. Maybe it's Kelsey or someone else from his team wanting to talk about the photo.

"Hey, you're early," he answers. "No worries, though, she's right here." He looks at me with a childish smile, then squinches his eyes closed as he holds out his phone. "It's for you."

I try to look at his screen to see who it could be, but it's already gone dark. I shake my head in hopes he'll take the phone back, but all he does is shove it closer. Defeated, I take it and hold it to my ear. "Hello?" I squeak.

"Kallie? Hi. Aw, it's great to meet you. You're the one who stole my son's heart, huh?"

If my eyeballs weren't attached, they would most definitely be falling out of my skull right now. Did he seriously just put me on the phone with *his mother?*

"Listen, honey," she says, "I'm going to get right to the point. I raised the kid, so I know he can be a dummy sometimes, but you gotta give him another chance, okay? Whatever he did wrong, I'm sure he's truly sorry. He's completely smitten with you, and I know he'll make it right. Just tell him how he blew it and make him prove to you he'll never do it again. You won't be sorry. He's a good kid, and he really truly lov . . . well, he really seems to like you. A whole bunch."

I have no idea how to respond, but I obviously need to say *something*, so I issue her a, "Thank you, it was great hearing from you," and cast Niles a bug-eyed glance. He smiles in response.

"Kallie, I'm going to tell you something," she continues. "He'll kill me if he knows I'm saying this, so just smile and nod and giggle as I talk so we don't let on, okay?" I mumble my okay.

"All I have heard out of him the past few weeks is Kallie this, Kallie that. It's a little weird because Kallie is his sister's name, too, haha. So, it's taken a little getting used to." I giggle, hoping it doesn't sound too fake. "The crazy thing is, he was with that Robbyn for a year, and she was nice enough, don't get me wrong, but I only spoke to her twice. Just twice. And *he* only spoke *of her* when things were going wrong. But with you . . . you're all he talks about. I'd never even know he was out on tour if I didn't ask about it. Every time we talk, it's always about you. You should probably laugh now." As instructed, I laugh.

"I saw your picture in the tabs. You are a beautiful girl. Your author photo is gorgeous, too. But what really gets me is the look on my son's face in that *Page Six* picture. I honestly don't know if I've ever seen him that happy. But, as of last night, he's a wreck all over again. I don't know why. He didn't say. But I hope you two can work it out. A mama likes to see her baby happy, no matter how old or how famous he gets. Do you feel me here?"

"I do," I breathe. I let my eyes wander over to Niles and every last bit of me melts into a heap. "Thank you for sharing your thoughts. Niles is really lucky to have you."

"Sounds like he'd be lucky to have you, too. I hope we get to talk again soon. And next time, I hope it's for happier reasons."

"Me, too."

"Good. Tell that kid of mine I'll check in with him tomorrow. You two do whatever it is you need to do. Have a good day, sweetie." And with that, she's gone.

And with that, my heart is wide open.

CHAPTER TWENTY-NINE
Pictures and Places

"Your mom? Really?" I try to look like I find it pathetic, but the smile that lets loose across my face tattles otherwise.

"Did it work?"

"It didn't hurt."

"Ha! Good. Now," he says, turning serious, "are you ready to talk to me?"

"Yes." And I am. I am ready to get this all out in the open and hopefully sorted through, and I'm ready to move on. I mean, I just talked to his mother. *His mother.* Who would do that unless they're one hundred percent serious about setting things straight?

He sighs a relieved sigh, then glances at the clock on the nightstand. "Hey, uh, wanna go for a walk? It's really nice out."

"Um, sure?" Again with the unexpectedness, but I guess that'd be a good chance to go somewhere neutral, before I unleash "the issue." "But, did you bring a hat and glasses? One tabloid pic for the weekend is probably enough."

"Left in a hurry this morning." He shrugs. "Besides, I don't care who sees us." He hands me my coffee and kisses me on the cheek. "You look great, as always. If the cameras find us, then lucky them."

So Mr. Private doesn't care about the cameras anymore, huh? Well, I do. I check myself in the mirror because a girl's gotta look good . . . just in case.

"I'm happy to see you're still wearing the earrings. I half expected you to throw them at me last night or something."

I reach up and touch them guiltily. If last night *was* the last time I was ever going to see him, I probably *should* have given them back. How shitty would that be, receiving some serious bling just hours before, then walking away for good?

"Do you want them back?"

"What? No! I'm thrilled you're still wearing them. That gives me . . . hope." He bunches up my hair and moves it behind my shoulders so my ears are in plain view. "You ready? Let's get some air."

We walk for two blocks, sipping our coffees, talking only about the places and people we see as we pass by. I'd be lying if I said we weren't getting stares. But I haven't seen any cameras. Not yet.

We round a corner and it's pretty clear that Niles knows exactly where he wants us to go. He tosses his empty coffee cup into the trash and reaches for my hand. The more we walk, the more populated the area becomes. We're walking through throngs of Sunday-morning meanderers, hand in hand. This is so weird.

"Niles? Oh my gosh! Is that you?"

From out of nowhere, a tall, beautiful girl, about seventeen, bursts through the crowd and rushes over to us. "Holy crap, wow!" she gushes. "It *is* you. Do you mind if I get a quick picture? Please?" She casts me an apologetic smile. "I'm so sorry . . . for interrupting."

"You're totally fine."

The girl hands me her phone, then smashes herself against Niles in preparation for her snap. "Do you mind? If not, I can ask my mom or someone." She waves toward a group of people who are all facing us with their phones held out, snapping pictures of their own.

"Of course I don't mind." I wiggle my hand out of Niles's and hold up the phone, feeling both jealous and exhilarated seeing Niles on the screen with another pretty girl. "Say cheese!" I chirp.

Oh my God, what a nerd.

The girl is smiling so big I think I could count every one of her teeth, but Niles pastes on the same smirk I've seen in a million other pictures. I'm once again fascinated by the distinct differences in his real versus rock star personas. It's like he's two different people.

"All set."

"Eek! Yay!" She bounces like she just won the showcase on *The Price is Right*. "Thanks so much."

"Sure! No problem!"

It occurs to me right then that if Niles and I are really happening, I'm going to have to learn really fast how to be congenial to all his fans. This one seems normal—albeit pretty excitable—but it should be interesting to see how I react to the super crazy, overzealous ones. I wonder how Robbyn handled it. I'm guessing she loved the attention as much as she hated the girls themselves.

"You guys are *so* amazing," the girl says, touching Niles's arm. "We all can't wait for the new album." She pauses, clearly not ready to walk away, then turns back to me. "Um, do you think I could get a pic with all of us?"

Without waiting for my answer, she motions for one of her family members to come over. "Here!" She passes her phone to another girl then reaches out her arms to gather Niles and me on either side of her.

"Smile big!" she squeals. "This is *so* going on Instagram!"

***

"Now do you see why I have a million hats?" Niles asks. We continue our trek through the crowds, with onlookers' eyes narrowing as we pass. Some people pay no attention to us at all. They must be natives, I decide. It's the people with maps and a thousand plastic gift shop bags looped around their forearms that seem to have their eyes on high alert for celebrities.

"It's gotta be a little exciting, though, right? Being recognized? It's a pretty big validation that what you're doing is resonating with people."

"Let's see how you feel when your movie comes out and you get all famous." He laughs. "Come on, this way." He pulls me gently so we scurry though a throng of people crossing the street. His pace has picked up big time. He's definitely on a mission.

Finally, he slows down just a bit as we break free from the sandwichy restraints of sweaty tourists. The sun is shining and our hands are still clasped. This feels good. *So good.*

But we still haven't had our talk.

"Can we sit somewhere?" I ask. Frankly, I'm surprised he hasn't re-initiated The Conversation. He was chomping at the bit back at the hotel, and now it's like the issue's totally off the table. He's not getting off that easily. We need to talk this through.

"Just a sec." His pace turns to a saunter, so I work hard to match it. I see a park just ahead. It looks lovely and peaceful and there's a bench with our names written all over it. I sigh a sigh that I hope is not bitchy, yet conveys that it's time to end our stroll. He completely ignores me and walks over to a random building.

"Isn't this a cool structure?" He touches the façade, then backs up a little, gazing up at it admiringly.

"Yeah, it's very NYC." *Now, let's get to that park.*

"It's a great little neighborhood. We're not too far from my place, actually." To be honest, I have no idea where we are. I have lost all sense of direction and could totally be standing in the middle of Central Park for all I know.

"Cute park right over there, too." He waves toward it. "Look at all the kids playing, while the parents sit and chat. Hey, some of the parents are even on their laptops. Wonder if any of them are writers?" A smile tugs at his lips. "Looks like a nice way to spend a Sunday, right?"

At face value, his words seem innocent enough. But the look he gives me as he turns his gaze my way tells me he has a really big reveal just waiting to explode from his lips.

I narrow my eyes and scrunch up my mouth—my invitation for him to spill whatever it is he's so desperately dying to spill.

"There's a two-bedroom for rent in there, Kallie," he blurts. "I saw pics online. It looks amazing. It would be a perfect second—or maybe someday primary—home for you and your girls."

Huh?

"It's a little pricey because the neighborhood is so awesome, but I would totally help pay for it. It's close to everything. Really great school just a block away. The park. Close to me . . ." He finally pulls his eyes away from the nothingness he'd been staring at throughout his sales pitch and lets them fall back on me. "Close to me."

"Niles."

"I know," he interrupts. "I know it's something you hadn't given much thought to, but how awesome would it be, really? You could come here whenever you wanted. Stay here the weeks Bub has the girls, bring them here on weekends. And if you ever moved here full time, they'd be right by the school. It makes a lot of sense, really."

He's right. It would be awesome. It'd be crazy and nuts and a whole lot irrational, but it would be totally, totally awesome.

If we were completely okay.

"Uh, we haven't had our talk yet," I stammer.

"I know, but I already said I was sorry, and I promised not to do whatever I did ever again. Even my mom promised." He gives me playful wink.

"Niles! You don't even know what you did! How can you be sorry? And how can you promise you won't do it again?" I know he's trying to keep this light, so I try, too, but I need to know that something like this is a one-time dealio, and that from here forth, we're all about being straight with each other.

He pulls out his phone, looks at the screen, and jams it back into his pocket. "We'll talk, I promise. But the realtor will be here any second. She was planning to head to church this morning, but I convinced her to meet us here instead." He looks so incredibly proud of himself.

"The realtor? You're having *the realtor* meet us here?" There are several people nearby, as usual, so I try to keep my voice down and not attract a lot of attention, but . . . What. The. Hell?

"There is no obligation here, Kallie. I just thought the timing was pretty awesome. I set this up last night. Before everything happened." He leans into me and hushes his voice. "I called her when I ran out to buy the, ahem, *supplies* that we sadly never used." He nudges me with his elbow; my heart lurches in response.

If I could kiss him and punch him in the throat all at once, I most certainly would. On one hand, I'm crazy pissed that he set this up without even telling me. On the other hand, I'm crazy *giddy* that he set this up without even telling me. I mean, how romantic.

Then, on another hand, I'm crazy pissed that he didn't cancel, given the questionable condition our . . . situation . . . is in right now. And on yet another hand, I'm crazy giddy that he didn't cancel, because this must really mean a lot to him and he must be totally sold on being with me for the long haul. Ah, confusion. The name of the game in our little relationship.

"Hey," he says, smoothing my hair. "I wanted this to be a fun surprise. I didn't mean to freak you out. But since we're a little, uh, pressed for time, let's just take the walk through and then I promise we'll hash absolutely everything out, once and for all. Okay?"

"Okay."

He leans in to kiss me, just as I hear a camera snap nearby.

"I think we just got shot," I whisper.

"I don't care," he breathes. "If you move here, they'll get used to us." He kisses me again, which is both electrifying and nerve-wracking. It's entirely possible these kisses will be documented all across the Internet. Where anyone can see them. Anyone at all. Man, this is going to take some getting used to.

"Hi, guys, sorry to interrupt," says a far-too-chipper voice from behind. "I'm Mindy." A petite little redhead even shorter than me extends her hand, first to me (impressive) then to Niles. "Huge, huge fan, Mr. Russell. Just had to get that out of the way." She winks to no one in particular and holds the door open for us. "This is a great property. It'll be perfect for you two. Let's go have a look."

My heart flies right up through my throat and settles itself onto the tip of my tongue. She thinks we're looking at this place to live in together. And Niles doesn't bother to correct her. He just holds on to my hand and pulls me along behind him as we trudge up the stairs to the second floor. The floor that contains the apartment my rock star crush is hoping to help rent for me. And my girls.

Holy cats.

As we hit the top stair and prepare to head into the apartment, the magnitude of this moment hits me like a tsunami. I've had a lot of surreal experiences over the past few weeks, but this one?

This one tops them all.

CHAPTER THIRTY
Home and Heartache

"Did you love it?" Niles pulls my hand up toward his chest so our arms are intertwined. "It was amazing, right?"

Of course it was amazing. It had exposed brick walls and wood floors, just like his place, and a gourmet kitchen and lots of light. The bedrooms were perfectly sized and the bathroom seemed downright huge by New York standards. It was quieter than I expected and it had a little postage stamp-sized balcony where Niles already envisioned himself grilling. It's perfect.

I try so hard to keep an even keel, but I can't. Glimpses of a maybe-life take over my mind. So much has unfolded over the past few weeks—so much more than I could have ever imagined—that I can't help but indulge in this wild fantasy, too.

"It's pretty damn perfect."

"Mindy thinks it will move fast," Niles says, his voice urgent. I can't help but know this—she said it at least half a dozen times as she showed us around.

"It's incredible," I bubble. "Of course it will move fast." I feel like a model at a post-fashion week buffet.

Niles stops in the middle of the sidewalk, spins me so I'm facing him, and says, "I think we should put in an offer, Kallie." He bites his lip, which I think I've seen him do, like, once. "Do you?"

I look around for a place—any place—that looks even remotely private. I find a teeny little passage between two buildings and yank him in. "This is crazy, Niles."

"I know."

"It *is* too fast, right?"

"Maybe. Probably. But who really fuckin' cares? Not me."

His smile is huge and his eyes are happy. I grab the back of his neck and pull his face into mine. Our lips know exactly what to do next. My stomach, not so much. It twists and turns and bubbles and plummets the entire time we kiss. If we were somewhere a little more private, things would definitely be getting very interesting right now.

"We should do this," I say, finally pulling away. "We should put in an offer. Oh my God! Ack! This is insane!" Niles laughs in agreement and pulls me into a hug.

"Let's call Mindy."

"Yes!" I squeal. "But first, we gotta settle 'the issue.' Just to get it completely off the table, okay?"

This should be easy because I've clearly all but forgiven every last bit of his initial deception. We are in such a big place in our relationship that what happened has really diminished in importance to me. He has shown me again and again how real this all is and how committed he is to making it work. All he has to do now is come clean, say he's sorry, promise that "upfront with each other" will be the name of the game going forth, and we can move on. We can rent that apartment and see each other any damn time we want and grill a freaking steak on a Monday night if we so choose. My dream life. Amped up by a hundred million percent. Coming true.

"Okay," he says. "Shoot."

"Okay." I let out a big breath. "Here we go . . . I'm just putting it out there, right? No holding back."

"Yeah, go."

I look at him and scrunch up my face. "Why did you use me, Niles? I know you'd never purposefully hurt me. So why did you do it?"

"Do what?" His eyebrows crinkle and the sunshine leaves his face. "What do you mean *use you*?"

"Use my story to write your album. You reached out to me to get to know me so you could find out all you could about my fangirl obsession. You had a list of a whole bunch of questions to ask me, all to get into my head. All so you could write a new album." I watch as his eyes widen. "Right?"

He swallows hard. "How did you know about that?"

"Your lovely ex, of course."

He shakes his head. "How did she know? I never said one thing to her about it. I never said anything to *anyone* about it."

"She sent me a picture of the notebook page with your handwritten questions all over it. Wanna see?"

"Yeah, I wanna see!" he growls.

I scroll through my photos (passing the *Page Six* picture that I saved) and hold out Robbyn's photo for his inspection.

"What in the hell?" He takes the phone right out of my hand and puts it so close to his eyes, he must be seeing double. "That notebook was hidden in a cabinet in my apartment." He turns to look at me. "Where did you find this?"

"I told you. Robbyn sent me this picture."

"She couldn't have, Kallie. She hasn't been to my apartment in over a month."

I hold my breath. I don't know what he's trying to imply, but I know damn well this photo came from Robbyn.

"She told me you were using me when she cornered me at the

197

after-party. That's why I was so upset. Then in the cab, I decided I didn't believe her. But then when we got back to your place and you, uh, *stepped out*, she sent a couple texts and the picture. This is her number, right?" I scroll through my recent texts and pull up Robbyn's. I watch Niles's face contort as he reads them.

"She frickin' broke in to my apartment," he says, handing back my phone.

"Sadly, I'm not surprised. But . . . um . . . can we get back to the main issue here? Please?"

"Kallie, I'm sorry. Yeah, I admit it. That's a legit piece of paper with my legit writing with the legit questions I thought I wanted to ask you. And yeah, I texted you because I couldn't come up with any fucking ideas for this new fucking album that every fucking person on Earth wants me to shit out right this fucking second. I was dry. Drier than dry. You know how it is sometimes, right? We've talked about this. Sometimes the inspiration just isn't there. So you gotta find it in unexpected places. And that's what I thought I might do with you."

I am not at all surprised by what he's saying, but somehow hearing him admit it is not as easy as I expected. Why not? Why does it hurt worse coming from his lips than it did when I heard (and easily forgave) it in my head?

"But I scrapped that idea, just like I told you yesterday morning on the couch. I got to know you. You were the anti- what I thought you were. Or what I thought you would be." He kicks at the wall with his shoe. "All this," he says, motioning around him. "The kisses and professions and apartments and plans? They're all real, Kallie. They're all where we really are. At least, that's where I *thought* we were."

His phone bloops, and he silences it with force. "I thought I proved this all to you many times over," he says, turning to face me.

"So why then, after all of this, are you still doubting me?"

"I'm not."

"Then call Mindy. Right now."

"Niles."

"What, Kallie? Call her."

"We'll call her in a sec," I say, touching his arm. "Don't get mad, okay? Let's talk."

"Mad? Why would I get mad?" He snaps his arm away. "Robbyn breaks in to my apartment, the girl I am seriously fucking nuts over thinks I'm slimy, and now instead of calling the realtor to put in an offer on an apartment together, we're talking about something shitty I did, that I admit to as being shitty, that I said I was sorry for, but is somehow still an issue." He flings his arms out and shrugs. "Hm, nope, nothing to get mad about here."

"Well, it *is* kind of something to talk about, right? You've told me again and again to talk to you, open up to you, be straight with you. Yet when I do—right before we're about to hit a very serious milestone in our very young relationship—you freak out?" I wrinkle my nose and shake my head. "I just wanted to put the issue to bed. So we can move forward without anything hanging overhead. I don't think I'm wrong to have done that."

He's quiet for forever, pacing a little, running his hands through his hair, generally looking like he's losing steam by the second.

Finally, he turns around to look at me. His eyes are sad and his forehead is all creased up. "Remember all those times I told you I was a piece of shit? Well, here you go. I guess this is just another example."

"Um, no. That is not true at all. And besides, even if it was, I already told you that I like shit." I'm trying to joke, to get him to smile, to lighten the mood, but his face is still flat.

"No, Kallie," he says, his voice soft. "See, this is what I meant.

199

This right here. Need a girl, use a girl. I guess that'll always be my M.O. I thought you were proof otherwise, because goddamn it, I really could see myself in that apartment with you, going to bed together, waking up in each other's arms. Shit, I even imagined myself making breakfast for you and your girls. Your freaking *girls*! But I have no business doing any of that. Because all I do is fuck with people."

"Niles, stop," I say. But it's too late.

"My mom seems to think that what I have with you is *so different*," he says with air quotes. "I thought so, too. But no one can deny my history. No one can tell me I'm not right for sticking to my 'no promises, no regrets' theory. I almost let that slide with you. I mean, renting an apartment for you and your *children*? That's a pretty damn big promise, right? And we all know I can't handle promises. Jesus, what was I thinking?"

"What you were thinking," I say, trying to catch his gaze, "is that this feels right. That this *is* right. And I agree, it absolutely is. I just needed to know that deception won't be part of the deal going forward. That's all." I feel a tear slip down my cheek. "That's all." I step toward him and at first it looks like he's going to allow it, but then he steps back.

"Well, Kallie, given my track record, I'd say that's not something you can plan on." He closes his eyes and that look of self-hatred—the same one I saw when he confessed all he'd done to Robbyn—is back. He looks ashamed, angry, surprised, confused. All at once. It breaks my heart.

I want to hold him, have him hold me, cry together, just for a minute, acknowledging that baggage is part of the deal and that we both have plenty of it, but it's nothing we can't overcome. I want him to tell me he has no doubts that he'll never hurt me again. I want him to be strong and self-assured that this will be perfect, with a little work. Or not perfect, but perfect enough. I want him to tell me it's all alright, and though my worries were valid, they're no longer relevant.

"I wanted to make love to you last night," he says, instead. "And again this morning. And again this afternoon. And then every chance I could get for the foreseeable future. But now I am so glad that didn't happen. I'm so glad I didn't wreck you, too."

"Don't talk like that," I whisper. I step toward him and this time he allows it.

"I want to make love to you, too." I tentatively put my hands on his shoulders. "Right now. Let's go back to your place and do what we both so badly want to do. And then when it's over, we'll tell each other that we love each other, just like I've been dreaming, because goddamn it, it's true. And then we'll both assure each other that being transparent will always be our first priority and that'll be that. We'll live happily ever after." He lets out a little laugh and tries to speak, but I interrupt him.

"You admitted that you initially used me, and now all you have to do is tell me you won't do it again. That's it. That's all you have to do." I swipe at the tears streaming down my cheeks as he backs away.

"Tell me that, Niles," I say, my voice rising. "Tell me that, then we'll call Mindy. We'll put in our offer, then we'll go back to your place and have crazy, breathtaking sex until we're too tired to move. Then we'll order in and make plans for where I'll meet you next on tour." I look at him, but his expression is blank. "That will be the beginning of our dream, Niles. We'll live a fucking dream! So just *tell me!*"

I am in full-on hysterics now, just like that. I know I'm pretty much begging and pleading. I know I sound desperate. I know I'm carrying on like a lunatic. But with every breath I take and every second that passes without resolution, I become more and more aware that I'm losing him. As I am standing here and we are breathing the same air, I am losing him.

Most people would tell me not to fold. They'd tell me to stand strong and be a woman of conviction. But the reality is, I used him, too. My book wasn't 300 pages of how amazing he is as an honest, loyal, committed person. It was 300 pages of me living in a fantasy world. It was 300 pages of me dreaming what my life would look like if I could design it and assign it to a fictional character.

There is absolutely no question that I used the poor guy a million times over. I used him to pacify my disdainful nights. I used him when I couldn't deal with the shit that came in and out of my head on a daily basis. Hell, I even used thoughts and images of him when I was feeling sexy and didn't want to go anywhere near Brad. And not only that, I used him for the benefit of my career, just like he was about to do with me. Except he never did. But, me? Yeah, *I* did.

So, who am I to talk? Just because I used him then, does that mean I'm going to be deceitful forever? No. Holy shit, no. But that's what I've accused him of. How did I not see that until now?

"Niles," I cry. "I used you, too, and I am so sorry. The book? It's the same thing." I want to explain it to him, but he's already closed me off. I can tell. There is no light in his eyes anymore. There isn't any sadness either. He's just blank. Absolutely, completely blank.

"Kallie. I'm not going to fool myself anymore. Or try to fool you. I am who I am. And I'll just hurt you."

"You won't. I know you won't."

"I do love you," he says, with a fire in his eyes. "And that's why I won't promise anything to you. I just won't. Because then I can't regret anything if, *when*, I fuck it up."

My knees go weak and every bit of my breath leaves my lungs. *He said it.* Niles Russell just said that he loves me. I heard it. It was not a book passage or a fantasy or a hallucination. It was real.

But now what? Now he's backing away from me instead of walking toward me. Where is he going? This is supposed to be the part where we hug and take each other's hands and walk back to his apartment so we can finally seal the deal. That's what's supposed to come next. But, it's not.

"I probably can't totally be without you," he says, "so I'm sure you'll get a random text from me here or there. Write back, or ignore them if you want. I get it."

My feet are frozen to the ground. He takes a few steps toward me, then quickly brushes his lips over mine. I feel his breath in my ear and hear his whisper down my spine. "I really do love you. I need you to know that."

Then, in the next breath, he's gone. My hand goes out to grab his shirt, to reach for his arm, to stop him. But he's gone. There is no more pleading, no begging, no rationalizing, no words. Just like that, he's out of reach, then out of earshot, and then finally out of sight.

What in the hell just happened?

CHAPTER THIRTY-ONE
Carry On

The plane ride home was tortuous. So was the cab ride. I refused to call Sara to pick me up so late, and besides, I have no interest in filling her in yet anyway—or maybe for the next forty years—so I managed on my own.

I burst through my door and heave my bags onto the couch. For at least the two millionth time since Niles left me standing in that passageway, I check my phone. There's not one bit of communication from him. No new emails, no new texts, no missed calls.

Why isn't he calling me?

I flop down on my floor and stare up at my ceiling. After so many flight delays, it's clear I should have just kept my original. It's 3:00 a.m. and I should be dog tired, but all I think about is how I should be with Niles right now, staring up at *his* ceiling. Or asleep, snuggled up next to him. Or, better yet, making love to him.

I reach for my phone and scroll to his number. I have to call him. I have to hear his voice. But wait, it's 3:00 a.m. Wouldn't that make me the Mayor of Crazyville? Yeah, for sure it would. And besides, I'm pissed at him. He left me there. All alone. In New York City, where a newbie finding her way around is like setting a two-year-old in the middle of a corn maze. It took me ages to find my way back to the hotel. (But not before I walked past what could have been our apartment, because that, of course, I easily found.)

My mind spins with memories of the past few weeks. It's hard to grasp that's all they are now. Memories. Is that really what we've become? How did that happen? How did we go from insta-bond to seconds-away-from-having-sex   to   let's-rent a-NYC-apartment-together to we'll-probably-never-talk-again, all in the course of a few weeks?

Oh yeah, I fucked everything up. At least that's what it feels like. But so did he. So there's that.

I scroll through the pictures on my phone. The last one was of Niles and me sneaking a selfie in the master bedroom of the apartment. Mindy was in the hallway waiting for us, and Niles and I had just exchanged knowing looks. Knowing that the apartment was a win and knowing that we'd make some beautiful memories there. Neither of us even had to say anything. Niles just reached for my phone, arranged himself beside me, stuck out his arm, and snapped the pic.

I study our faces. They're full of hope and excitement and anticipation of what's to come. We look so natural. Like any normal couple about to make a big decision together. In this pic, I'm not an author and he's not a rock star. I'm just Kallie and he's just Niles. And we're so uncomplicatedly happy.

I can't help myself. I call him.

"I was hoping you'd call," he answers. "I just didn't think it'd be at three a.m." He laughs a little, his voice hoarse and sexy.

I try to speak, but nothing comes out. It suddenly occurs to me that I have no idea what I want to say.

Thankfully, his tongue and brain are working better than mine. "Are you home? Like, home-home?"

"Yeah."

"Good. I was worried about you. I'm so sorry I left you alone like that."

Though I *should* give him a good tongue lashing for leaving me stranded, then not even texting to check in on me, I have no interest in talking about my crash course in New York City foot travel, horrific (and multiple) flight delays, or creepy late-night cab rides. I want to talk about us. I want to tell him what he didn't let me tell him this afternoon. I want to set things straight and make a game plan for making this right. No pussyfooting around. I want to get down to business.

"I miss you already," I whisper. I barely hear myself, so I'm not sure if he heard me either.

"Trust me," he says, almost as softly, "I miss you more."

My heart pangs as I dig my fingers into the carpet beneath me. "If that's true," I sniff, "then why am I here and you're there?"

There's a long silence. So long that I wonder if the call got dropped. But then he says, "We're getting back on the road at ten sharp. I suppose I should get some sleep. Thank you for calling. I'm glad you're okay."

"I'm *not* okay," I protest, because playing it cool is absolutely not on my agenda. I knew going into this call that I had no hope for keeping my composure, so I'm just putting it all out there. Because, really, what do we have left to lose?

"I know, Kal," he says, quietly. "I just meant that I'm glad you made it home safely." I hear him breathing, and I swear I hear a sniff, too. "I'm not okay either. Not even close."

"We need to fix this, Niles. We shouldn't be sad like this. It's just proof of how much we really do love each other."

"I'm too broken to be fixed, Kallie. You and your girls? You need so much better than me."

Those terrible—and completely untrue—words are like BBs penetrating through the tin can that is me. I cannot stand to hear him talk like this. Why is he so, so hard on himself? Why can't he see that his past doesn't have to define his future? Why can't he realize that one mistake doesn't mean he doesn't deserve me? Why am I failing so hard at helping him understand this?

"You're better than you give yourself credit for, Niles. So much better."

There's another silence, and it hangs there for ages, like fog over a lake. "I need to go," he says finally, his voice shaking. "Thank you for . . . all the wonderful memories." Then he pauses again, just for a beat and says, "I love you."

I try to answer back. Tell him that I love him, too. Tell him that I don't care about his past or how awful he thinks he is or how much he feels the girls and I need someone better. I try to say anything at all to keep the lines of communication open, but it's all for nothing. He's gone and "Call Ended" glares back at me from my phone.

I allow a new wave of tears to wash over me as I grab a throw pillow from my couch and hold it in my arms. I fall asleep, just as is, on my floor. I wake up at least once an hour and my mind immediately goes to Niles, but I don't move. I stay there on the floor, fully dressed, a crumpled mess with airplane hair and smeary mascara. Doing anything to make myself more comfortable seems too self-indulgent and I want to make myself pay. Pay for using him, pay for hurting him, and pay for inadvertently confirming the POS viewpoint he has of himself. And, of course, pay for sabotaging our future.

Finally, at 9:00 a.m., with stiff muscles, crusty eyes, and a phone that stayed silent the rest of the night, I get up.

What am I gonna do next?

***

Showers were made to renew the soul; I am convinced of it. While standing under its heated, pulsing comfort, I make a plan for how I'm going to tackle the day, because Lord knows that's as far ahead as I can think right now.

I'm going to email Lucy to tell her that Niles and I are keeping to ourselves for a while. I won't offer explanations and I won't make it sound like it's do or die. I'll just be succinct and matter-of-fact and professional. That'll take care of that. For now.

Then, I'll sit my butt down and work on Book Two. This is dangerous, maybe, because I have no idea what will pour out, given what's transpired over the last couple days. But I need to get some thoughts out, some words on the page. I need to sort through some of the stuff that will surely dominate my thoughts, maybe forever, and see if there's any inspiration I can pluck from it all. Writing is my therapy and I need it now more than ever.

I'll stay glued to my keyboard for as long as necessary, ignoring the rest of the world, until my mind is empty for that moment. Then I'll get up and clean this apartment. With all my jet-setting and rock star loving, I have neglected it to within an inch of its life. The flowers Niles got me over a week ago are testament to that, as they sit, wilted and rotty-stemmed in the vase on my table.

Or maybe I'll just sit here and cry. Because that's what I really want to do.

I look at my phone and will it to ring. It doesn't. I look at my door and wish for a knock on the other side. There isn't one. I look at my couch and long for it to be cradling Niles's bum, like it had when he came home with me the day after we met. It isn't.

I think about how I am going to write when just days ago I was sitting on Niles's rooftop, with the New York City skyline and hot kisses as my inspiration. Now, I'm alone, staring at the walls of this lonely apartment, with not a single morsel of inspiration to be found.

Oh God, oh God, oh God. What am I thinking? I can't just sit here. I'll go mad. And I'll no doubt have to start coming up with answers for all the questions that will surely be fired my way once people figure out I'm home.

Nope, there is no way I can stay here. I need to get out. And not just out, as in out for groceries. I mean out, as in totally away from here.

Where can I go?

I think about the next leg of Niles's tour. Baltimore tonight, then Virginia Beach, then a couple dates in North Carolina.

North Carolina. Where my girls are.

My crazy mind can't help but piece together a plan. What if I hopped on a plane to go see the girls? I've been wanting to. In the beginning of this whole Niles whirlwind, I entertained thoughts of going to see them but, alas, got a little, well, sidetracked. Maybe this is the perfect time. I'll rent a cabin in the woods and spend a couple weeks down there. Toward the end of my book, Emily had rented a cabin in the woods so she could write, so I'll totally channel my inner Emily and get some work done, too. Yes, this is perfect!

For the first whole week I'll write until my fingers fall off and my butt cheeks go numb. I'll see the girls for a few days during week two and we'll enjoy a little mommy-daughter time together in a neutral place. That'll help chop up our long summer apart and give Brad a little break, too. And maybe, since I don't exactly expect that Niles will surprise me there like Nash surprised Emily, I'll sneak into one of his shows just to see him perform again. I won't stalk him after or even tell him I'm there. I'll just admire him from afar, as I did before any of this happened. Just watch him and indirectly be with him, since I can no longer actually *be with him*. Yes, this is good! I'm loving this idea.

I head straight to the cabin rental website and sift through my options. I click through picture after picture of nature-infused coziness and can't believe my luck when I find a place about an hour from Brad's parents. It's absolutely darling and close but not too close. I'm smitten. What's more, the concert venue Niles is playing at is a couple hours in the other direction. Not wild about the aspect of highway driving to get there, but maybe I'll just spend the night in town that night. Sounds perfect. I'm in!

I close my eyes and my mind immediately sets me on the cabin's quaint little front porch, where I'll type away for hours on end. Honestly, I can't think of anything more heavenly, unless Niles was seated in the chair next to me, working on his album. Now, *that* would be heavenly. And then we'd sneak little peeks at each other, and after we caught each other's eye and tossed out some overly hokey eyebrow raises and air kisses, we'd head inside and then, well, you know.

Whoa, girl. C'mon back. Focus, focus, focus.

I close my eyes again and shake those gutterific thoughts from my mind. This is serious. If I'm going to do this, I better get my shit together before I chicken out.

Okay. Next stop, StubHub. I poke around for a ticket to Niles's show, resisting the urge to grab a front-row spot and picking one in the eighth row instead. Still close, but not likely to be discovered from the stage. Even though I *do* kind of want him to see me. Or do I? Yes and no. More yes than no. Ugh, this is ridiculous.

So what happens if he does see me? Will it be weird? I imagine maybe a little. Will we smile at each other? Exchange knowing looks? Will I throw him off or make him mad? Will he send Zeke over afterwards to invite me backstage where we'll make up and pretend that none of this yuck ever happened? Or will I go totally unnoticed and he'll leave the stage, head to the after-party without me (or worse, with someone else!) and I'll head back to the cabin and cry myself to sleep yet again? Seems like all I do these days is cry. Do I really want to do something that will surely take me for a spin down The Road of Tears once more?

Yeah, okay. Maybe I shouldn't go to the show.

But I have to. I absolutely have to.

I buy the ticket and say a silent prayer that fate will intervene and what is meant to happen, will. I can only control so much. I can put myself in his path as much as I always have and see what happens from there. It's worked before—whether I intended for it to or not—and I have to have faith that it will work again. I can't imagine we'd have gone through all this for just a few weeks' worth of memories. There must be more in store for us. There's gotta be more in store.

And judging by the subject line of the email that just came in from Lucy, I have to believe there is.

CHAPTER THIRTY-TWO
Take Flight

Lucy's freaking out. I can tell by the tone of her email. There are new photos making the rounds, this time in CelebFeed. Eek! (That's my eek, not hers.) If we want to be savvy, she says, and get some great mileage out of these photos (translation: Kallie, if you have any brain cells at all) we should get them posted to my fan page by the end of the day.

"Something simple," she types, "like 'Look who's read (and approved of) my book.' Fun and cheeky. People will adore that. We still have the *Page Six* pic to play with, too. Oh, and some shot a fan posted to Instagram. When was that? It's totally cute. Anyway, what do you think? I know you're traveling today, so call me when you can. I have a meeting with the marketing department at the publisher this morning. I wish you could've stayed in town to meet them."

Me, too, Lucy. Me, too. I almost did stay in town. Forever.

As my heart twists, I close her email and scour CelebFeed. She didn't include a link, so I'm on my own. It doesn't take long to find them, and when I do, I just about lose my mind.

It's hard to digest that it's really us. But the girl in the photo is wearing exactly what I was wearing yesterday and same for the guy.

There are my diamond earrings and there is Niles's amazing hair. And there are our lips, caught in a kiss, right outside the apartment. I knew it happened. I heard the camera snap. That's when Niles said if I lived there, they'd get used to us. At that time—just *yesterday*—that was the plan. Now, there are much different words needed to tell this story.

The other photo was taken during the same timeframe, but we're simply talking, gazing at each other as though there was not one other person or issue in this world aside from us, right there and right that second. Just like the one from the after-party, both of these new pictures are gorgeous. They tell the story of a couple who obviously loves each other in a crazy way. Of two people who wouldn't care if the entire universe fell apart around them, as long as they were together.

It's suffocating.

My next instinct is to call Niles, but I know I shouldn't. Surely his publicist has gotten to him by now, and maybe he's told her we're not together anymore and this just all needs to die down.

But it feels like this is a statement from the universe somehow. A there-is-no-way-you-two-are-done-yet statement. I mean, I've been stalking Niles for three years and I honestly don't think I've seen him in CelebFeed more than once, and that was just a round-up post from Coachella last year. And Robbyn only showed up on fan blogs and pics that the band posted themselves. There has to be a reason people suddenly care about his love life . . . and the fact that I'm part of it. Could my book be the alluring factor in this equation? Holy cow, what if it is?

Once again, I let my better judgment fly out the window and text Niles. I figure that's better and safer than calling, since he could be in the middle of something, or maybe he hasn't even seen them yet. He'll probably appreciate a little warning before I just dive right in.

As I wait for his response, I stare at the photos some more. I am so conflicted. On one hand, I feel like I'm texting my boyfriend, who just happens to be a rock star, about some photos that were snapped. On the other hand, I feel like I'm talking to a complete stranger with whom I just happened to be photographed kissing. It's so weird.

I burst into a cold sweat as I wait seven lifetimes to hear back. What is taking so long? Is his phone turned off? Is he ignoring me? Is he looking up the pictures? Hell, maybe he's totally blocked me!

Finally, he sends a quick, "Heard but have not seen. One sec." I wait some more, my fingers a shaky mess as they absently trace the bridge of my nose. This is so unnerving. What will he say?

My hopeful little heart takes over and reminds me how he reacted to the pic in *Page Six*. He loved it. Asked me how I felt about it. Thought it said a lot. Used it as a device to get me to see that we belong together. For sure these new photos will affect him the same way. God knows they just about knocked me on *my* ass. Maybe this will be the prod he needs to get over his insecurities and see that we really are meant to be.

My phone's bloop pulls me back into the present . . . where I'm prepared to see just about anything other than what I really do see.

"Great. We're fucked. I gotta call Kelsey. She'll prob say to ignore them, but if I can get them yanked down, I will."

What? Yanked down? No! Leave them there. And no, we're not fucked! This is great. This is a wake-up call, Niles. Don't you see it?

"They're beautiful," I type, hoping I can reach him like he reached me the day *Page Six* came out. "Do you like them?"

There's a too-long pause, which seems to be a center point in all our conversations of late, before he finally responds, "They're incredible. But that doesn't matter anymore."

My heart plummets.

I could and should fight back. I should say that yes it does matter, and then ask why he's being so blind to that. I should say that he's making this way too cut and dry, that all that fighting he did to win me back just a day ago is what's representative of us, not this horrible mindset he's created about himself. I should tell him to snap out of it, give himself a break, realize that two have tangoed here and that none of this has to be this way.

But that's not a conversation we can have over text. So instead, I break out the big guns and put it as plain and simply as I can.

"Niles," I type, with tears streaming down my cheeks, "I love you."

There's no response.

***

I can't get on the plane fast enough. Between my bombed conversation with Niles, yet another deluge of accusatory texts from Brad, and ducking the local news crew that tap-tap-tapped on my door, calling out that my story is so exciting and they'd love to hear how it all unfolded, I know that getting away from here is the only logical thing. I packed for all of five minutes, recycling my personal stuff from New York and adding a few outfits. At this point, if I sit around in my pajamas for the entire two weeks, that would be completely acceptable. Who's going to see me anyway?

I'm thankful that not many people are headed to North Carolina right now, because I have a whole row of three to myself. I smash myself against the window and stare out over the tarmac. Some nights this view is so exciting. Today, it feels so very, very lonely.

I know I'm torturing myself, but I wedge in my earbuds anyway. I should watch a movie or listen to something (or someone) totally different, but I can't. Because if I can't hear Niles on the phone or whispering in my ear, I'll have to hear him the way I always have: crooning in my ears with passion clawing through his voice.

I scroll to the playlist I made with all of his songs—from his own albums, from albums he was featured on, all of them—and go right to my fave. "The Sadder Side of Midnight" has no musical introduction—it's just his voice a cappella, clear and strong and commanding, right off the bat. Then the music swells, but he never lets you go; he grabs you from that very first note and holds you for three and a half minutes without ever letting you slip away from him. It's magical. I could listen to it for hours.

With my eyes shut and my mind zoned out, my body vaguely senses that the aisle seat in my row is now occupied and that there is a set of knees swinging their way toward me. I drag my gaze to my new seatmate, straightening up when I realize this person is clearly intent on speaking to me . . . and that she's clenching a book in her hands.

My book.

"Miss Reagan?" Her eyes gleam, but her face is sheepish. "I am so sorry to bother you, but I just really had to say hello." She holds her book out to me and flips to the back, where my author photo smiles back at us. (Surreal, much?) "I read this in one sitting. I loved it so much. What a fun story!"

Her voice has turned giddy, and I'm immediately roped in. "Thank you!" I wiggle my butt cheeks back in my seat so I'm straightened up even more. "It was so much fun to write. I'm really glad you enjoyed it."

A pen materializes from out of nowhere, which she taps on the book. She holds them both out. "Would you sign this please?" She looks at me hopefully, the gentle-but-there creasing around her eyes tattling that's she's likely right around my age. "My name is Erin. You know, in case you want to write a message."

"Of course!"

I settle the book into my lap while my tummy does that oh-my-

God-this-is-so-awesome fluttery thing. I cannot believe this is happening. Someone is asking *me* for my autograph? In a random experience? How freaking cool! Yeah, I've signed lots of bookplates and plenty of ARCs for reader contests, but I've yet to have a fan stop me somewhere other than at a bookstore signing. I feel like a rock star.

Ugh. A rock star.

"So, uh, the Nash character?" she says. "He was based on Niles Russell, I take it?" She giggles and wrings her hands before setting them in her lap. I look at her quizzically. How would she know that?

"I saw the CelebFeed pics this morning," she bubbles. "Very nice." She raises her eyebrows in approval, which makes me want to both squee and cry with this poor, unsuspecting stranger. She, just like Lucy and Sara and Katherine and God knows who else, could see the love between Niles and me just by looking at those pictures. Dammit, Niles! Can't you see what you're throwing away?

"Were you already dating when you wrote it? Or is this something new?" She looks at me in horror as her cheeks instantly flush to crimson. "Oh my gosh, I'm so sorry if that's too pushy. I'm just a huge fan of you both. You guys have got to be the cutest couple on Earth. Seriously. But forget I even asked that. I was way out of line. I'm sorry."

I decide right then and there that I adore this human being, no matter how sad what she's saying makes me. I'm thrilled that this is my very first random fan experience. She's sweet, she's sincere, and she seems to really understand how someone can be such a huge inspiration creatively. The only problem? I'm just going to have to tread lightly, so I don't mistakenly confirm or deny anything about Niles and me.

"It's okay," I say with a smile. "Really. And to answer your question, I just recently met him. We became . . . very good friends."

"I'd say so." She leans forward and hushes her voice. "Are you meeting him down in Raleigh? Because I have tickets to that concert. It'd be totally hilarious if we crossed paths again there."

Hm, yeah. Totally hilarious. Except I won't be laughing. At all.

"Um, I don't know." And that's true. Because I have no idea how it's all going to go down yet. "I'm heading down for a writing retreat mostly. So I guess I'm not sure yet."

If her smile is any indication, this is even more exciting to her than me meeting up with Niles. "I'd *love* to attend a retreat someday, too." She fiddles with the seat tray in front of her for a moment, then pulls her eyes back to me and turns so she's as sideways as she can get.

"You know," she says, her face turning serious "I wasn't going to say anything, but I really want you to know . . . I've started a book of my own. I'm less than half done, but I have to say you've inspired me to not only finish it, but to pour all of my passion into it as well. So, thank you for that. Really."

She looks down at her hands, then noticing they're empty, holds them out for the return of her book. "Maybe I'll have a dream-come-true story of my own someday. But without the whole Niles Russell component. Unfortunately." She laughs as I hand back her book. "Thanks so much. For this"—she holds up the book—"and for the inspiration. I'll leave you alone now."

"Thank you for reading, Erin." I hold out my hand. "And for coming over to say hello. It was really great to meet you. Good luck with your writing." I squeeze her hand, sending a grin charging across her face. I can tell I've made her day. Just like she's made mine.

"Hurry up with book two," she says, standing up. "Your fans are already getting impatient." She gives me one last grin and disappears down the aisle.

Now that she's gone, I can't help but beam. Like really, really beam. I've inspired her. She just said so. She's a writer, too, and she's been inspired by me to both finish the book and do it with passion. What an amazing, amazing feeling.

I know someone else who had that exact same effect on me, and look what's happened now. A completed book, an agent, a book deal, and now a possible movie deal. All because of passion. All because of inspiration. All because of him.

Whatever my writing future holds—and now the inspiration I spread to others—all started because of him.

CHAPTER THIRTY-THREE
Out of the Woods

Getting myself around in the mountains wasn't something I gave much thought to when I booked my cabin. But given the winding road stretching out in front of me, I most definitely should have.

I've been at this stop sign for ages, fully convinced my hands are shaking so badly there's pretty much no way I won't steer myself into a guardrail. When it's clear I can't put it off any longer and I'm sure there's not another soul around, I inch up the road, staring straight ahead so I don't freak myself out even more. I can see that once I get to my spot, I'm not leaving again until someone sends a pack mule up after me. No, really. I'm serious.

When I finally reach my cabin—my seriously adorable cabin—I thank every religious and nonreligious deity there is for my safe arrival and tumble out of the car into the fresh mountain air.

Though there's beauty all around, the first thing my eyes fly to is the porch where I hope to spend a good amount of time. I can't help but notice the two rocking chairs, looking all cozy and inviting. I make a mental note to remove one of them, so I don't feel so lonely, but decide against it when I remember that the Law of Attraction would tell me to leave it there, so that a "visitor," ahem, would have a place to sit if "he," ahem, were to come visit.

I run my hands along the backrests of each of the chairs, then walk into the tiny cabin. I look around for a bouquet of flowers or a card like the ones Niles had surprised me with before. Like somehow he had figured out I was coming here and pulled out his best Nash moves in an effort to win me over again. But, duh, of course, there's nothing. I check my phone, and though there are two new emails from local news personalities and a zillion new notifications to my social media pages, there's nothing from him there either. No texts, no voicemails, no nothing. Maybe there's just spotty reception where he is. Yeah, I'll go with that.

Ugh. Okay, enough Niles talk, Kallie! Time to get over this. I came up here to write, and dammit, that's exactly what I'm going to do.

I settle into one of the rockers and fire up my computer, reminding myself how exciting this is. For years, I've wanted to do this. Just plant myself somewhere, with no distractions and no obligations, and just write, write, write. Like Emily.

My word count tracker shows I'm a little over half done with this book, pre-edited, of course. If I dedicate most of the day and night to writing, only taking breaks for quick workouts or hikes in the woods, I'll be nearly done with the first draft by the end of the week. Then, I'll play with the girls for a few days, come back to my book with fresh eyes for another few days, then head home. This is perfect.

And hopefully this will help boot Mr. Russell loose from my brain as well.

Until I see him at his show, that is.

Annnnnd, great. Here we go again. In one split second I've opened the thinking-about-Niles floodgates once more. Because I can't *help* but think about what's going to happen when I see him. Maybe we'll have made up before then, and we'll be right back to awesome, just like we were before this all went down. It could happen. Right?

221

Unless he's back with Robbyn. Seriously, why hasn't that thought occurred to me yet? I've been so busy boo-hooing over all this that I've forgotten what a huge piece of the puzzle she is. That big, huge, giant biyatch is the reason this all got started. She sabotaged the incredible relationship we had going by planting seeds of doubt within me, not to mention breaking into his apartment and meddling as much as she could. She is to blame for every bit of this. And she should pay.

But wait. Niles hates her now, right? And he must especially hate her since she's a class-A crook. But what if he doesn't? What if he's somehow forgiven her and now *she'll* be the one moving into that apartment with him instead of me? Augh, I can't handle this!

I look at my phone and scroll to her text. There's her number. Now's my chance. Niles isn't around to stop me; no one is around to hear. I can rip her a new one and no one will be the wiser. She has it coming to her. She deserves it.

But I'll say my piece and then what? *No one will be the wiser.* What's the point of that? I have a much, much better revenge idea. I am *so* creating a character like her in my book and doing some very, very bad things to her! Gotta love that perk of being a writer.

I notice a stick on the floor and kick it so it skids across the porch. I pretend it's Robbyn's face and feel the slightest bit satisfied. My glee doesn't last long, though, because with the incessant buzz of hungry mosquitoes, I realize my outdoor writing time is quickly dwindling, and if I'm going to count Day One as a success, I better get going.

I turn my attention back to my laptop and type a few notes. *Robbyn character: Name is Bertha. Fired from job. Broken up with. Pants split in yoga class. Hit by bus.* There, that should suffice. I can hardly wait to get to a chapter where I can work that in. How fun will *that* be?

After checking my texts and emails yet again, and with not one other procrastination device at my disposal, I reread the last few pages I'd written.

And my heart breaks into a thousand pieces.

Because those pages, after all, were written atop Niles's roof. And on his couch. While everything was going right and everything was amazing and my creative juices were in full swing.

I stare at my screen and freeze. How can I keep writing this story? How can I get myself back into that frame of mind? That's what my readers want from me. They want fairytales and romance and little bits of conflict that are quickly resolved and massaged into happy moments and even happier endings. They want love and lust and trust and excitement. They want what Niles and I had. Until yesterday.

I slam the lid of my laptop closed and walk to the edge of the porch. I look all around and don't see a soul. I'm not sure how far apart each of the cabins are—probably not very—but at this point I don't really care. I stand at the edge of the porch, dangle my toes over and close my eyes. I'm loud and wobbly and weepy and overcome with so much . . . *everything*.

Somehow my mind decides that now would be an excellent time to take stock in all I've managed to accomplish lately. So, let's see. Failed marriage? Check. Failed rock star romance? Check. Feelings of motherly inadequacy as I allowed Jilly and Alana to be hundreds of miles away while I followed my one-time rock star lover all over the East Coast? Check, check, and check.

And now I'm holed up in a cabin in the mountains, a mere hour away from them, without so much as letting them know. Oh wow, that's outstanding. Where do I sign for my Mother of the Year award?

Oh, and let's not forget how shitty of a best friend I am. I still haven't called Sara back, and frankly, I have zero inclination to do so. I'm a shitty client, too, since I'm sure my message to Lucy earlier was so cryptic she doesn't even know what to make of it. And again, now I'm up in the mountains with spotty Wi-Fi and phone reception, and she could be calling or emailing me for all I know . . . but I wouldn't even know.

And now, possibly the worst thing of all. The most terrible, horrible, insanely baddest thing of all: I can't even write. My one motherfucking saving grace. The one thing that makes all the shit in my life seem somewhat-kinda all right. The one thing that sets my mind straight when it's wonky and helps me work through whatever ails me. The one thing I felt I was actually good at these days. I can't do that either.

My fans are waiting for Book Two. But I can't even imagine that I'll have anything to give them. How can I? My life is totally different now. I mean, there was never any pressure with Book One. It was just me telling a fantastical story. Now, these people want a follow-up. And it better be good, or they'll abandon me and find new characters to love. And just like that, I'll be yesterday's news. Just. Like. That.

Oh my God, I totally understand how Niles must be feeling about his new album.

I'm only four feet off the ground, but it feels like miles. Not only do I understand Niles's creative struggles, but I also know how he must've felt that night on the bridge. He was obviously in a much darker place than me, but I understand how very, very excruciating failures are. And how hopeless you feel when you don't know where to start in order to fix them. Which one do you tackle first? How do you do it? Can you do it alone? If not, why not?

I stand and teeter, cry and shake, heave and finally collapse to the floor. The once-upon-a-time me who once upon a time felt in control of everything—or at least of some things—is gone. Where did she go? And how do I get her back? I don't know anymore.

I honestly don't know.

***

I can't say I'm dying to do it again, but sleeping on the cabin's porch was a kinda-cool experience. After flipping out like that last night, the last thing I wanted to do was hunker down in a teeny tiny cabin, so I brushed my teeth, chiseled the cry-dried makeup off my face, and grabbed a blanket and pillow from the adorably rustic bed. I think I covered every square inch of the porch, alternating between sleeping upright in the rocking chairs and rolling up in the blanket burrito-style on the floor. I'm pretty sure I would've come face-to-face with a raccoon or three, but I squinched my eyes shut tighter whenever I heard what I presumed to be scampering claws. I'm all about the great outdoors, but that's pushing it.

The sunrise is staggeringly beautiful as I sit with the blanket draped around my shoulders, appreciating every moment of it. Yesterday was rough. From start to finish—aside from my encounter with Erin—it was very, very rough. But today is a new day. Today, I will slay my dragons and conquer yesterday's demons. This day might not be perfect, but I will put one proverbial foot in front of the other and make it be better than yesterday.

Because sometime during the night, through a haze of muddled thoughts and half-dreams, I allowed myself to admit that I'm a good writer. With or without Niles Russell's influence. For sure, this sounds ridiculous because if I weren't a good writer, I wouldn't have gotten published, right? Well, that rationalization doesn't matter when you're an artist. You can create something gorgeous one day, then two breaths later hate every single thing you've ever done. It just goes with the territory, and it can be very debilitating when you let it.

Like with Niles and his new album.

But instead of freaking out like he did, I've decided to turn this completely around. Erin says my fans are getting impatient for Book Two. So, I'm going to give them Book Two. And it's going to be the best damn book I can write because I'm going to take all the good and the bad that's happened over the past few weeks and craft it into a story people can relate to—but with the much flashier personalities and circumstances of Nash and Emily.

This book doesn't have to be a journal of the experiences between Niles and me. It just has to be a story I want to tell and that others will want to read. That's it. Nothing more, nothing less.

So, I'll do it.

I sit on the porch and flip open my laptop's lid, positioning my fingers over the keys so the magic can begin. It doesn't. I reread some of my particularly inspired earlier paragraphs. Still nothing. I get up and run three laps around the cabin, thinking maybe I just need to get some blood flowing. I try to draw inspiration from the trees, the birds, the rustling of critters in the woods. Zip, nada, nothing, zilch.

What the heck is wrong with me? Why can't I get my shit together? It's just a story. It's just words. I know Nash and Emily better than I know Niles . . . or myself.

Or do I?

What would my readers want right now? Love. They'd want love. Maybe some hope and a dash of passionate excitement.

But what am I experiencing right now? Heartache. And lots of it.

Super.

Okay, sitting here is useless. Maybe a walk to the little coffee shop I passed on the way up will help. I head inside to spruce up and grab some cash. Out of habit, I reach for my phone and check for messages. I must finally have good reception because there are plenty from the usual suspects (Sara, department stores, coupon sites, and now the local media), but none from Niles. I notice there is a voicemail, though, and figuring it must be Lucy following up on an email (which asked me to call her so she can debrief me on the marketing meeting), I dial in.

I hold the phone with my shoulder and pull the door closed behind me, growing more excited about my impending coffee walk by the moment. (Coffee! Yay!) My excitement doesn't last long, though. Because although the voicemail is scratchy and barely audible, there is no question I hear a panic stricken male voice gasping into the phone pleadingly and hauntingly.

"Kallie?" it says. "You need to get here immediately. It's Jilly. She's been in an accident."

CHAPTER THIRTY-FOUR
Baby, Mine

I play the voicemail again. And again. And once more. There is no mistaking—it's Brad's voice and he's telling me that our daughter is hurt. Oh my God.

With hands so shaky I can barely poke the keys on my dial pad, I call him back. My ears are met with incessant ringing, but no human voice to interrupt it. I immediately consider which hospitals are near Brad's parents' and grab my car keys in preparation to leave.

But without Brad answering, I have no idea where to go. Why isn't he answering?

Wait. What if he's just messing with me? Maybe he got really drunk last night and decided to yank my chain. That's probably why his voice sounds so weird. And who knows what time this voicemail came in? Maybe this is his way of getting back at me because of those photos. He knows that the one thing that will punch me in the gut is my children. He wouldn't do that, though, would he? Maybe. The way he's been talking to me lately, I guess it's not out of the question. And I swear, if that's what this is, I'll strangle him with my bare hands. I absolutely swear I will.

I dial his number again and again, until he finally picks up, breathless.

"Kallie, poor Jilly." He's definitely crying. This must be for real—and really bad.

"What's wrong with her?" I fire. Every nerve in my body is shaking. My lips can barely move.

"We were horseback riding. You know how she loves that. He bucked and she fell off. She hit her head on a fence post on the way down. Knocked her out cold. Taking X-rays for broken bones. She's in rough shape, Kallie."

As a parent, there is nothing worse than hearing your child is hurt. And not knowing the extent of it is crippling. Is she conscious now? Is her body broken? All I can think about is my itty-bitty seven-year-old, one of the smallest in her class. There's no way she could come out of a fall like that unscathed. This is serious.

"Where is she? Which hospital? Is she conscious now?"

"Duke. They took her right to Duke. And no, she's not conscious. How fast can you get here? Where the hell even are you?"

I pause.

"I'm here," I say, the guilt rising to the top of my voice. "I'm about an hour from your parents. Let me Google directions to Duke and I'll be there as soon as I can."

"Wait, what? What do you mean you're an hour from my parents? You're here? In North Carolina?" With every sentence, Brad's voice rises higher and higher.

"I just got here last night. Rented a cabin in the woods to get some writing done. I was planning to call you next week. To meet up with the girls."

"So you're telling me you're in the fucking mountains right now and you didn't bother to tell us? Oh wait, that shouldn't be a big surprise considering you've been all over the East Coast and the only way we knew *that* is because the big mouths at home saw it in the freaking tabloids!"

"Brad . . ."

"And you were going to call us *next week*? What exactly were you going to do the other week? Oh yeah, write. Pfft. I highly doubt that. More like you were going to tag your rock star boyfriend where no one could see you or take your pictures and splash your lovesick faces all over the fucking Internet."

"*Brad!*" I don't know if I expected him to be thrilled that I'm nearby or what, but I certainly didn't expect him to flip out. And I really, really didn't expect to discuss Niles right now. My freaking daughter is injured. Christ.

"You really are a piece of work, Kallie. What happened to you? You are *not* the girl you used to be."

I blink in disbelief. Well, no shit I am not the girl I used to be. That was the exact reason for ending our marriage. But none of that is here nor there right now. Not one bit.

"Brad, our daughter is hurt. Can we concentrate on that please?"

"Right, keep denying it, Kallie. As if I haven't seen and heard all about your steamy little romance. It's sickening."

"I'm not denying anything, Brad. What I *am* saying is that I do not give one single fig about any of that right now. I want to get off this phone and get in the car to see my daughter. Now, text me later with her room number. I'll be there as soon as I can."

I hang up on him and immediately Google directions to the hospital. I stagger out to my car, only narrowly remembering to grab my purse on the way. I try so hard not to cry because I know tear-clouded eyes are not good while navigating down a mountain road. My fears are so secondary, however.

Getting to my baby is all that matters.

***

I walk into her room and see her little body, all tucked into a sterile bed that's not her own. Her blonde hair, which has gotten even lighter from the summer sun, frames her face on the pillow beneath her. There's an IV running into the top of her little hand and machines that are making pumping and bleeping sounds. Her eyes are closed and her face, though scratched and puffy, is sweet and peaceful.

"Baby girl." I reach out my hand, but am afraid to touch her. She looks so fragile, as if a gust of wind could shatter her into pieces.

"You made it," Brad says, walking in behind me. He extends his arms like he wants to hug me, but drops them immediately.

"She looks awful," I say, looking up at him. "What's going on?" I want to ask prodding questions, get more details, formulate intelligent sentences, but as usual, my tongue does not cooperate.

"Couple broken ribs, possible fractured pelvis. Arms are fine, surprisingly. The big worry is the blow to her head. They're keeping her heavily sedated for now until all the tests have come back."

My poor, sweet little daughter.

Brad moves closer to me and puts his hand on top of mine, which is resting on the bedrail. It's warm and scratchy, just like I remember. "I'm glad you got here as fast as you did. She needs her mama."

Those words send my tear ducts into overdrive. She does need her mama. Thank God I was close. Thank God I could get here so quickly.

"What now?" I ask. "What's next?"

"More testing, more waiting. That's all they can do."

I wiggle my hand out from underneath his and run the backs of my fingers along my daughter's cheek. "She's such a good girl," I whisper. "She's a fighter. She'll be just fine." I feel tears slip down my cheeks and make no effort to wipe them away. "Right, Jilly?" I sniff. "You're going to be just fine, sweet love. Right?"

Brad turns me and pulls me into a hug. I want to resist it, but I don't. It feels odd but comfortable at the same time. I allow my face to rest against the same grubby T-shirt he's had for years and squeeze my eyes shut in an attempt to stop the tears. I envision my daughter springing up in bed, healthy, and raring to go. I envision all of this being a dream. A bad one. I envision walking out of here, holding her hand, setting us free from this nightmare.

"What do you see in him, Kallie?" Brad whispers, interrupting my thoughts.

"What?" I try to pull away, but he pulls me in closer.

"Is he really worth losing your family over? We miss you."

"Brad . . ." Is he seriously bringing up Niles right now? I can't believe this.

"I can't help but think this was maybe meant to be. Our daughter getting hurt while you're only two hours away. This has to be a sign. Or some cosmic intervention or something. Don't you see it that way, too?"

I straighten up as though someone just poked me with a cattle prod. "Do I think that our daughter getting bucked off a horse is a sign that we're meant to be a family again?" Though I wish it wouldn't, my voice rises. "No, I don't! How could I? This has nothing to do with us, Brad. She's a sweet little girl whose body is a broken mess. How does that have anything to do with you or me or Niles or anyone? It doesn't!"

I pull away from him and sink down into the recliner that flanks Jillian's bed. "You lambaste me over text for weeks, and on the phone just two hours ago, and now you're trying to tell me this is a sign that we should all be together again?" I shake my head. "Unbelievable."

He doesn't respond.

"Our daughter is what's important right now, Brad. This really is not an appropriate time to talk about anything else."

"I bet if you think about it long enough, you'll see what I mean." He rests his hand on my shoulder. "She needs you home. We all do.

You got to live your little fantasy. You got to follow him around like a puppy, have your picture all over the Internet, and make all the small-town mothers jealous. Now it's about time for you to come back to us."

"Brad," I say quietly, "there really is no us." I raise my eyes to meet his, expecting to see anger. But he looks nothing but sincere. My heart tugs a little.

When he again says nothing in return, I shake my shoulder from his grip and stand. "Can I have some time alone with her?"

"Of course. Alana and my mom are in the waiting room. I'll go sit with them." I nod. "And Kallie?"

"Yeah?"

"You don't need to make any decisions right now. Just think about it."

I close my eyes in an effort to show him exactly how much I want to be having this conversation right now. Or ever. I'm livid. How can he even be thinking this way at all, let alone when our daughter is lying here, unconscious? And why on Earth would he think I'd flip a switch and come crawling back? Why would he even want me? He truly seems to think that Niles is the impetus behind our split, but that's simply not the truth. There's so much more to it. How have I failed in showing him that?

I open my eyes and narrow them. "Can you go? And send Alana in after a few minutes. Please?"

"Yeah. Sure." He tries to put his hands on my shoulders again, but I've already turned away from him.

When he's gone, my eyes take in my daughter, lying still, completely oblivious that her mother is by her side. I should have been with her all along, shouldn't I? I should have seen the horse getting agitated, yelled for Jilly to hold tighter, zoomed through the air to catch her with my SuperMom arms. What kind of mother am I?

"I'm so sorry, my love," I whisper. "Mama should have been there." I squeeze her little hand and swear I see her eyelids flicker. "Atta, girl. Come on back to us, Jilly. You can do it. We need to get you out of here." I pull my fingers gently through her hair. "It's time to get you out of here."

CHAPTER THIRTY-FIVE
Dream Weaver

I am certain that I no longer know my own name. For the past two days and nights, I have not left Jillian's side. I sleep in the recliner next to her bed, eat cafeteria food in her room, and brush my teeth in the tiny attached bathroom. I've been encouraged to shower, to head to a hotel for a good night's sleep, to join Brad, Alana, and Brad's parents for lunch in a restaurant. I refuse it all. I refuse to leave.

"Mom, please come get a burger with us," Alana pleads. I feel awful. I don't want her to think I'm choosing Jillian over her, but I am very superstitious and feel like if I leave Jilly's room for more than fifteen minutes at a time, something will go wrong.

"Maybe tomorrow, sweets." I tug at one of her curls and it springs back into place. I pull her into a hug and notice her hair needs a good scrubbing and detangling. I should take her back to Brad's hotel, wash the bejeebies out of it, and condition it with a good hair masque. I *should*. But I can't. Not yet. Maybe when Jillian makes some progress. I shove the guilt out of my mind and usher the whole brood out the door to go get their bite.

I settle into my recliner and grab my phone. It's been on absolute fire with texts, calls, voicemails, and emails. After two days of noncommunication (four days, really, since reception was pretty spotty in the mountains), I stare at my device like it's a python. But I know I have to deal with it.

I scroll through everything, my heart leaping when I see the only name that would make it react that way. It's just a quick text, saying hi. No really, that's it. It literally reads, "Just wanted to say hi. So hi." With a smiley face. Of course.

I'd be flat out lying if I said I haven't thought about him since I've been here. My primary focus, obviously, has been my girls. But through the long days and sleepless nights, with catnaps as my only source of rest, my mind has gone all sorts of places with all sorts of people. I've had dreams of telling Lucy that I quit all this madness, that maybe I'm not cut out to be a professional author after all. I've had dreams that I told Sara I wanted to date Jack and that she should break up with him so I can have him (what?!). I've had dreams that Brad and I reunited and patched up our little family, just like he wants. And, of course, I've had dreams about Niles. Dreams of us together and dreams of us apart. I like the together ones better. I really, really miss him.

I notice that his text was from early yesterday morning. How did I miss it? What should I do about it? Do I respond? Do I tell him that I'm here in North Carolina and that my daughter is in the hospital, unconscious and broken?

No, of course not. I may miss him, but I have no business letting my head and heart go anywhere near him right now. My priority is my daughter. I'll catch up with him later.

It occurs to me that tonight is the show I should've been going to. It would have been my chance to see him again. To hear him, to be in the same room with him. Maybe, in some weird way, Brad is right. Not about us coming back together as a family, because no matter how many pleading glances he gives me as we stand at Jillian's bedside or how many times he tries to lure me away with him and Alana, or how many times his mom tells me how nice it is to see us all together again, I absolutely know it will never happen. We're different people in different places. Well, maybe not him, but I am. There's no dancing around that, despite how much he wants to.

But maybe missing Niles's show *is* that one last confirmation that he and I are just not meant to be. I'd been letting my mind trick itself into believing we'd reconnect there and then we'd be back on track, just like that. That's not going to happen now. It's out of my control. I'd placed a lot of faith in fate, thinking that if I did everything to put myself in his path, the rest would work itself out. Well, now I'm not going to be in his path. And now there's no way anything can be worked out. How could it?

Oddly, this revelation kind of puts me at peace. That's one less thing I have to worry about. Although I am still hopelessly in love with Niles, there is no denying that I cried more with him, for him, and because of him than at any other time in my life. I felt like a weepy middle schooler most days. I didn't even cry that much over my failed marriage. He brought out emotions in me that made me think and feel way too much. Maybe it's better for me to be single and in my own world for a while. If I focus on my career and my daughters right now, that's probably not a bad thing. I can still love him; I'll just have to love him from afar.

With that "decision" made (not like it was a decision that needed to be made—he'd already made it for us), I work my way through my other calls and obligations. I fill Sara in on Jillian's condition, my whereabouts, my status with Niles, and my decision to be alone. Although she should be mad at me for being so incommunicado, she's exactly as compassionate as she needs to be.

"I'll come stay there with you," she says. "Ben's got the kids this week. I can come until Saturday."

"Aw, God, I love you so much for that. But I'm okay. You stay there. Just keep your phone handy in case I call." I laugh a little and cast a glance at my still-sleeping daughter. "She's just a shell, Sar. You wouldn't even believe it if you saw it."

"Honey," she says. "Does Niles know?"

"No. We haven't talked at all."

"But he sent you a text?"

"Yeah."

"Why don't you answer him? I bet he'd want to know."

"Why? We're not together anymore. And plus, he's got enough to worry about."

"Kallie, he still cares about you. If he didn't, he wouldn't have texted. I'm sure he'd want to know."

I have to believe that what she said is true. He must still care about me, right? That type of intensity doesn't go away in less than a week. If I still love him as much as I did the moment he walked away from me, wouldn't he still love me, too? Probably. But maybe not.

"I can't be concerned about that right now, Sar. I'm not going to mess up his tour mentality. And he's trying to write an album. And besides, what's he gonna do about it? Nothing. I'm here with my injured daughter, and what? Maybe he'll call and offer an ear and I'll have no idea what to say to him since he doesn't have kids and has no idea what it's like to go through something like this. It's pointless and it would just complicate matters. Things are just as they should be right now. Best to just leave it all alone."

"You do know the CelebFeed pics are still up, right?"

"For real? Are people still talking, or is everyone over it?" I've gotten the emails and social media pings. I already know the answer.

"Is everyone over the photos of you and a rock star all over the Internet? Uh, no. Not even. They've been picked up by other sites, too. Lots of them. Niles's publicist, what's her name?"

"Kelsey Graves."

"Well, Kelsey sure as hell didn't get them down. They're everywhere."

This might explain why a bunch of the younger nurses have been giving me the hairy eyeball every day. They must recognize me—although, I look *nothing* like the Kallie in those photos right now. I sigh and pull at my hair. It's so knotted and disgusting, I'm almost starting to think about doing something about it.

"Don't worry about pictures or gossip or any of that other bullshit right now," Sara says. "Just take care of your baby. The rest of it will all shake out in time. Hugs to you, my love."

I send her hugs back and plant my rear right back into the recliner that's become my best friend. I drift off to sleep and my mind revisits my last day with Niles. Except in this version, we call Mindy and secure the apartment. Then, we go and make love in it.

Because we can.

***

The shower feels amazing. I'm surprised I don't clog up the drain with all the grease I've washed from my strands, though. I didn't realize just how disgusting I was until I saw myself in the bathroom mirror. So gross.

Naturally, I don't have much to work with. No body wash, no color-safe conditioner, no extra rich body whip. When I left the cabin, I grabbed whatever my hand caught as it flailed around aimlessly. Apparently, I didn't grab the good stuff.

I burst out of the bathroom and am shocked to see Brad sitting on the bed, flicking through channels. He is supposed to be at the hospital with Jillian. That was the deal. I wasn't going to leave unless I knew he'd be there.

"Brad, what the fuck?"

"What? We're good. My mom's there. No worries." He doesn't look even the slightest bit bothered that he totally reneged on his promise.

"You were supposed to stay with her! That was the deal!"

"I wanted to talk to you. I promise I'll make it quick."

"Talk to me later, Brad. This is really not a good time." I motion toward my towel-clad body.

"I've seen you naked before, Kallie. Like, many times."

I shoot him my laser eyes because now I'm hot. Like, hotter than hot. "I came here for a little peace, Brad," I spit. "I really needed some time alone. I thought I could trust you to do what you told me you'd do, but instead, you come here and stalk me because you want to talk?"

My face has got to be redder than a stoplight. I can just about feel the spit flying out of my mouth as I speak. Brad just sits there. And stares.

"I want some freaking privacy, please!"

He jerks his eyes away and shuts off the TV. "I'll get us some coffee and be back in fifteen minutes."

"No way. Do not come back here. You need to get back to the hospital. Please."

He stares at me a moment, then shifts his weight and stands up straighter than I've seen him in years. "Are you in love with him?" he asks, looking me dead in the eyes.

The words hit me like a dumbbell to my chest. I cannot go there with him right now. Maybe not ever. I mean, how many times have I seen or read about confrontations like this in movies or books? And of those times, how many of those conversations actually ended well? There is absolutely no way for either party to come away feeling good. There just isn't.

"I am not discussing this with you, Brad. It doesn't matter what

I do or don't feel for anyone else. That's not the point. It never was."

"Does he love you?"

I close my eyes, trying to do everything I can not to fling my fist into his face. "What don't you understand here? What I'm doing now is none of your concern. If there were a chance for us, I would tell you. But there's not. So, please. Please let it go, okay? Jillian needs us to be strong, and if we're fighting on the sidelines about something that doesn't need to be fought about, we're not doing our best for her. Right?"

"You're making a big mistake, Kallie. I know I'm not perfect, but I'm a good guy. I love you so much and I always have. I'd do anything for you."

I breathe in and let this register for a minute. He'd do anything for me, huh? Really?

"If that's true, then why didn't you? Why didn't you take the time to talk to me? To ask me what was going on in my life and in my head? Why didn't you ever romance me or have fun with me and the girls or let me in on your life a little? We existed together, Brad, but for years there's been no love. No excitement. Nothing of interest, nothing to look forward to, no reason to stay. This isn't something new."

I look at him, half angry, half sad. This is not the first time we've had this nearly exact conversation. Why does he refuse to admit there is no one to blame but ourselves?

"I need to get back to the hospital," I say. "So, please, can I have some privacy?"

"Just make love to me, Kallie," he says, stepping toward me. "Let me show you how committed I am to making things right. Please?" He reaches out to touch me or pull my towel away or something, I'm not sure. I back up from him until I can't go any farther, but he's still moving toward me. I fear for a second that he's going to try to overtake me, but he doesn't. With a crushed face and the posture of a bullied kid, he finally steps back.

"Get out of here," I growl, shooting my finger toward the door. I'm shaking so hard I feel like a pine needle in a windstorm.

"This is so unbelievable," he says, backing his way out of the room. "We had it all. And you're pissing it away."

He shakes his head, and as he inches out the door, he gives me one last look of disappointment. One I'll probably never forget.

CHAPTER THIRTY-SIX
Do My Eyes Deceive?

Thank God he's gone. Even when the specialists come in to tell me that the swelling around Jillian's brain is improving and they'll start letting her come to on her own, I'm glad he's not here to hear the news with me.

He left town straight from the hotel after our "talk" and drove back to his parents' house. Said he needed to grab some more clothes and that he wanted to visit Alana (who went back with Brad's dad upon my insistence that she needed a good shower with her special curly-girl shampoo). I know that was his way of slinking away, knowing he made an ass of himself, and checking out long enough to pull himself together. That's fine. God knows we need the space.

I sink back into my beloved recliner, a thousand weights lifted off my shoulders. My daughter is improving. My ex is gone for now. It's a new day and the sun is peeking through the gloom that has dominated the past several days. I'm feeling optimistic for the first time in a week. And it feels really good.

I glance at my laptop sitting on the floor, neglected and lonely. I've used her to check emails only when my phone was breathing its last battery-supported breaths. She looks sad, and I pick her up (I've always called my computer "her" and "she." Doesn't everybody?) and cradle her in my lap. "I'll use you soon," I tell her, rubbing my finger along the perimeter of the apple on her lid. "I'm finally getting the itch to write again. I think."

I lean my head back and think about the next chapter I'll scribe. Being away from Book Two for a few days has been good. The state of panic I was in back at the cabin seems to have lifted, at least a little. I haven't written a single word since I've been here, but I'm at least thinking about the whos, the hows, and the whats. From my little recliner paradise, I settle in and create different scenes in my head, different dialogue chunks, different stakes. I think about this so long and hard I fall asleep sitting up, my head slumped forward onto my chest.

Lord knows I've had plenty of wild dreams while in this chair, but some seem more vivid than others. Like the one I'm in the middle of now. This thing is multi-sensory and seriously messing with my head. Because I actually smell a familiar smell and hear a familiar voice— namely my *favorite smell* and my *favorite voice*. I feel calm and on fire all at the same time, just like I do whenever I'm with him. Though I want to keep dreaming so I can experience it longer, and maybe figure out a way to incorporate it into my writing, my eyes pop open against their will.

I gasp.

"Hi," says the voice. "I've missed you."

***

I can't even believe what—who—I am seeing. I stand up so fast, I give myself a head rush and fling my arms around his neck.

"Niles!"

"What's going on?" he asks quietly, nodding toward Jillian. "Why didn't you call me?" I can tell he's trying not to, but he looks genuinely hurt that I didn't call.

There is so much to discuss, I really don't even know what to say to him first. Truly, all I want to do is hug him. Now, with him standing here in front of me, I feel like the last week has not even happened. All the sadness and tears and feeling sorry for myself and accusing myself of being a self-sabotaging ninny . . . it's all gone. I feel alive again. How does he *do* that?

"Is she okay?" he asks, redirecting my attention.

"She will be." A thankful smile washes over my face. "How did you know I was here?"

"Kelsey told me." He looks over his shoulder at Jillian again, then back at me. "She looks exactly like you. Talk about a mini-me."

"We've heard that once or twice."

He smiles and runs his hand down my hair. "You look so tired. I wish I could've been here for you."

"You're here now."

We face each other, holding hands, our eyes glued to one another as I fill him in on the entire story, from my plane ride fan encounter to my quickie cabin sleepover to my endless days in the hospital room recliner. When he finally gets the chance to talk, he tells me that Sara is the one responsible for Kelsey finding out I was here, and subsequently getting ahold of him. I make a mental note to thank them both so hard. Like, *so* hard.

During our entire conversation, one nurse after the other comes in to monkey with this machine or that, then scurries right back out, her eyes big and her smile bigger. It's so obvious they're coming in just to scope out my visitor, and there's no hiding who he is since he's already dressed in tonight's show clothes. It's kind of weird getting all this attention in the middle of a very serious situation, but I'm just happy he's here. Celebrity or not, I adore this man and having him here with me makes me feel content and at peace.

After we've debriefed each other on the necessities, Niles sits down on the recliner and pulls me into his lap. He looks worried that Jillian will suddenly come to and bust her mom canoodling with another guy. I love that he's concerned. It's as considerate as it is cute.

"We're good," I assure him. "She's not going to wake up anytime soon. Plus, we'll see her stir first, I'm sure."

This seems to appease him. He visibly relaxes, running his hand up and down my back, just like he used to. I forgot how amazing his touch feels (well, no, I really didn't, but my skin still melts under his hand just like it's the first time, anyway). We sit in silence for a moment, while my head continues to reel from the fact that he's here. I thought we were over. I thought missing his show was the ultimate sign that we weren't meant to be. But now here he is, underneath my legs, and it feels perfect. Right. Exactly as it should.

"I can't even tell you how much I've missed you," he says quietly, shifting so he can look up at me. "Did you miss me, too?" He makes duck lips and I can't help but giggle.

"So much."

"I'm so sorry," he says, "for absolutely everything."

"Me, too."

I drop my face, aiming my lips toward his, just as I had been dreaming they'd do once again. Once they connect, every single neuron in my body zooms back to life. He feels as amazing as always. His warmth, the light scratching of his stubble against my chin, the strength in his kiss. It's like we haven't missed a beat—like we're kissing on a rooftop, or on a blanket by the Charles River, or in the back of a grimy NYC cab. My hand travels toward his hair and my tongue prepares to explore his once again. But before we can get there, before we can hand ourselves back over to each other, we hear a voice from behind. And not just any voice. A seriously pissed-off voice.

"Classy, Kallie," Brad roars. "I heard all the little nurses at the station whispering about a celebrity being here but I refused to believe it'd be your little rock star boyfriend because I thought you were bigger than that. Looks like I was wrong."

I leap off Niles's lap, half guilty and half pissed off. What is he doing back here so soon? Before I can say a word, he saunters in and looks right past me to size up Niles, who is now standing at my side.

"Got an email from someone claiming to be your girlfriend," he says, holding out his phone toward Niles. "Told me you'd be coming here. Did you know he has a girlfriend, Kallie?"

Robbyn!

"Again, I didn't want to believe that your sorry ass would have the nerve to show up here, but it looks like your girlfriend was right." He puts his phone away and folds his arms across his chest. "Get out of my daughter's room, asshole. Now."

"Brad!" I shoot him a scathing look.

"What? It's bad enough this little pretty boy prick stole my wife and is standing in the way of us getting back together. I'll be damned if I let him get his hooks into my daughter, too."

His voice is so loud, I'm afraid the entire floor will hear him. "You need to stop," I loud-whisper. "Jillian will hear you."

He completely ignores me and fires again at Niles. "I *said*, get out of my daughter's room."

I glance at Niles who is stone-faced and tense. It's clear he's doing everything he can not to blow a fuse, and I admire the hell out of his self-restraint. If I were him, I'd have punched Brad right in the throat by now.

I reach for his hand and he grasps mine back, hard. "She is my daughter, too, Brad. Niles does not need to leave. If you don't like him here, then there's the door." I nod toward the hallway but don't take my eyes off Brad. I am not backing down.

"You," he says, ignoring me again and taking a step closer to

Niles, "should seriously be ashamed of yourself, dude. You broke up a happy family."

Niles shifts, but still doesn't say a word.

"We had it all and you killed it, just like that. You came along with your punk ass and your 'uber-unique voice' and my wife falls all over herself for you and writes a goddamn book about you. Then she kicks her family to the curb and starts following you all over the goddamn country. It's disgusting." His eyes look directly at Niles, who is glaring right back.

"And now you probably fuck her on a daily basis then roll over and pass out. Is that right, Kallie?" he taunts, ripping his gaze away from Niles and fixing it on me. "Is he a good lover, Kallie? Does your rock star boyfriend sing when he hits you in all the right places?"

That does it. Niles's hand tries to leave mine; I barely hold him back.

"Shut up, Brad!" I hiss. "You are completely out of line!"

He faces Niles again, nostrils flaring. "I'll say it one more time, man. Get out of my daughter's room. Now."

"I will," Niles says, his voice measured and calm. "But for the record, I did not break up your marriage. You did that all by yourself." He leans in to kiss me on my cheek. "I'll be outside. Take your time." He drops my hand and walks out of the room. My heart trails after him, but my rage stays right here.

"What. The hell. Was that?" I snarl. "How *could* you?"

"How could *I*? I'm not the one bringing my newest bang-buddy into my unconscious daughter's room, Kallie. Right under the nose of her father—your husband—no less."

"*Ex*-husband!"

"Right. Well, thanks for that reminder." He narrows his eyes again. "You know, he's just as pansy-ass as I thought he would be. Didn't even stick up for himself. He knows what a tool he is for breaking up a family, I guess. What do you see in that schmuck, anyway?"

"What I see," I say as calmly as I can, "is a man who is so respectful and confident in himself that he didn't need to fight with the Neanderthal that was trying to break him."

I tip my head back, and knowing I'm about to say something that will crumple Brad into bits, I breathe, "I loved him before. But I love him even more now."

I turn on my heel and allow my shoulder to bump Brad as I walk out. "Oh, and by the way," I say, spinning back around and nodding toward Jillian, "our beautiful baby girl is going to be okay."

CHAPTER THIRTY-SEVEN
Smokin' Hot

"Hey! You lighting up back there?"

I'll get my answer as soon as I walk behind the giant pine tree that Niles's shoes are peeking out from beneath, but since a plume of smoke is in the exact same vicinity, I'm guessing he is, in fact, spending a little time with the Marlboro man.

"I might be," he says with a guilty smile. He flicks his cigarette to the ground and smooshes it until it's out. "Been a little, uh, on edge lately. Sorry."

"On edge? That would define me in my *best* moments over this past week."

"Kallie . . ."

"I am so sorry about what happened in there, Niles. Really. I don't know what I expected, but that was worse than I ever imagined it would be."

"Ha, please. I'm the last person you need to apologize to. Like, Robbyn seriously emailed him? What is she, a fucking detective now?" He pops a mint into his mouth. "Looks like we both scored big in the crazy-ex department, huh?"

"Pfft, understatement of the century. I just never expected to want to strangle someone I used to love so much, you know?"

"It happens," he says. "Let's just make sure it never happens to us."

A serious look crosses his face as he moves toward me, tentative at first, then with the full Niles conviction that's defined some of our most heated moments. It feels so amazing being in his arms again. Like there's nowhere else either of us should even bother being. We stand like this for ages, calming down until our breaths even out to match each other's. I feel so at peace, I don't ever want to break free.

"You feel so good," he says. "God, I've missed holding you."

Chills spread over my entire body. He missed me. As much as I missed him. Despite all the bullshit that's gone down over the past week, we both know what we need. Each other.

"Niles?" I ask, my stomach tangling into a knot.

"Yeah?"

"Maybe it's too soon to ask this, but . . . what's next for us?"

"What's next," he says, "is that I kiss your lips until they just about fall off."

And that's exactly what he does. My tongue doesn't care that his is muddled with cigarettes and breath mints. The two of them expertly reacquaint themselves and our recently slowed breath quickens again, just like always. I don't care that I'm standing outside a hospital, hiding behind a tree like a high schooler. I don't care if every photographer this side of the Mississippi snaps our pic. Hell, I wouldn't even care if my 95-year-old great-grandma set up a folding chair to watch. This is a moment I wasn't sure would ever happen again. But it is. And it's magical.

"I can't—and seriously don't want to—live without you," he says, when he finally pulls away. "Maybe we don't know what that's going to look like yet, but I know without question that whatever I do, I'm happier when I'm doing it with you."

251

I'm guessing my face totally reflects the joy I get from hearing that because he "boops" me on the tip of my nose and says, "Thank you, Kallie. Thank you for setting my sorry ass straight and reminding me I don't have to be the head case I long ago pegged myself as." He sticks his chin out and looks down his nose at me. "I certainly indulge in my funks sometimes and can be a real dummy. Just like my mom said. I'm sorry."

"She told you?"

"She told me." His little-kid smile breaks through.

"You know, just yesterday I told myself I'd be okay alone for a while. I was all convinced that us being together wasn't meant to be and I was prepared to fly solo." I pull my eyes away from the parking lot I'd been talking to and let them rest on him. "But you had to go and ruin that now, didn't you?"

"Really? You think you want to give up flying solo for little old me?" He holds me out in front of him and bats his eyelashes mockingly, making me burst into a laugh that is probably way too loud for the moment.

"If you're gonna keep making ridiculous faces like that then, no, maybe not," I giggle.

"Okay fine, I'll stop. But you do know that I'm going to need to go back to talking to you every day, right? Well, more like multiple times a day."

"That's fine," I deadpan, as if we're in negotiations.

"And you'll need to come see me on tour stops still. Whenever Jillian gets better, of course."

"Can do."

"But, above all, I need you to keep writing." He looks at me like a teacher would look at a student. "I mean it, Kallie. Your talent is astounding. I know you think all your success is somehow due to me, and hey, I am super happy and flattered that I could inspire it, but the true execution is all you, my dear. *You* wrote the book, *you* poured your heart out, *you* snagged an agent and a publisher, and *you* are on the verge of a movie deal. You, you, you. Not me." He pokes me playfully in the shoulder with every single "you," then pauses for a moment, looking like he's just had a major revelation. "Or maybe it's a *combination* of you and me. And that's why it worked so well."

"Yes," I say, as chills race down my arms. "That's exactly what it is. The combination of you and me."

"Do you know that I have gotten more writing done in the past week than I have in months?" He holds out his phone so I can see his notes page, which does, indeed, contain *a lot* of words. "Care to wonder who inspired *me*?"

"But we were . . . apart."

"And my heart was raw. Emotions everywhere. No offense, but I kinda felt like a chick most days." He smiles and nudges my shoulder again. "I told you, you do some crazy shit to me, Kallie Reagan."

"Well, good. I don't plan on stopping."

As he shimmies his phone back into his jacket pocket, I take him in again. The way his shirt hangs on his frame, the way that one little wisp of hair scuttles across his forehead from the wind, the depth of the gray in his eyes when the sunlight catches them just so. I love this person and every bit of the quirk and awesome that comes along with him. And I know we just more or less stated that we're going to pick up where we left off, but what I need to know is, are we packing up all the other stuff and putting it away? There was a reason we got to this point. Is that all behind us now? Are we free to move forward? Are we good? I can't make assumptions anymore. I have to know.

"So, are we, like, *fixed*?" I ask, looking up at him. "Just like that? I mean, that seems kind of easy, right?"

"Why make something good be hard? But no, we're not fixed yet. You need a promise that I won't be a jackass again. That I won't use you and that I'll always be honest with you. So . . ." he drops his head and looks up at me, "you have that right now, Kallie. I promise I won't hurt you like that ever again. Or in any way. I'll be honest and open and won't bottle everything up like I may occasionally be known to do." He smiles and rests his hands on my upper arms, squeezing them gently. "I'll be as straightforward as I've always asked you to be with me. *I promise.*"

"Gasp! Did Niles Russell just make a *promise?*"

"Yeah. He did."

With that, my heart swells and bursts into a million flecks of glitter. He said it. He said exactly what I wanted—and needed—him to say. What I begged him to say in the alley right after we looked at the apartment. And not only did he say it, he capped it off with a promise. A promise!

I close my eyes and let this all sink in. We *can* go forward now. Nothing hanging overhead, nothing standing in our way. This is really, really it. I could not be happier even if Ed McMahon resurrected and handed me a million-dollar Publishers Clearing House check.

"We good?" he asks, squeezing my arms even tighter.

"Yeah, we're good. Really, really good."

He lets go of my arms and smooths my hair away from my face. "Upfront and honest. We'll be the poster couple for it."

"*Couple,*" I repeat, as chills cover every inch of my body yet again. "We've never actually said *that word.* Sounds nice, doesn't it?"

"Most definitely."

His phone buzzes wildly, and after reading the message, his face falls flat. "My driver is on his way. I gotta roll. Unless you want me to stay with you. Because I absolutely will."

"I know you would. But no. Your fans are waiting for you, so go give them one helluva show. Just call your *biggest fan* when you're done, okay?"

"You know I will." He pulls me into another hug, then runs the backs of his fingers along my cheek.

"Are you sure you want to do this?" I ask. "We really do have a whole lot stacked against us."

"Kallie," he says, his eyes penetrating mine, "the only things stacked against us are the things we allow to be stacked against us. Do you hear me?"

"I do."

"Good." He leans forward and kisses me on the forehead. "I love you, Writer Girl. So much."

My heart squeezes tight. Tighter than tight, really. Because, finally. *Finally,* after all the starts and stops and one of us saying it at one moment and the other saying it at another moment, *finally* I am able to look him in the eye and say it right back to him with absolute, no-holds-barred conviction.

"I love you, too, Rock Star."

CHAPTER THIRTY-EIGHT
It's Time

"Well, cabin, it was great staying with you for, what? Eleven seconds?"

Jillian's improving rapidly, but until she's discharged to a rehabilitation facility, I am packing up shop and staying at a hotel near the hospital. Going days on end without a shower is no longer my jam and sleeping in what was once my beloved recliner has caused me to feel like I could be cast as the fifth Golden Girl. No thanks.

I feel so sad saying good-bye to the cute little rocking chairs I planned to spend my days in. This was my big chance to pen my next book from a mountain-view porch. To be still and enjoy nature. To regroup and remind myself that, "I got this." But you know what? It's all okay. Because when I got here that very first night, Niles and I were no more. Today, as I pack up, things are exactly the opposite.

I blow it a kiss (because, you know, cabins totally "get" that kind of human-esque love) and hop in my car, no more used to the winding drive than I was on Day One. My phone bloops as I round a bend, but I don't dare give it a look until I'm safely on flatter ground. When I finally get to the stop sign at the bottom of the hill, I peek and see it's a text from Lucy.

"Please call me when you get a chance." That's all. Cryptic, but very intriguing.

Because although Lucy's been a dream, sending occasional emails inquiring about Jillian's condition and telling me to take all the time I need on Book Two (though I know she'd love to get reading it so we can move things along in a timely manner), she hasn't asked me to call her this entire time. Not once. So this must be . . . something. But what?

Of course, my mind goes into overdrive. Why does she want me to call instead of email? What could she have to say that would necessitate a non-digital interaction? Will she finally start giving me heat about getting stuff done? Does she want to suggest (again) that Niles and I make the "big announcement" that we're dating, given that she never knew we temporarily bit the dust?

Or, could she possibly have news? Like the news to end all news? I can't stand it. I gotta know. I pull over and dial her number from a parking lot.

"Kallie, how's Jillian?" she answers, her voice oozing concern. "She's improving, right?"

"For sure. Sitting up now, talking, being her normal, chatty self. Still lots of pain and still really weak, but I think it's only a matter of days before we get her out of the hospital and over to rehab."

"Perfect. Because I might need you to come to New York pretty soon, if you can. You know, to meet some people."

Ack! People? What people?

"Oh yeah? Tell me more."

"Sales of your book have picked up in a very big way. And the marketing department wants to meet with you in a very big way. Obviously, the media is totally onto you guys, but whether you and Niles officially announce your relationship or not, we have some great ideas for promoting you that will put you in a prime spot for

Book Two's release. And maybe that movie deal."

"Um, any news on that yet?" Even though I am thrilled, thrilled, thrilled for the extra marketing support and the news of the uptick in sales, I'm not even going to pretend I'm not a little sad the movie deal wasn't the primary reason for her call. Does that make me a horrible person? Oh man, it does, doesn't it? I'm rotten.

"I think your time in New York will be well spent. So I'll be in touch with details soon. Sound good?"

I can't tell if she's being coy or if she's totally avoiding my question because the whole movie prospect has actually fallen flat, so I just tell her "sounds good" and then promise her I'll write my face off while I'm holed up in the hotel. She chirps an encouraging approval and I'm left feeling more determined than ever to finish Book Two and knock it out of the park.

So, that is exactly what I do. Every second that Jillian does not need me, I'm typing. I type in her room, in the hospital's (and, eventually, the rehab center's) cafeteria, in the hotel room, outside on a bench, and even on the ground next to the tree where Niles and I declared ourselves "fixed." I churn out pages and pages of story, each word finding its birth from my deepest feelings over the last month. I've never written so fast. I've never been so focused. It's as though if I don't get these words out, I'll spontaneously combust.

And it's a really good thing I've been so busy writing, because not seeing Niles is really starting to be a drag. At first, it was okay. I was still riding high from our last meeting and my daily drip of "I love yous" and other such lovey-dove statements. But now we're closing in on two weeks here and my little heart can't handle much more.

But thankfully, the days are flying and so are my fingers across the keyboard. Finally, as I prepare to type THE END, my insides bubbling with pride because I know in my heart of hearts that Book Two is a win, I finally get *the call* from Lucy.

"Kallie?" she squeals. "Are you ready?"

She doesn't have to utter another syllable. I know what she means. And yes, I am ready! Hell yes, I. Am. Ready!

"When?" I literally sit down just to keep from passing out.

"I can get a ticket for you to fly in Thursday night. We'll spend Friday together. If you can stay the weekend . . . well, I hope you can stay the weekend."

I consider this for a moment. *Can I* stay the weekend? Can I really be gone four days? That seems like a lot. But this is business. It's totally different than flying somewhere solely to be with Niles. And speaking of Niles, I wonder where he will be that weekend. Does he have a show booked that night? I rack my brain, trying to remember. I used to know his schedule so well, but now with all that's going on, all the days run together and I'm usually in the dark until he tells me where he is when he calls.

"Can I, uh, ask Niles where he'll be that weekend?" I know I sound like a lovesick teenager, but I gotta know if he'll be in town. And if he won't be, maybe I'll just stay in NYC for Friday night then fly to wherever he is on Saturday. If I have a chance to get away for a few days, I better make the most of it.

"Sure," she says. I can't read her voice, though. It's not an excited "Sure!" like I'd expect from her. It's more like a, "Suuuuuure?" with a question mark.

I promise to let her know how long I'll stay as soon as I can, so I immediately dial Niles, who picks up the first nanosecond it rings.

"Niles!" I screech. "I just talked to Lucy!"

"Annnnnnd?"

"New York! On Thursday! Eek! She wants me to stay all weekend, but the important question is, where are *you* going to be? Maybe I can finally meet you somewhere!" I am so excited hearing these words come from my own lips, I can't stand myself. Two weeks (and by then, three weeks) is obviously my absolute limit. I am friggin' dying over here.

"Oh man, I'm so sorry, Kal. I have to go home next weekend. Like home-home. To Colorado. Family anniversary party. I thought I told you."

"Really?" I whine.

"I wanted to invite you to come, too. But well, you know. Jilly."

My breath catches. Because while I'm totally heartbroken that I won't get to see him, I'm also absolutely giddy that he just called my sweet daughter "Jilly." That's the first time he's ever done that. Seems so personal. My mind flashes back to him talking about wanting to make breakfast for all of us in the New York apartment. I can see it as if it's happening right this moment.

I wish it *were* happening right this moment.

"Niles, I can't take this. My poor little heart is barely beating over here. When am I going to *see* you again?" I swear if behaving immaturely were a sport, I'd be medaling in it right now.

"Soon, I swear. We'll work something out very, very soon." He sounds bummed, but there's also a lilt of hopefulness there. It's hard to read him completely. "I can't stand not kissing you. My lips are sad."

"Mine are sadder."

"We'll celebrate," he says. "Get your business done in New York, then we'll celebrate big. Okay?"

"Yeah, we will. Bigger than big!"

CHAPTER THIRTY-NINE
Seal the Deal

You'd think I'd told him I was jetting off for a month of parking my ass on the beach, the way Brad reacted to my travel news. Telling him that it's "for work" did not help my case either, since he'll always insist that's what lead to our demise.

Despite my best efforts otherwise, I let his disapproval and ridiculous accusations of being an "unreliable mom" wear on me the entire week. While I packed, while I finalized plans with Lucy, while I wiggled my diamond earrings in, in an effort to look like I'm someone who deserves to be signing a movie rights contract. But now that I'm getting ready to de-board in New York, I vow to push it out of my mind. This is my moment. This is probably the biggest thing I'll ever face in my career. This is the granddaddy of all awesomeness.

But, I still feel kinda shitty.

Should I have left Jillian? She's doing great. She'll probably be discharged from the rehab center early next week. When I asked her if she minded that I was heading to New York for a couple days, she looked at me with bright eyes and said, "Can you bring me home an American Girl doll?" Not, "Mom, you're horrible for leaving," or "Mom, please don't go." She just wants a doll. So simple. I wish adults could be like that.

I make my way through JFK in a haze, plotting when I should call her next. Miracle of miracles, my bags are already sailing in front of me when I get to the claim area, so I grab them and decide I'll call en route to the hotel.

Since Lucy told me she'd booked a car for me (a car! Squee!), I look around for a driver holding a sign with my name. I spot him right away and dutifully follow him outside into the warm New York night. *Now,* I'm starting to get excited. There really is something so magical about this place. I look around at the lights. The cars. The people. There's activity everywhere. There's hope. There's promise. There's life.

And I'm part of it.

You know what? Screw Brad. Screw his judging ways, screw his insecurities, and screw his nerve to disrespect me. I am a smart woman who knows how to run my life. Yeah, my job's not conventional. Yeah, my boyfriend's not either. And yeah, my life isn't going to fit neatly into the package others expected from me. So what? And while I'm at it, screw Robbyn, too. She can meddle and be as psycho as she wants. I'm done letting these people have any sort of control over me. This life is short. I'm not getting any younger. I'm living the hell out of my time here on this earth and I don't give one single fig what others think. *I will not allow these people to be stacked against me.*

So there.

I can't stop the smile that now nearly splits my face in two. I throw my shoulders back with great dramatic flair and walk toward the car like the lady boss I am. The driver takes my shoulder bag and opens the door for me. "Whenever you're ready, Miss Reagan."

I offer him a smile while I grab my phone out of my purse. If I hurry, I can catch Jilly before she leaves her room for physical therapy. Now, where's her number? Why can't I find her number? It should be the first one to pop up.

I can't make the poor driver wait for me forever, so with my eyes still on my phone, I toss my purse into the back seat and prepare to scramble in.

"Hey, watch your purse, lady. You almost hit me in the face!"

My pulse stops. That voice! It's a voice that came out of nowhere, but it's a voice I know so well. So very, very well.

I poke my head into the car and see the greatest sight I can imagine. He is seriously like a vision sitting there, looking all sexy in his black pants, smoky blue V-neck T-shirt, and a white unbuttoned button-up layered over top. There is no way what I'm seeing is real.

Except that it is.

"Oh my God!" I squeal, launching myself along the car's seat until my chest slams into his. "Niles, what are you dooooing here?"

"Surprise! Ready to celebrate?"

I'm dying. Like, seriously, seriously dying. This cannot be happening.

I don't care that my feet are partially dangling out the door. I don't care that the driver is waiting patiently (or impatiently) for me to get the rest of the way in so he can close the door and take off. I don't care that any passersby who cared to could look in and see us. I cover Nile's lips with my own and hold on for dear life.

"You . . . are . . . supposed . . . to be in . . . Colorado," I say, between smooches.

"I'm a good fibber." He punctuates the statement with another kiss.

I finally tear myself away and wiggle into place, gluing myself so close to him he's nearly pinned against the door.

"You seriously made that up? You're not going to Colorado?"

"Nope. That was a big old lie just to get you here for the whole weekend."

"You rat!"

"Hey, Lucy was in on it, too. I cooked it up, she helped execute. The timing couldn't have been more perfect. It's all . . ." he trails off and stares at me for a second. "It's all meant to be, Kallie."

I drop my head against his shoulder, fully appreciating the magnitude of this moment. I thought I was coming here strictly for business. And *huge* business, it is. Instead, I get to do business *and* I get to see my boyfriend. My rock star boyfriend who loves me as much as I love him.

"I'm sure you remember when Nash surprised Emily in a car in LA," he says.

"Of course." God, I love him for remembering that.

"He took her to dinner, which was nice. But I have other plans I hope you'll like even better."

I look at him through giant eyes. "Care to share details?"

"You'll see soon enough. But for now, let's listen to some tunes. We have a bit of a drive." He hands me his iPod. "Go ahead, get it started." He nods at his device, which has a playlist called "Kallie in New York" all cued up. Aw.

I push play, unsure how my fingers are even working. My hands are shaking, my breath is irregular, and I feel like I'm a living, breathing pile of sweat. This is seriously the most romantic thing I've ever experienced in my entire life. Or was it the nighttime picnic at the Charles River in Boston? Or maybe the rooftop wine, dessert, and writing sesh at his apartment? Or possibly even the gifting of diamond stud earrings at the after-party? So many options, so many options.

Lucky me.

The first song is "The Sadder Side of Midnight," the one of his I listened to on the flight down to North Carolina. The one I could hear over and over and over for the rest of my life. "I know it's your favorite," he says. "Someday I'll sing it to you when we're alone, just

264

the two of us. But for now, we can maybe just do some of this . . ." He leans into me and kisses me so slowly, so passionately, and so deeply I lose sense of everything else except him and me. I think about nothing but this moment, how he feels and tastes and how amazingly well we fit.

We kiss through the entire song, and are jarred back into reality when the next one starts. It's one of those songs that you know you know, but totally can't place . . . like it was in a movie or something. It's decidedly '70s-ish, but its title isn't obvious to me until I hear the chorus. But the second I do, my head whips toward him and smiles erupt on both of our faces.

"'Go All the Way?' Really?" My cheeks flush so badly I bet you could see the red even in the darkness of the car.

"What? You don't like this song?" He is failing so hard at pulling off the innocent look, and it is totally, totally adorable.

"I like it just fine. But are you trying to say something specific, Mr. Russell?" I wiggle my eyebrows and give him my very best sexy smile.

He answers by putting his hand on my knee and slowly dragging it up until it's high on my thigh. "Take it how you will."

We seriously can't get out of this car fast enough. I don't know where we're going, but it better not be much farther away. And it better be private.

I don't even hear the next song. I am so focused on keeping my cool despite the fact that his hand lingers on my leg. I allow mine to travel up and down his leg, too. We chat about Jillian and my trip, I call her quick to check in, and then Niles drops a bomb. A bomb of the very best type.

"So . . . Robbyn's moving to LA," he says, looking at me as though he's just won a new car.

"She's *what*?!" I shriek.

Incredulous. Joyful. Relieved. Ecstatic. All of those emotions live in my two simple words.

"Kelsey pulled some strings. Robbyn will be working for her firm's West Coast division. She leaves in two weeks." He holds his hand up for a high five. "Up top!"

My hand flies up to meet his and my head falls back until it hits the back of the seat. I haven't heard such sweet news since the docs told me Jilly's going to be all right.

"This is so amazing. Seriously, unless you told me Brad is moving, too, this night couldn't get any better."

Niles gives me the side-eye and a super sly smile. "Oh, but it will."

I shiver.

Finally, after seventeen, maybe twenty years of driving, we round a corner in a neighborhood that's looking really familiar. My head feels like it's on a ball joint as it swivels around, taking in my surroundings.

"Hey, is this . . ." I turn toward Niles, but by the time my eyes reach his, no further words are necessary. He's already in full grin.

"We're here, Mr. Russell," the driver says, his reflection speaking to us via the rearview mirror.

"You can leave the bags right outside the door," Niles answers, handing him some money. They continue talking business for a moment as I sit dumbfounded. I can hardly register any of this.

When they finally stop talking and I finally find my voice, I look at Niles and say, "Seriously. What are we doing here?"

He answers by reaching into his shirt pocket and cupping a key in my hand.

"Welcome home, Kallie."

***

Just like the last time we were here, I trail behind Niles as we make our way up the stairs. And just like last time, he's holding my hand.

But *unlike* last time, we're here alone. There is no Mindy.

It's just us.

"I can't believe this." I've said this at least fifteen times since we left the car. And it's true. I absolutely can't believe it.

I'm so shaky, Niles has to help guide my hand to insert the key. "This is our place now," he says, his hand resting on mine. I look at him, trying to ask him to explain more, but my words don't come out.

"Since we didn't put in an offer when we first saw it, someone else got it. But the first buyer backed out and the minute I found out it was available again, I pounced. By then, I didn't care what it would take." He touches my cheek. "I had to have you back. I had to get over myself long enough to realize that some things are bigger than just me, and I had to get you back. I figured securing this apartment would be like an invitation for the universe to comply. And I was right."

That's all the explanation I need. Now, it's time to go inside. Inside our place. Ours.

I push the door open slowly and am greeted with dim lighting and the incredible scent of an Italian feast. There is music going and a small table set for two.

"Come on in." He tugs me hard enough to dislodge my feet, which have somehow become frozen to the floor as I take this all in. "We'll eat in a bit. Let's look around."

He leads me into the living room, which has no furniture other than two beanbag chairs—one princess pink and one ocean blue— and a gloriously large TV. "I want you to pick out the décor in here, so I didn't touch a thing. Well, except for those ultra sophisticated chairs, of course."

"The girls will love them."

"That was my plan."

Tears flood my eyes as I follow him back into the kitchen, my hand still grasping his as if I'd somehow get lost if I let go.

"I got enough necessities to get us through the weekend." He motions toward the fridge. "Bare bones, though. I don't know how much time we'll have to cook." He turns to me and raises his eyebrows.

Whatever is he suggesting?

We walk down the small hall, where I see a few towels and basics in the bathroom, a blank slate of what will be the girls' room, and the little outdoor deck where we'll surely have a nightcap or three.

And a steak. On a Monday. Just like we'd dreamed.

Finally, we reach the end of the hall, where we're greeted with the closed door of the master bedroom. "Open it," he says quietly.

I turn the knob and nudge the door open. My breath disappears when I see candles everywhere, lining every inch of a gorgeous dresser and the two nightstands that flank the incredibly outfitted bed.

"Niles," I breathe. "How did you . . ." I turn to face him.

"You like it?" he asks, his eyes searching mine.

"It's unbelievable."

"You get to decorate most of the place . . . but this room needed to get done first."

I try to smile, but he has other ideas for my lips. We kiss in the doorway for ages, migrate to our left until I'm pinned against the closet door, and finally stumble our way around until we're hovering near the edge of the bed. Our lips have not left each other's, not even for a second.

"Oh my God, Kallie, this is killing me," he breathes. "Please," he traces my lips with his finger, "please tell me it's finally time."

I answer him by stepping back and unbuttoning my shirt. I watch his chest rise and fall as he watches me undress. When I'm done, I take his right hand and wrap it around my waist. He pulls me in close and we kiss again, our breath barely stable enough to keep us upright.

After getting all his shirts off—and silently cursing his love of layering—I take his hands and pull him down onto the bed. He looks at me as he runs the backs of his fingers along my jaw. "You sure you're ready? This is as big as it gets."

With that statement, the intensity of the moment charges through the air. He's right. This *is* as big as it gets. After this, the deal's been sealed. An apartment can be sold. Earrings can be given back. Pictures can be taken down. But sharing one body . . . that's something that can never be undone. I don't know what the future holds, but I do know that this is right. Right here, right now, in a bed that is ours and an apartment that is, too, it's right.

And that's all I need to know.

Tears spring to my eyes and I do nothing to hide them. "I've never been more sure."

He kisses my chest and neck, working his way up and down until he's covered almost every inch. "You're so perfect for me," he says to himself as much as to me. Every single nerve ignites, even more than they already were. This is sweet, it's hot, it's everything I dreamed. And more.

As he works his way back up my neck, his kisses soften and he pushes himself up on his arms. "Kallie?" he whispers, dropping his forehead until it rests against mine.

"Yeah?"

"I'm gonna try to do everything I can to make you happy and I'm gonna try to be my best for you and treat you the way you deserve to be treated, but . . ."

I put my finger over his lips. I know what he's saying. Or trying to say. Or even more accurately, being careful *not* to say.

I tilt his chin so that our eyes are back in line. He's gorgeous. He's peaceful. He's absolutely perfect for me, too. With tears pooled in my eyes, I brush a bit of hair from his forehead, kiss him gently, and as I position myself underneath him, I look him in the eyes and say, "No regrets."

EPILOGUE
Starring Roles

The cute little blonde reporter sits across from us, her legs crossed and her upper body leaning way too far forward. I want to tell her to sit up, but that would be rude.

"So, guys," she bubbles, "you two are quite the hot little couple. Grammy dates. The Billboards. Niles showing up on the set of Kallie's movie . . . which we all can't wait to see, by the way." She tilts her head and smiles. "You've even been spotted hanging out at a little park in New York City with Kallie's girls."

She looks at Niles, then back at me, then at Niles again. "Your fans can't get enough of you two." She shifts in her chair. "And I think they're kind of wondering what might be next. Especially given Nash and Emily's 'leaked' fairytale wedding that's supposedly coming at the end of Kallie's second book." She sizes us both up, finally sits up straight and says, "Any *special plans* coming up for the two of you?" She winks.

I can't look at Niles. If I do, I will totally lose it. Knowing him, he's staring her dead in the eye, giving zero clues one way or the other.

Ever since our coupledom became legitimately "public," I've been the representative of "us," for better or for worse. Questions are always deferred to me, while Niles hangs back and lurks in the shadows he so loves. Nope, he won't give her what she's looking for. This question will definitely have to be mine.

I toss a fleeting glance at my inner right wrist, where something so little tells so much. If the reporter got a good look at it and did a little probing she'd quickly learn a thing or two.

Our entire story, really.

Because where I had once contemplated tattooing *Muse* (the name of one of the songs from Niles's new album, inspired by guess who), I'd gotten something else tattooed instead.

NP ~ NR.

To the naked eye, it signifies Nash Pringle and Niles Russell. The hero in my books and my hero in real life.

To us?

No Promises ~ No Regrets.

"You know, we're just taking it day by day, Jodie Lynn," I say, flashing her a smile. I reach my arm out and take Niles's hand in mine, rubbing my thumb across the spot on his finger where a ring may or may not be someday.

"And today is a damn good day."

THE END

About the Author

Liberty Kontranowski is a romantic women's fiction author who adores all things lovey-dovey with a pinch (or more) of hubba-hubba. When she's not at the keyboard, she's taxiing around her three boys, knocking back craft beers with the hubs, blogging, fangirling, and dreaming up more fake people. She also spends an inordinate amount of time drinking coffee and dreaming of the day she can bid adieu to far-too-wintry Michigan and move to a place where she can write with her toes in the sand.

Acknowledgments

Who do you thank when you knock Item Numero Uno off your Bucket List mere days before your fortieth birthday? *Lots of people.*

First, a huge thank you to all of the writers, lyricists, musicians, artists, entertainers, and otherwise creative people out there. Keep shining your light, each and every day. Don't hold back. You bring such beauty into the lives of so many and we need you. Thanks for making it so easy for us to fangirl. And to the creative who inspired me to carry on . . . I thank you the most.

To my editor, Samantha March. Thank you for your commitment and enthusiasm, your expertise and sharp eye, and, especially, for believing in me and this story. Your passion radiates and it's been such a pleasure working with you. A million thank yous for helping to make this dream come true.

To my bestie, Jodie Lynn Boduch. I would not be at this place if it weren't for your steadfast friendship, tough love, mad beta skillz, and never-ending support. Fate brought us together and I'm so thankful we've figured out how to rock this long-distance friendship game.

To Matt and Sheri. You knew about this story idea before pretty much anyone else and you were crazy enough to egg me on. Now look. Thank you for seeing me all the way through to this big MoMent. *wink*

To every single person who has supported me throughout this journey. Every message and comment of encouragement goes straight to my heart and fuels me. Thank you, thank you. To Laura Chapman for taking my vision and turning it into a real book cover. To Kim, Jill, Lauren, and the entire #amwriting tribe — you're awesome and a continual source of inspiration. And speaking of inspiration, Theresa Weaver . . . girl, your bravery and beautiful soul know no bounds. You're amazing.

To my Aunt Joy and all of the incredible Girl Bosses out there. You are the very definition of turning passion into purpose. You make me believe I can do it, too. What a gift you're giving.

To my favorite angel up in heaven. My mother. My best friend, still and always. I miss seeing you every day, but you do an exceptional job letting me know you're always here. I hope you know how much of your caring soul you left with me. I love and miss you. So very much.

To my husband, Jim, and our three amazing boys. Every single thing I do in this life, I do for you. You make me want to be my best and I am so fortunate that you're part of my Happily Ever After. I love you with my entire heart.

To my new readers. What can I say? I love you already. Let the fangirl party begin!

And, finally, to all the dreamers out there. Whatever your goal, get after it. Life is fast and precious. Waste no time thinking. Just make it happen. As the plaque on my desk says, *"Life is a Story. Make Yours a Best Seller."*

28715141R00155

Made in the USA
Lexington, KY
19 January 2019